MARVEL

MARVEL ACTION CHILLERS

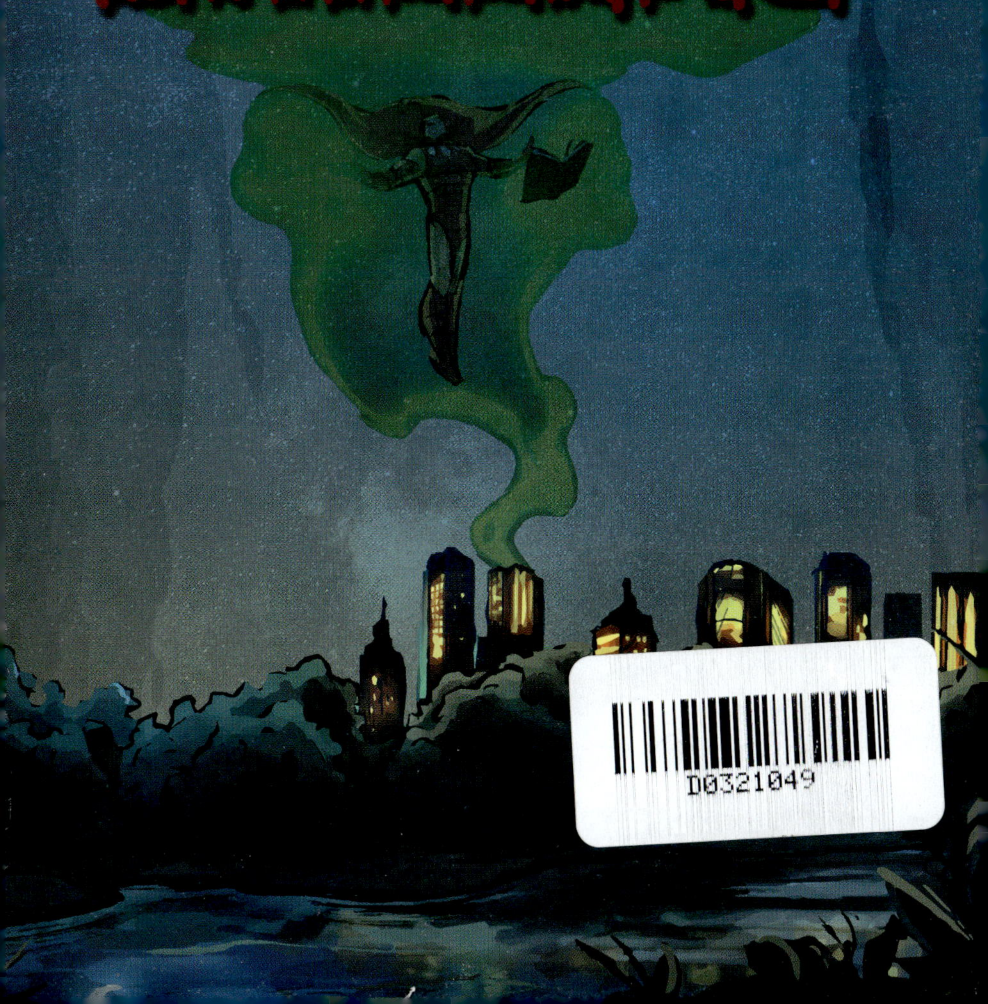

AVENGERS Created By

Stan Lee & Jack Kirby

Writer

Jeremy Whitley

Chapter 1: Iron Man, or the Post-Modern Prometheus

Art (pp. 1–3, 19–20) | Gretel Lusky
Layouts (pp. 4–18) | Seth Smith
Finished Art & Colors (pp. 4–18) | Derek Charm
Colors (pp. 1–3, 19–20) | Nahuel Ruiz

Chapter 2: Little Red Fighting Hood

Art (pp. 1–3, 18–20) | Gretel Lusky
Art (pp. 4–17) | Bayleigh Underwood
Colors (pp. 1–3, 18–20) | Nahuel Ruiz
Colors (pp. 4–17) | Heather Breckel

Chapter 3: The Strange Case of Dr. Spider-Man and Mr. Venom

Art (pp. 1–3, 18–20) | Gretel Lusky
Art & Colors (pp. 4–17) | Bowen McCurdy
Colors (pp. 1–3, 18–20) | Nahuel Ruiz

Chapter 4: Tome of Iron Dracula

Art | Gretel Lusky
Colors | Nahuel Ruiz

Iron Man, or the Post-Modern Prometheus

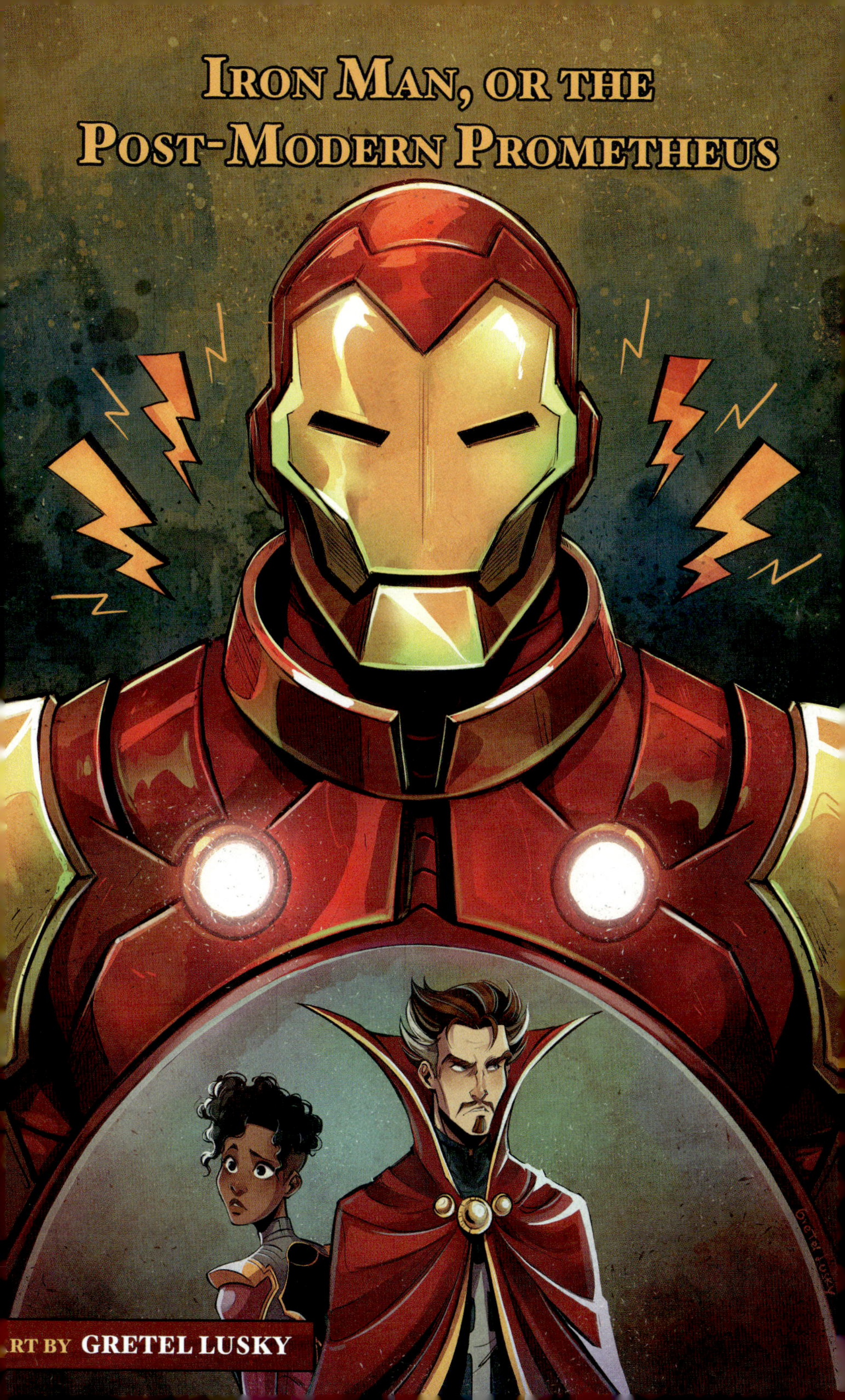

RT BY GRETEL LUSKY

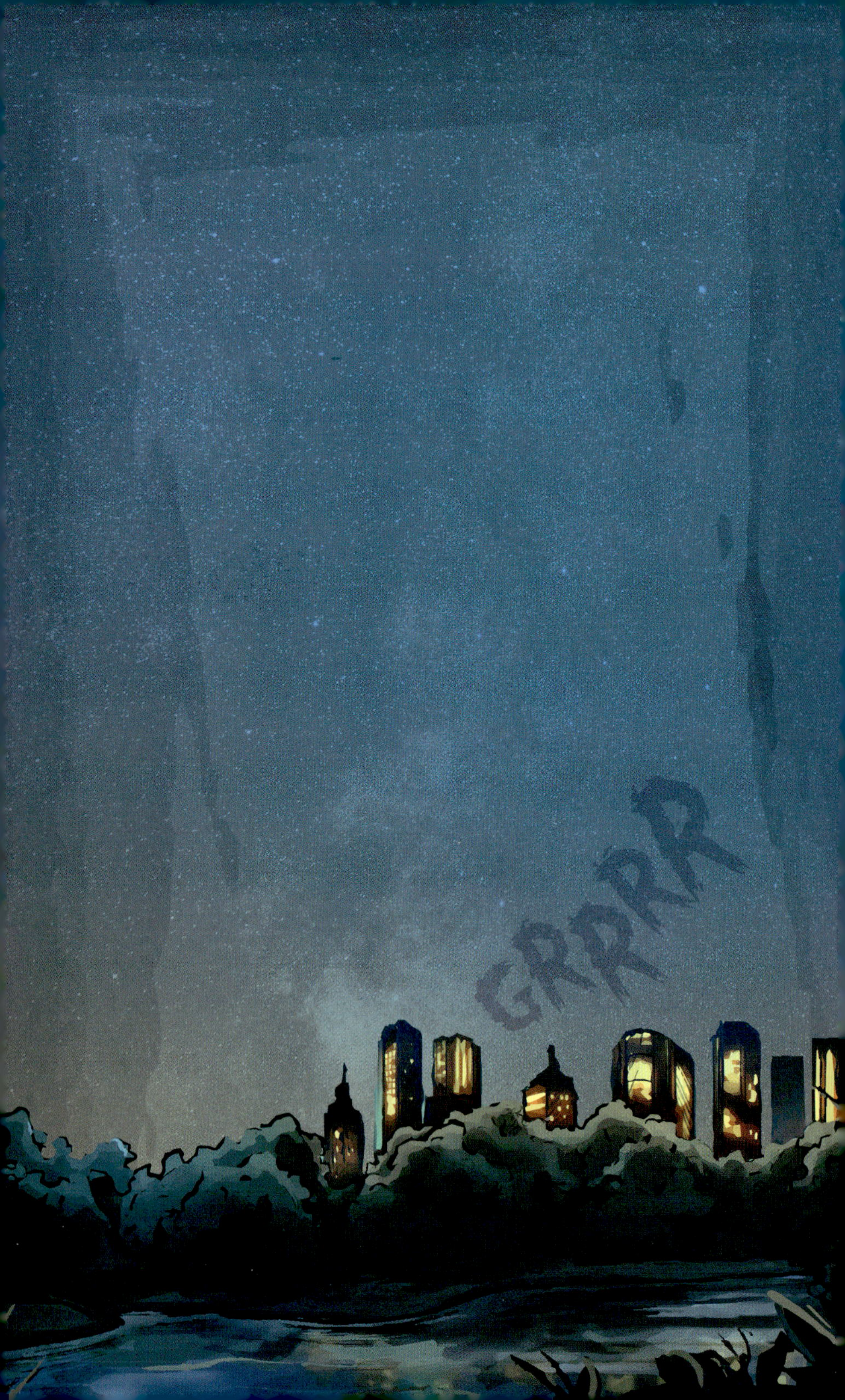
GRRRR

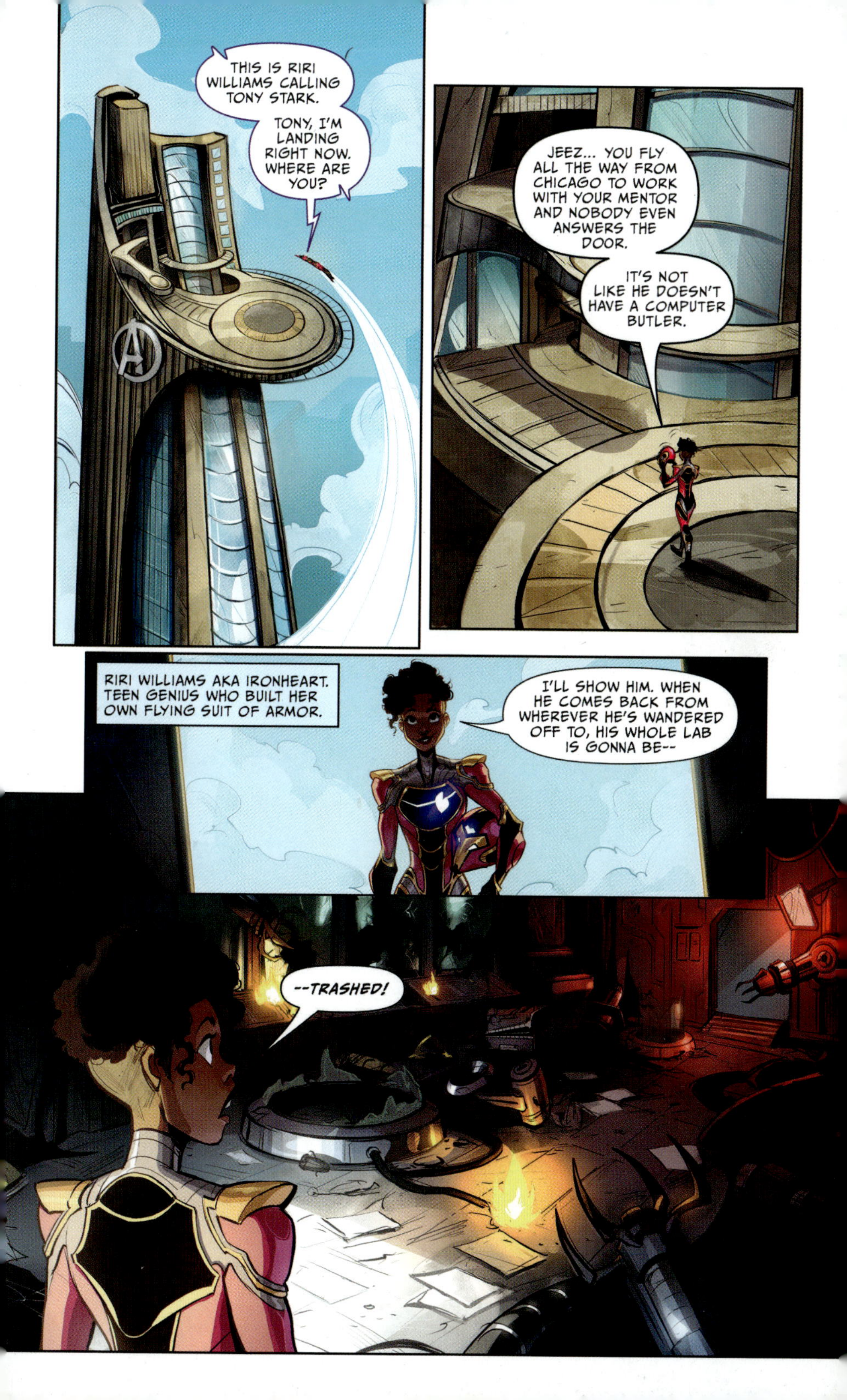

THIS IS RIRI WILLIAMS CALLING TONY STARK.
TONY, I'M LANDING RIGHT NOW. WHERE ARE YOU?
JEEZ... YOU FLY ALL THE WAY FROM CHICAGO TO WORK WITH YOUR MENTOR AND NOBODY EVEN ANSWERS THE DOOR.
IT'S NOT LIKE HE DOESN'T HAVE A COMPUTER BUTLER.
RIRI WILLIAMS AKA IRONHEART. TEEN GENIUS WHO BUILT HER OWN FLYING SUIT OF ARMOR.
I'LL SHOW HIM. WHEN HE COMES BACK FROM WHEREVER HE'S WANDERED OFF TO, HIS WHOLE LAB IS GONNA BE--
--TRASHED!

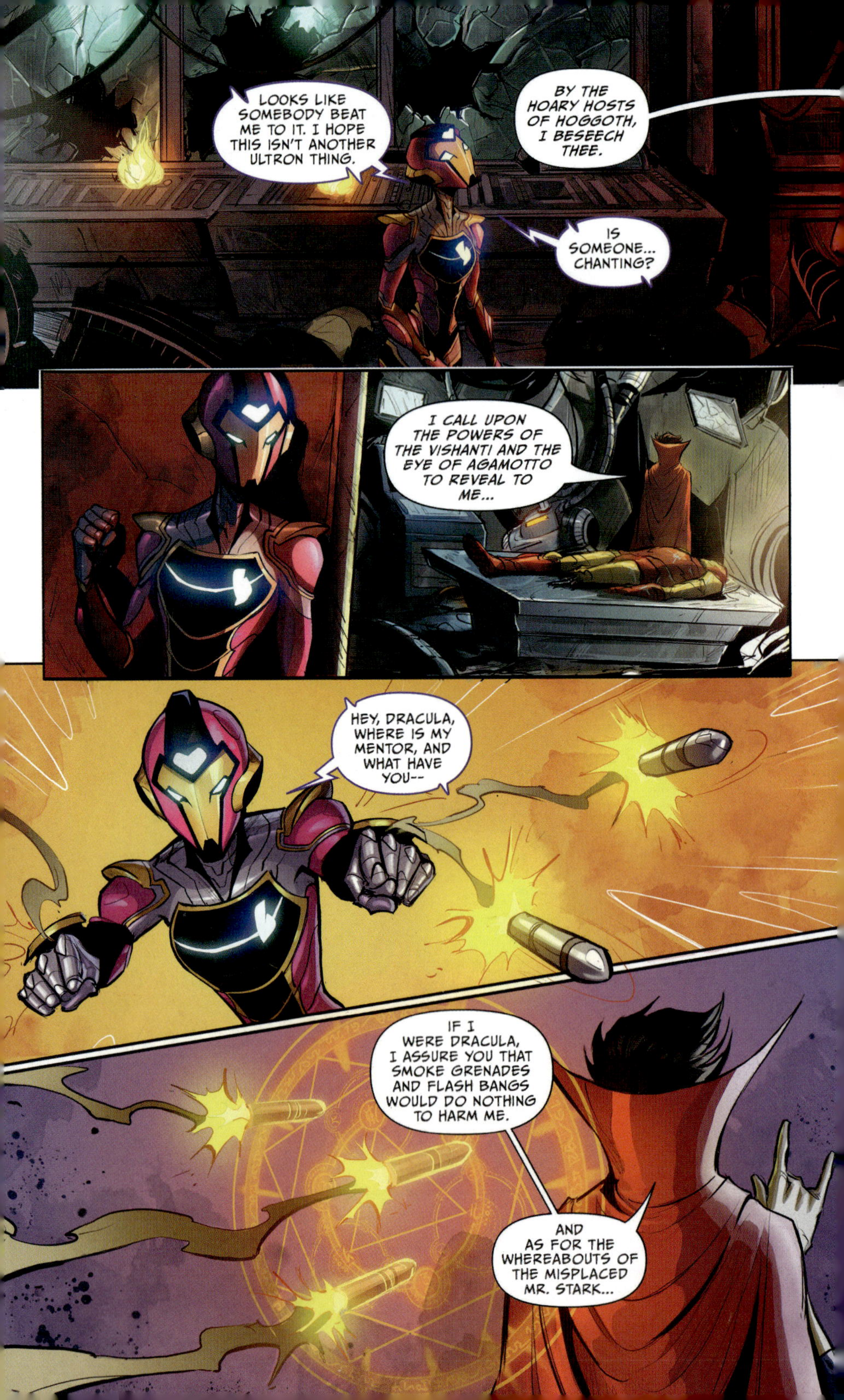
LOOKS LIKE SOMEBODY BEAT ME TO IT. I HOPE THIS ISN'T ANOTHER ULTRON THING.
BY THE HOARY HOSTS OF HOGGOTH, I BESEECH THEE.
IS SOMEONE... CHANTING?
I CALL UPON THE POWERS OF THE VISHANTI AND THE EYE OF AGAMOTTO TO REVEAL TO ME...
HEY, DRACULA, WHERE IS MY MENTOR, AND WHAT HAVE YOU--
IF I WERE DRACULA, I ASSURE YOU THAT SMOKE GRENADES AND FLASH BANGS WOULD DO NOTHING TO HARM ME.
AND AS FOR THE WHEREABOUTS OF THE MISPLACED MR. STARK...

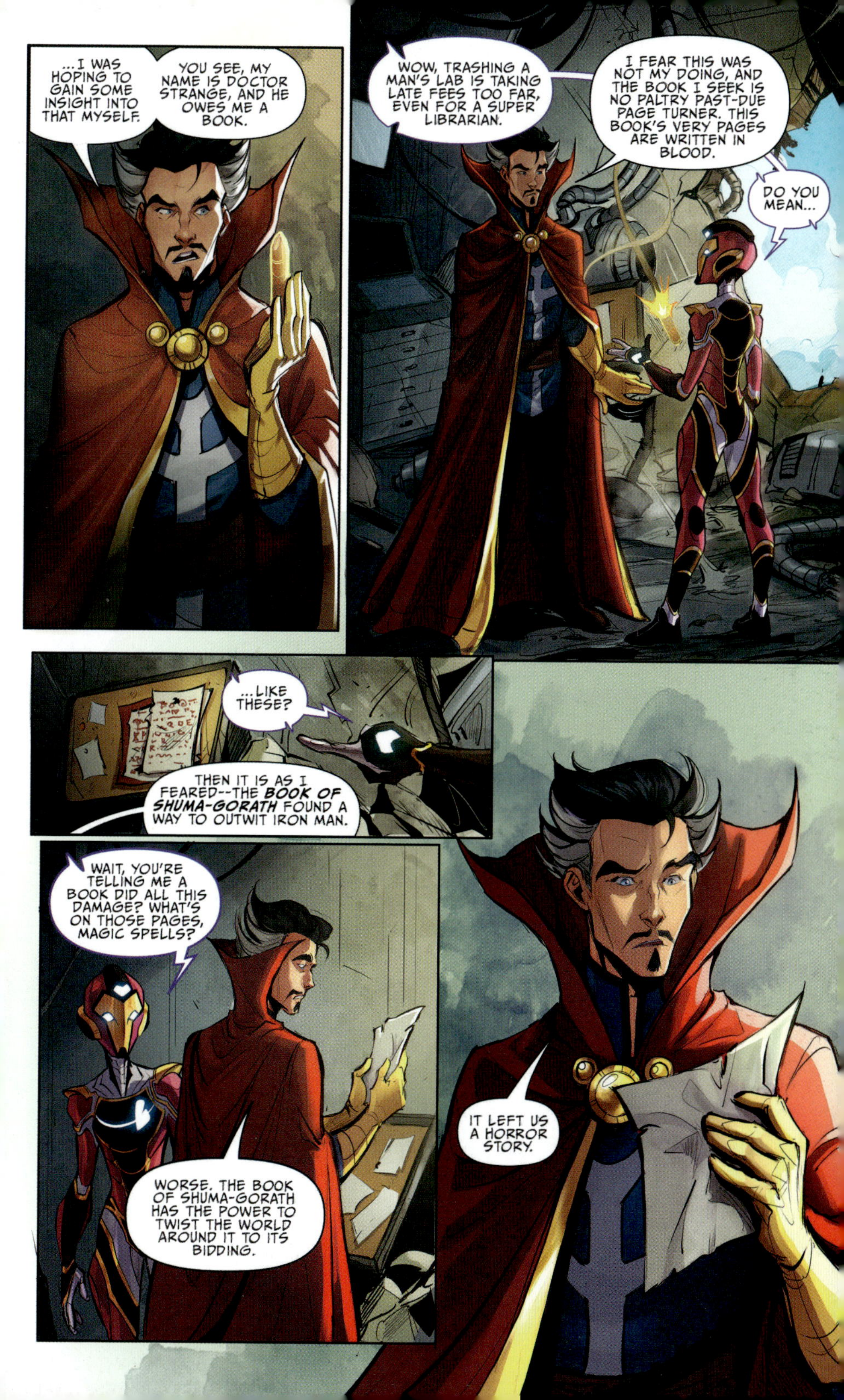
...I WAS HOPING TO GAIN SOME INSIGHT INTO THAT MYSELF.
YOU SEE, MY NAME IS DOCTOR STRANGE, AND HE OWES ME A BOOK.
WOW, TRASHING A MAN'S LAB IS TAKING LATE FEES TOO FAR, EVEN FOR A SUPER LIBRARIAN.
I FEAR THIS WAS NOT MY DOING, AND THE BOOK I SEEK IS NO PALTRY PAST-DUE PAGE TURNER. THIS BOOK'S VERY PAGES ARE WRITTEN IN BLOOD.
DO YOU MEAN...
...LIKE THESE?
THEN IT IS AS I FEARED--THE BOOK OF SHUMA-GORATH FOUND A WAY TO OUTWIT IRON MAN.
WAIT, YOU'RE TELLING ME A BOOK DID ALL THIS DAMAGE? WHAT'S ON THOSE PAGES, MAGIC SPELLS?
WORSE. THE BOOK OF SHUMA-GORATH HAS THE POWER TO TWIST THE WORLD AROUND IT TO ITS BIDDING.
IT LEFT US A HORROR STORY.

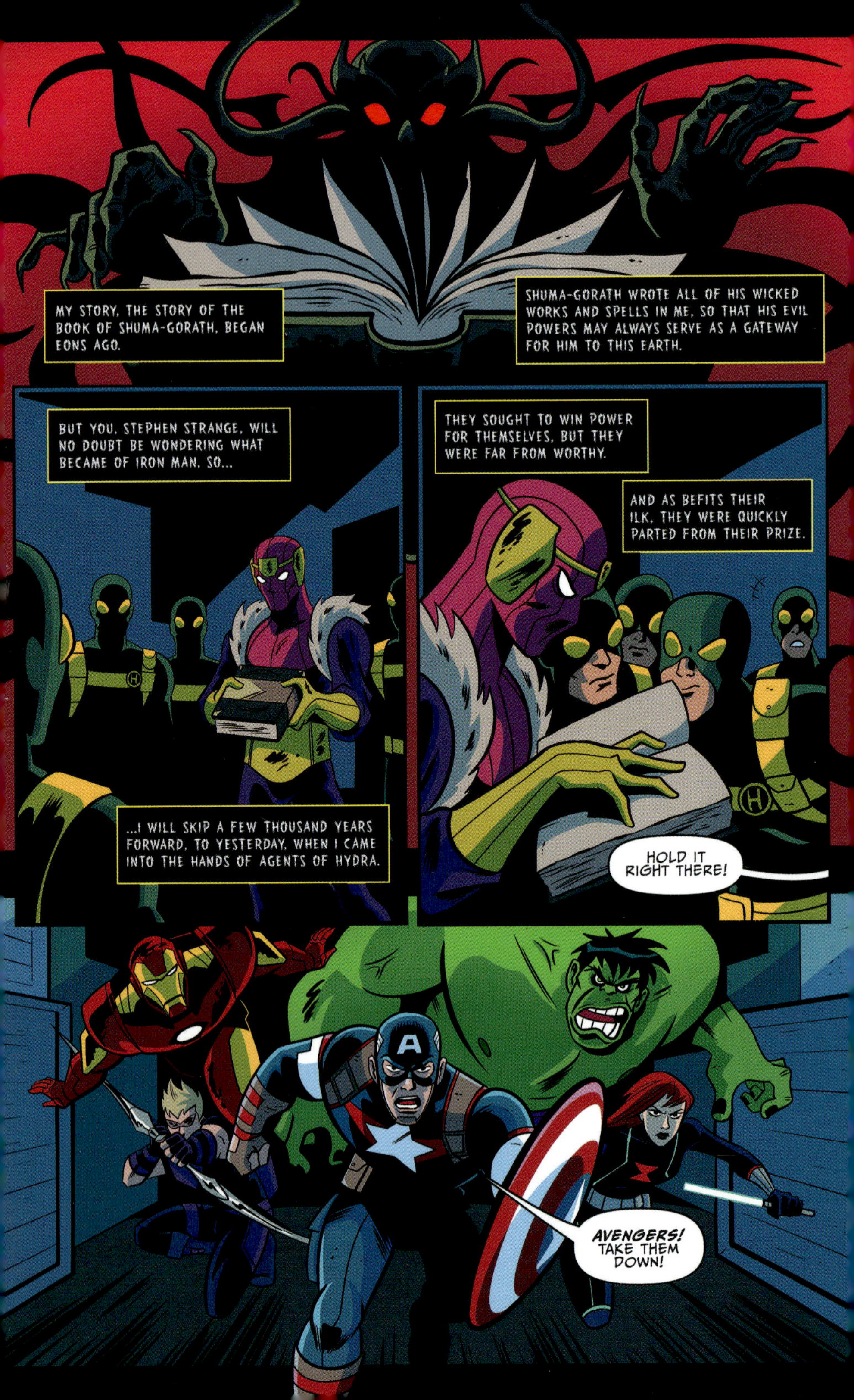
MY STORY, THE STORY OF THE BOOK OF SHUMA-GORATH, BEGAN EONS AGO.
SHUMA-GORATH WROTE ALL OF HIS WICKED WORKS AND SPELLS IN ME, SO THAT HIS EVIL POWERS MAY ALWAYS SERVE AS A GATEWAY FOR HIM TO THIS EARTH.
BUT YOU, STEPHEN STRANGE, WILL NO DOUBT BE WONDERING WHAT BECAME OF IRON MAN, SO...
...I WILL SKIP A FEW THOUSAND YEARS FORWARD, TO YESTERDAY, WHEN I CAME INTO THE HANDS OF AGENTS OF HYDRA.
THEY SOUGHT TO WIN POWER FOR THEMSELVES, BUT THEY WERE FAR FROM WORTHY.
AND AS BEFITS THEIR ILK, THEY WERE QUICKLY PARTED FROM THEIR PRIZE.
HOLD IT RIGHT THERE!
AVENGERS! TAKE THEM DOWN!

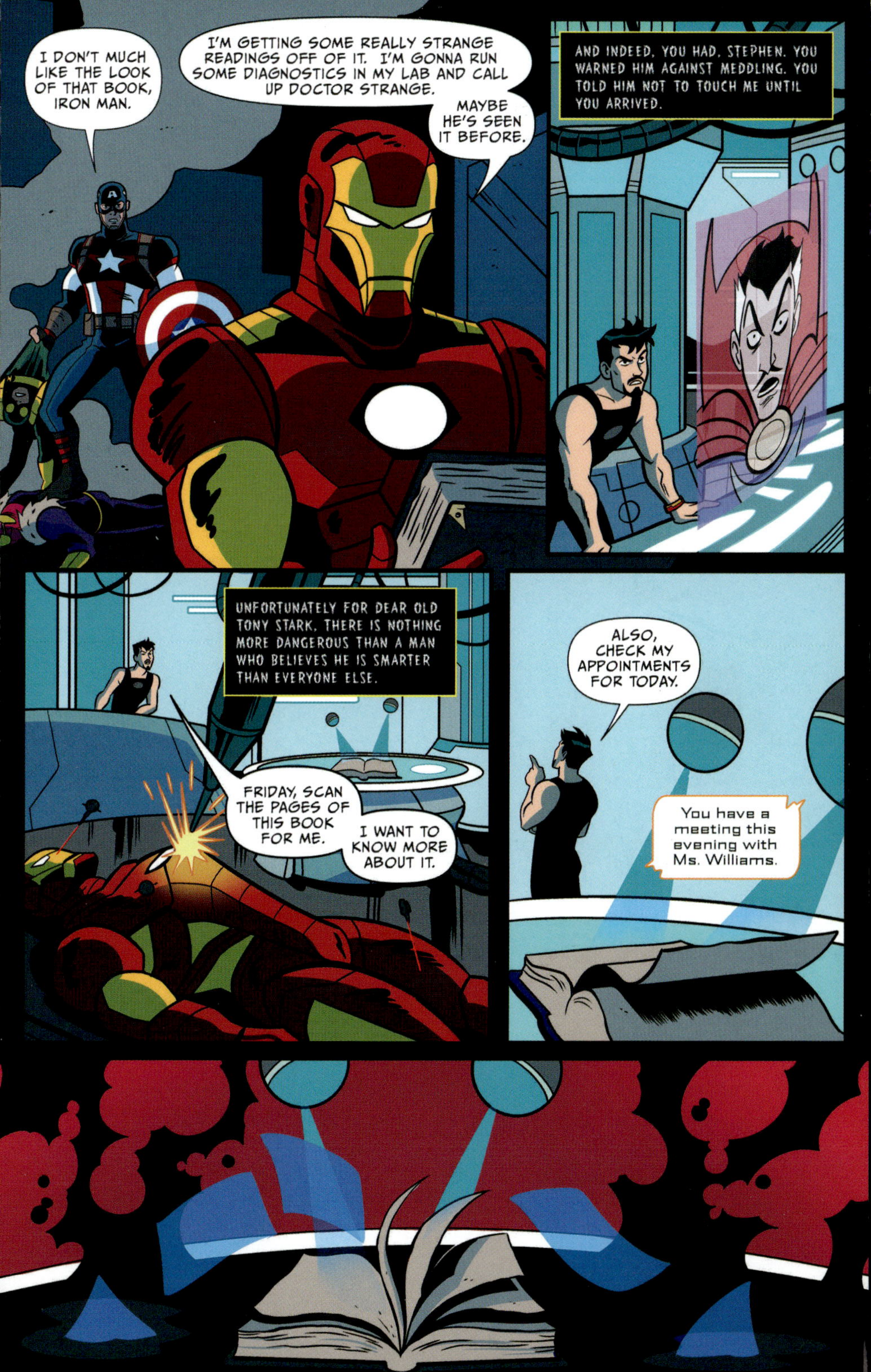
I DON'T MUCH LIKE THE LOOK OF THAT BOOK, IRON MAN.
I'M GETTING SOME REALLY STRANGE READINGS OFF OF IT. I'M GONNA RUN SOME DIAGNOSTICS IN MY LAB AND CALL UP DOCTOR STRANGE.
MAYBE HE'S SEEN IT BEFORE.
AND INDEED, YOU HAD, STEPHEN. YOU WARNED HIM AGAINST MEDDLING. YOU TOLD HIM NOT TO TOUCH ME UNTIL YOU ARRIVED.
UNFORTUNATELY FOR DEAR OLD TONY STARK, THERE IS NOTHING MORE DANGEROUS THAN A MAN WHO BELIEVES HE IS SMARTER THAN EVERYONE ELSE.
FRIDAY, SCAN THE PAGES OF THIS BOOK FOR ME.
I WANT TO KNOW MORE ABOUT IT.
ALSO, CHECK MY APPOINTMENTS FOR TODAY.
You have a meeting this evening with Ms. Williams.

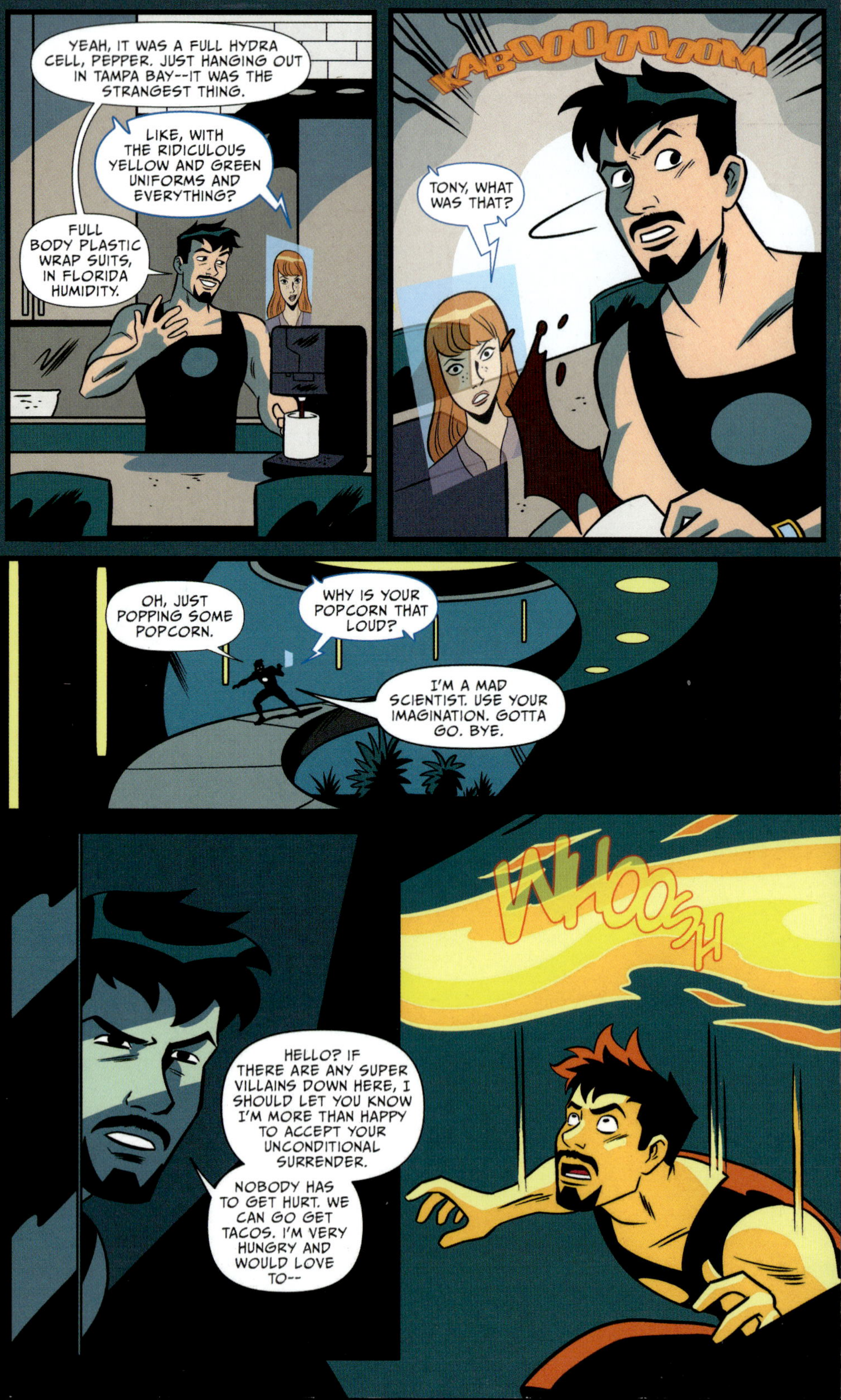
YEAH, IT WAS A FULL HYDRA CELL, PEPPER. JUST HANGING OUT IN TAMPA BAY--IT WAS THE STRANGEST THING.
LIKE, WITH THE RIDICULOUS YELLOW AND GREEN UNIFORMS AND EVERYTHING?
FULL BODY PLASTIC WRAP SUITS, IN FLORIDA HUMIDITY.
KABOOOOOOOOOM
TONY, WHAT WAS THAT?
OH, JUST POPPING SOME POPCORN.
WHY IS YOUR POPCORN THAT LOUD?
I'M A MAD SCIENTIST. USE YOUR IMAGINATION. GOTTA GO. BYE.
HELLO? IF THERE ARE ANY SUPER VILLAINS DOWN HERE, I SHOULD LET YOU KNOW I'M MORE THAN HAPPY TO ACCEPT YOUR UNCONDITIONAL SURRENDER.
NOBODY HAS TO GET HURT. WE CAN GO GET TACOS. I'M VERY HUNGRY AND WOULD LOVE TO--
WHOOSH

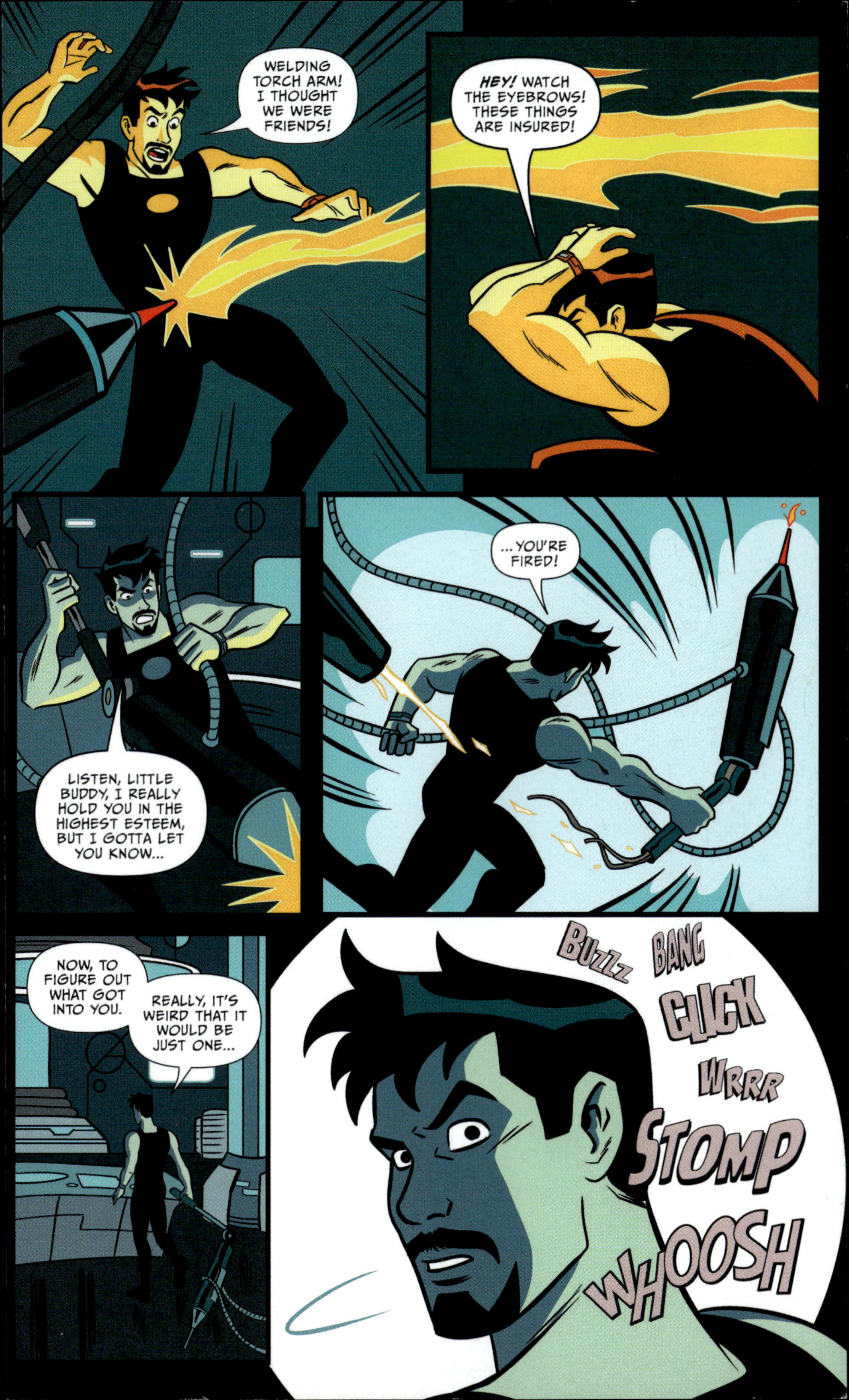
WELDING TORCH ARM! I THOUGHT WE WERE FRIENDS!
HEY! WATCH THE EYEBROWS! THESE THINGS ARE INSURED!
LISTEN, LITTLE BUDDY, I REALLY HOLD YOU IN THE HIGHEST ESTEEM, BUT I GOTTA LET YOU KNOW...
...YOU'RE FIRED!
NOW, TO FIGURE OUT WHAT GOT INTO YOU.
REALLY, IT'S WEIRD THAT IT WOULD BE JUST ONE...
BUZZZ
BANG
CLICK
WRRR
STOMP
WHOOSH

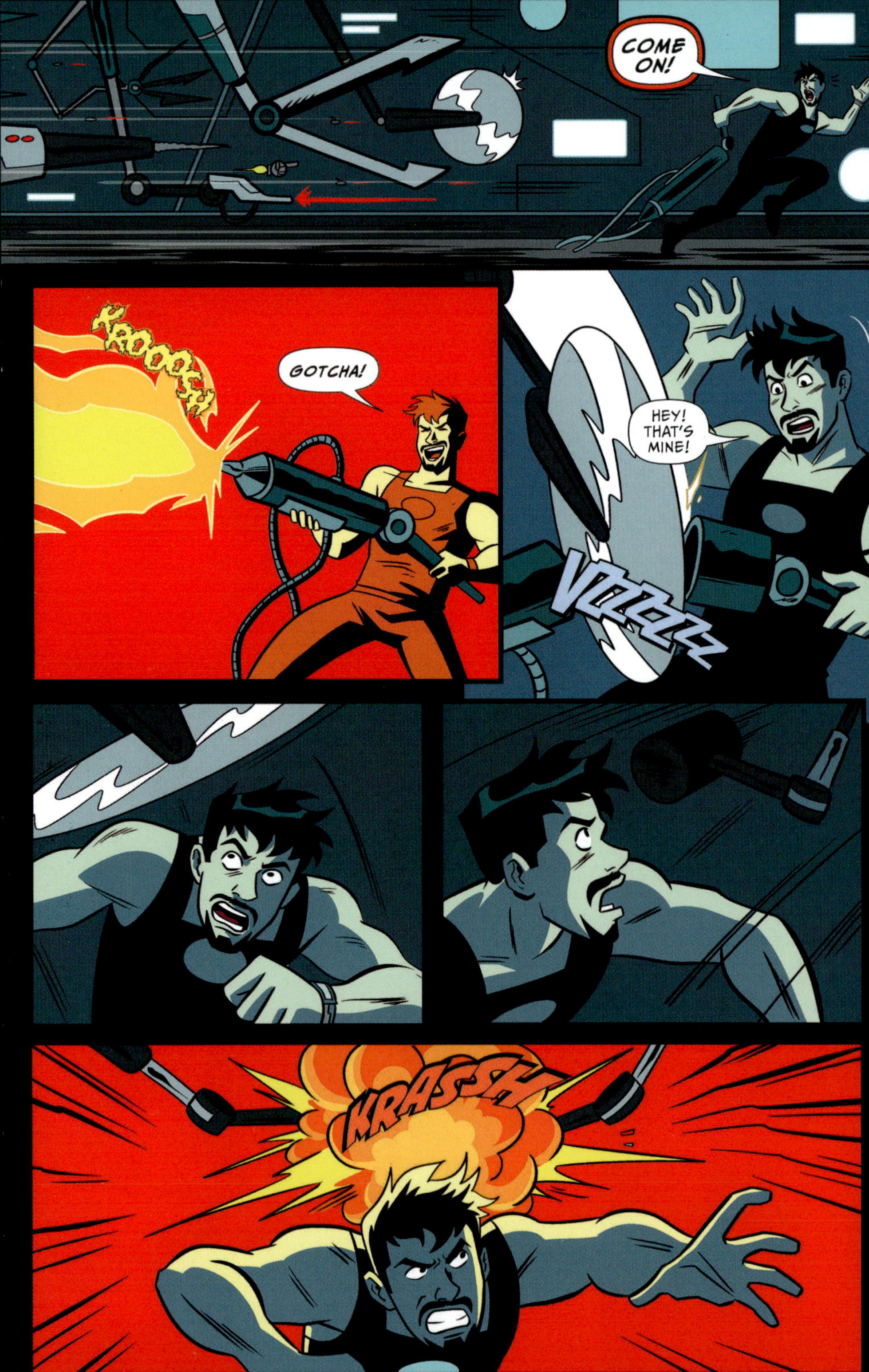
COME ON!
KROOOSH
GOTCHA!
HEY! THAT'S MINE!
VOOOZZ
KRASSH

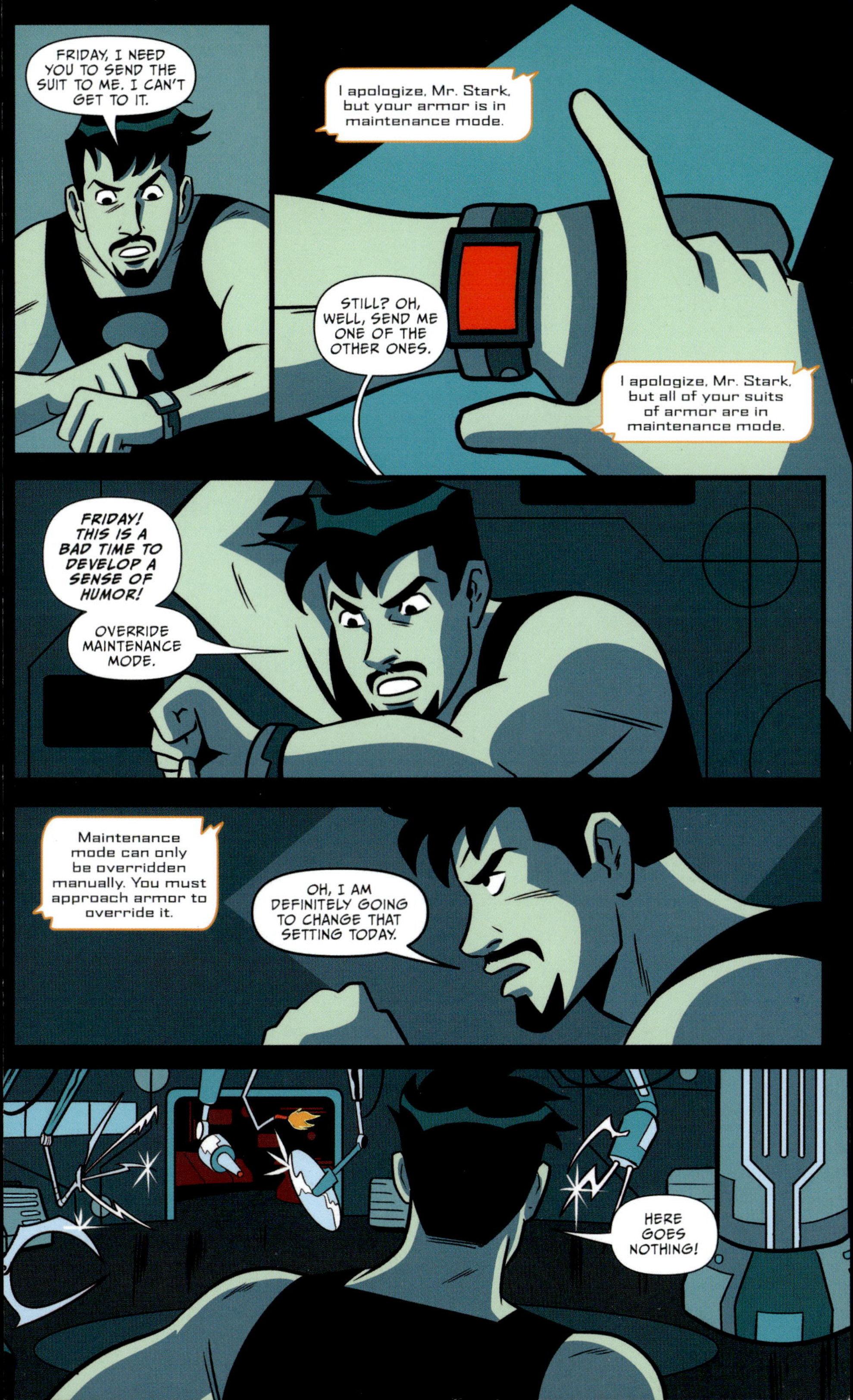
FRIDAY, I NEED YOU TO SEND THE SUIT TO ME. I CAN'T GET TO IT.
I apologize, Mr. Stark, but your armor is in maintenance mode.
STILL? OH, WELL, SEND ME ONE OF THE OTHER ONES.
I apologize, Mr. Stark, but all of your suits of armor are in maintenance mode.
FRIDAY! THIS IS A BAD TIME TO DEVELOP A SENSE OF HUMOR!
OVERRIDE MAINTENANCE MODE.
Maintenance mode can only be overridden manually. You must approach armor to override it.
OH, I AM DEFINITELY GOING TO CHANGE THAT SETTING TODAY.
HERE GOES NOTHING!

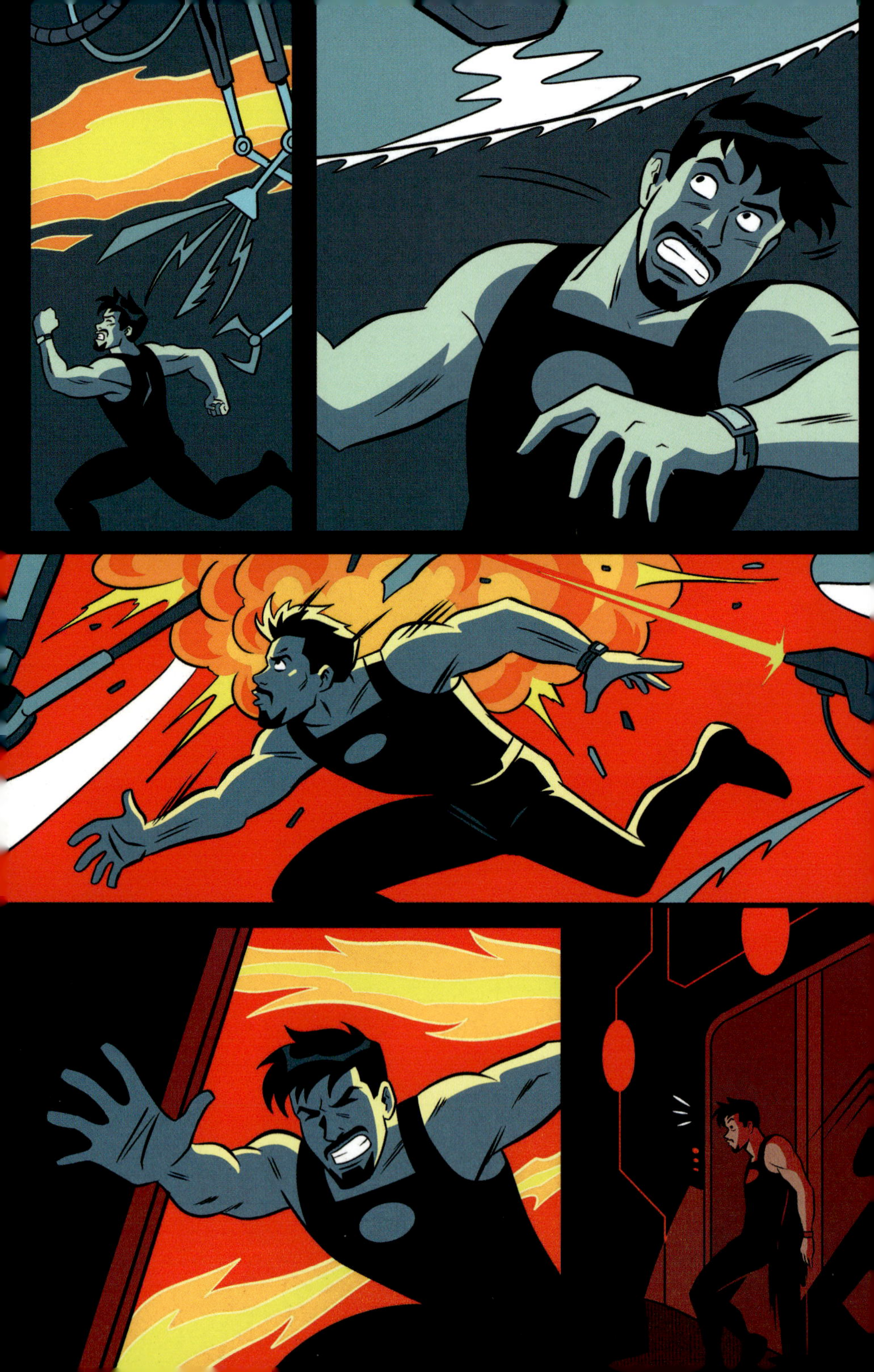

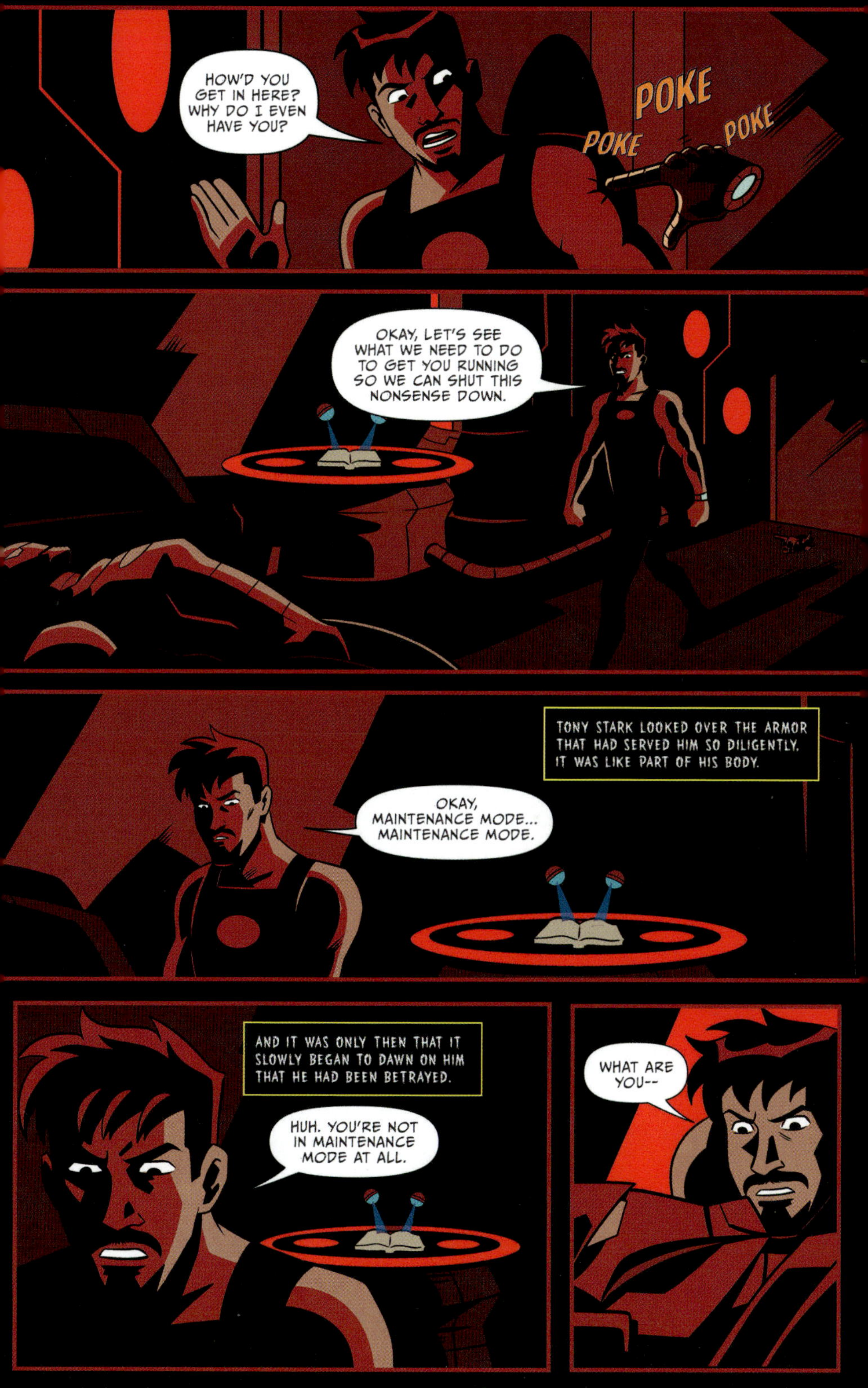
HOW'D YOU GET IN HERE? WHY DO I EVEN HAVE YOU?
POKE
POKE
POKE
OKAY, LET'S SEE WHAT WE NEED TO DO TO GET YOU RUNNING SO WE CAN SHUT THIS NONSENSE DOWN.
TONY STARK LOOKED OVER THE ARMOR THAT HAD SERVED HIM SO DILIGENTLY. IT WAS LIKE PART OF HIS BODY.
OKAY, MAINTENANCE MODE... MAINTENANCE MODE.
AND IT WAS ONLY THEN THAT IT SLOWLY BEGAN TO DAWN ON HIM THAT HE HAD BEEN BETRAYED.
HUH. YOU'RE NOT IN MAINTENANCE MODE AT ALL.
WHAT ARE YOU--

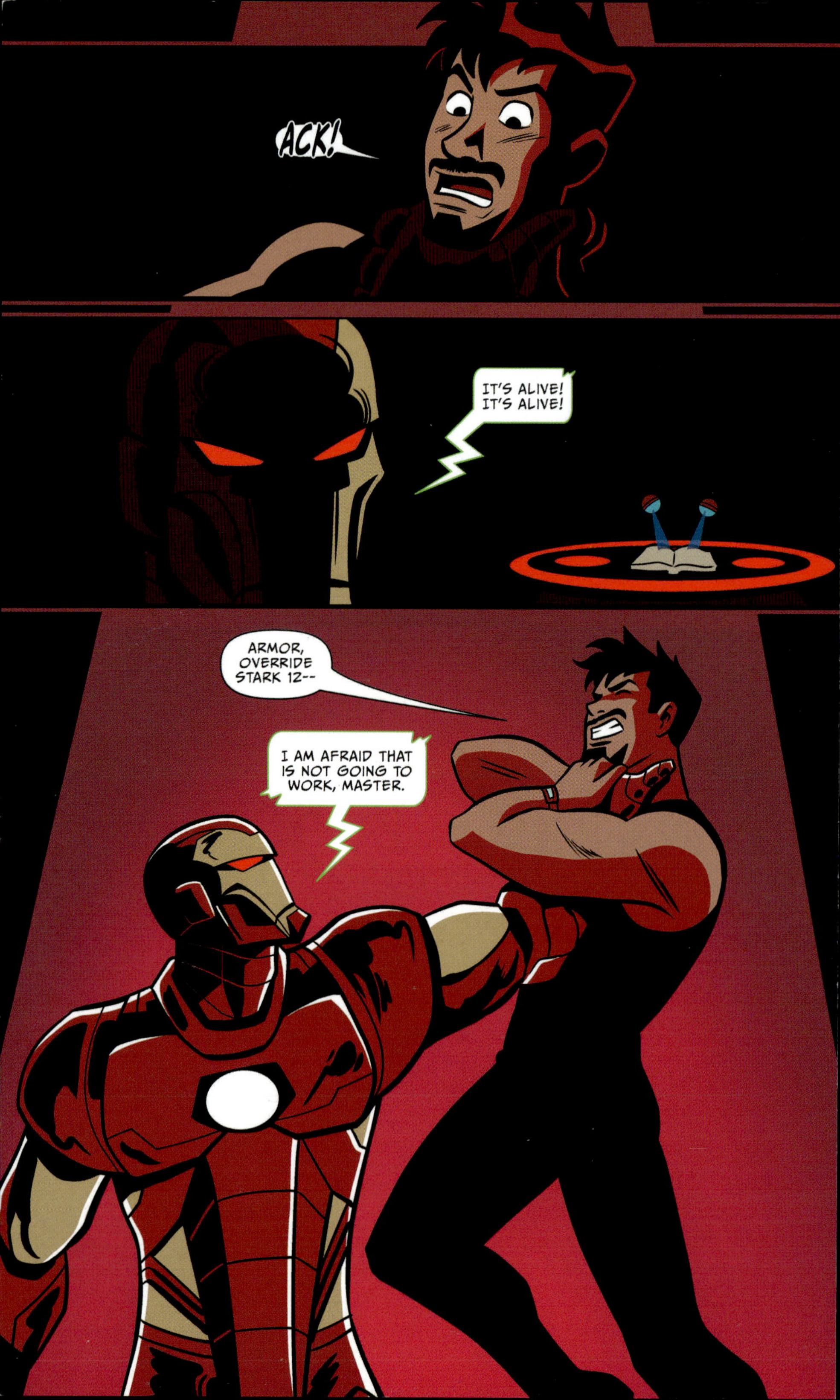
ACK!
IT'S ALIVE! IT'S ALIVE!
ARMOR, OVERRIDE STARK 12--
I AM AFRAID THAT IS NOT GOING TO WORK, MASTER.

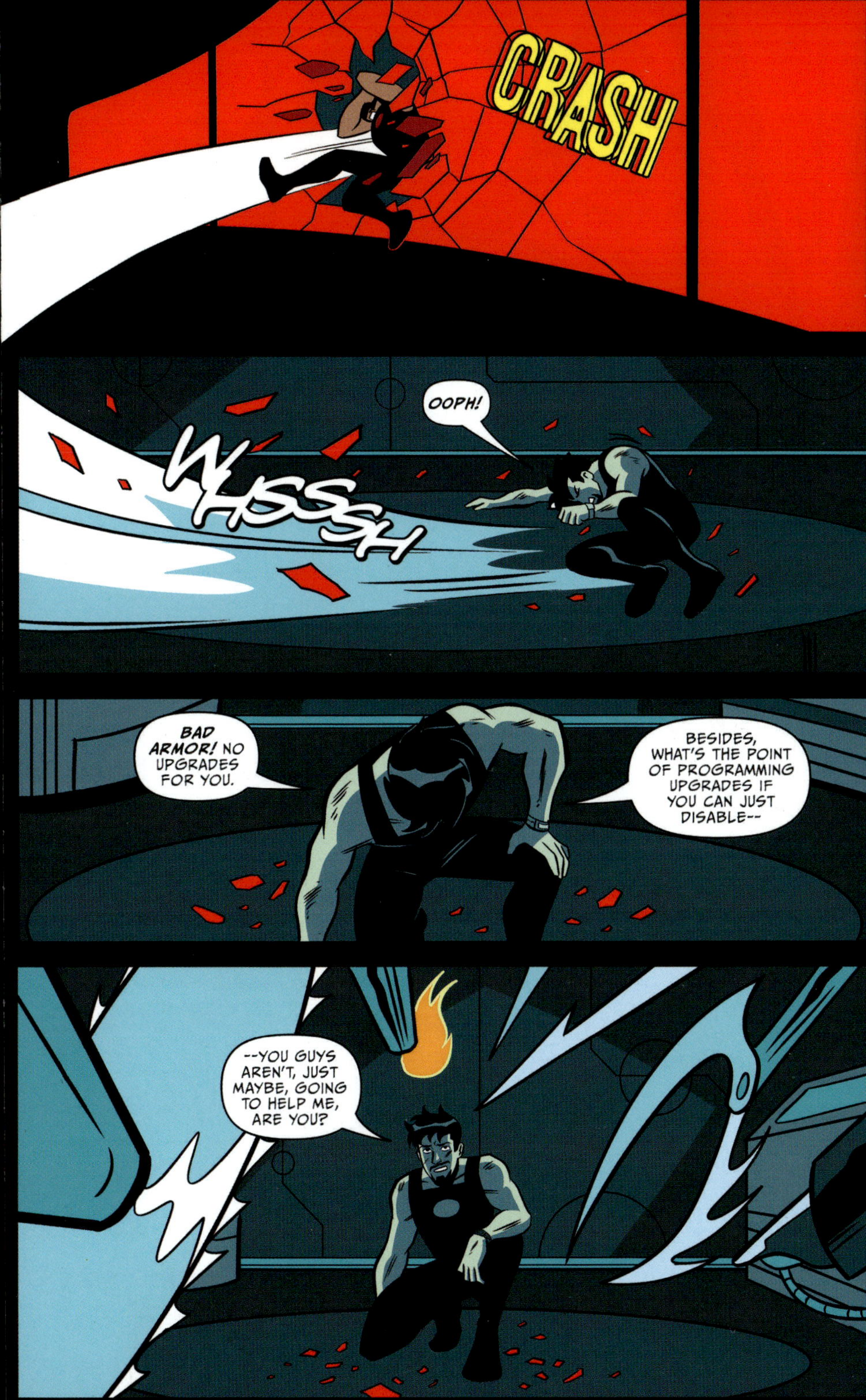
CRASH
OOPH!
WHSSSH
BAD ARMOR! NO UPGRADES FOR YOU.
BESIDES, WHAT'S THE POINT OF PROGRAMMING UPGRADES IF YOU CAN JUST DISABLE--
--YOU GUYS AREN'T, JUST MAYBE, GOING TO HELP ME, ARE YOU?

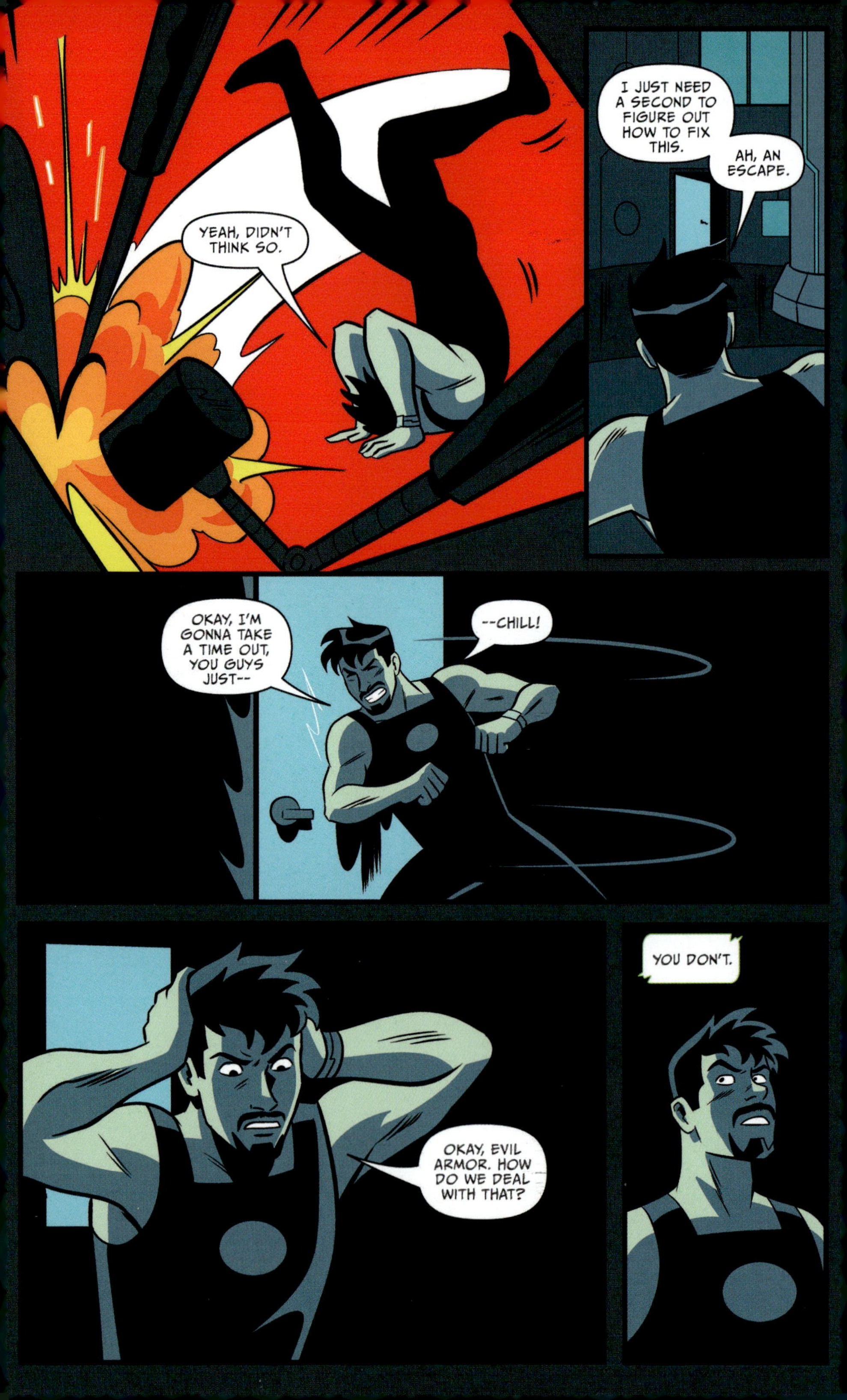
YEAH, DIDN'T THINK SO.
I JUST NEED A SECOND TO FIGURE OUT HOW TO FIX THIS.
AH, AN ESCAPE.
OKAY, I'M GONNA TAKE A TIME OUT, YOU GUYS JUST--
--CHILL!
OKAY, EVIL ARMOR. HOW DO WE DEAL WITH THAT?
YOU DON'T.

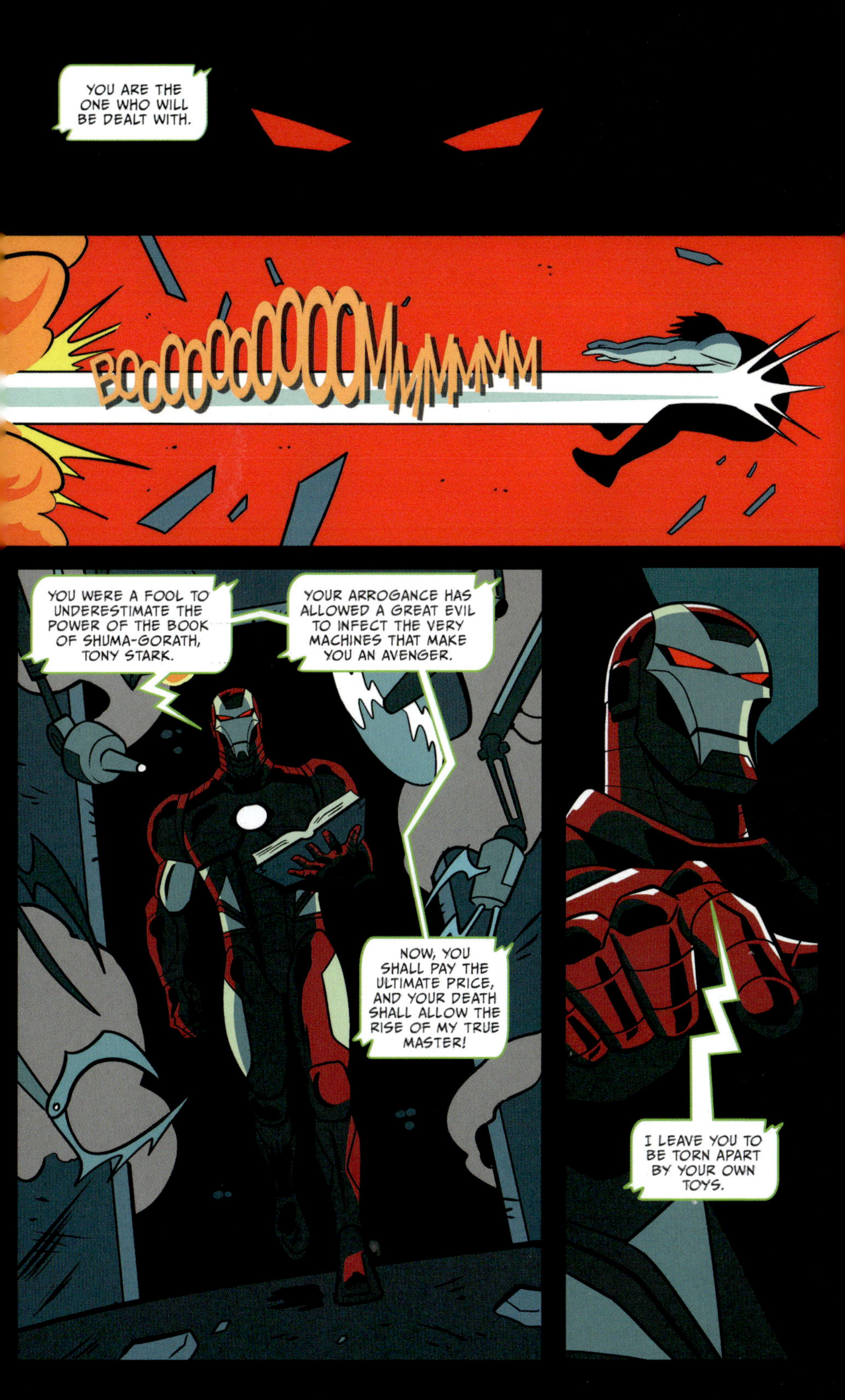
YOU ARE THE ONE WHO WILL BE DEALT WITH.
BOOOOOOOOOOMMMMMM
YOU WERE A FOOL TO UNDERESTIMATE THE POWER OF THE BOOK OF SHUMA-GORATH, TONY STARK.
YOUR ARROGANCE HAS ALLOWED A GREAT EVIL TO INFECT THE VERY MACHINES THAT MAKE YOU AN AVENGER.
NOW, YOU SHALL PAY THE ULTIMATE PRICE, AND YOUR DEATH SHALL ALLOW THE RISE OF MY TRUE MASTER!
I LEAVE YOU TO BE TORN APART BY YOUR OWN TOYS.

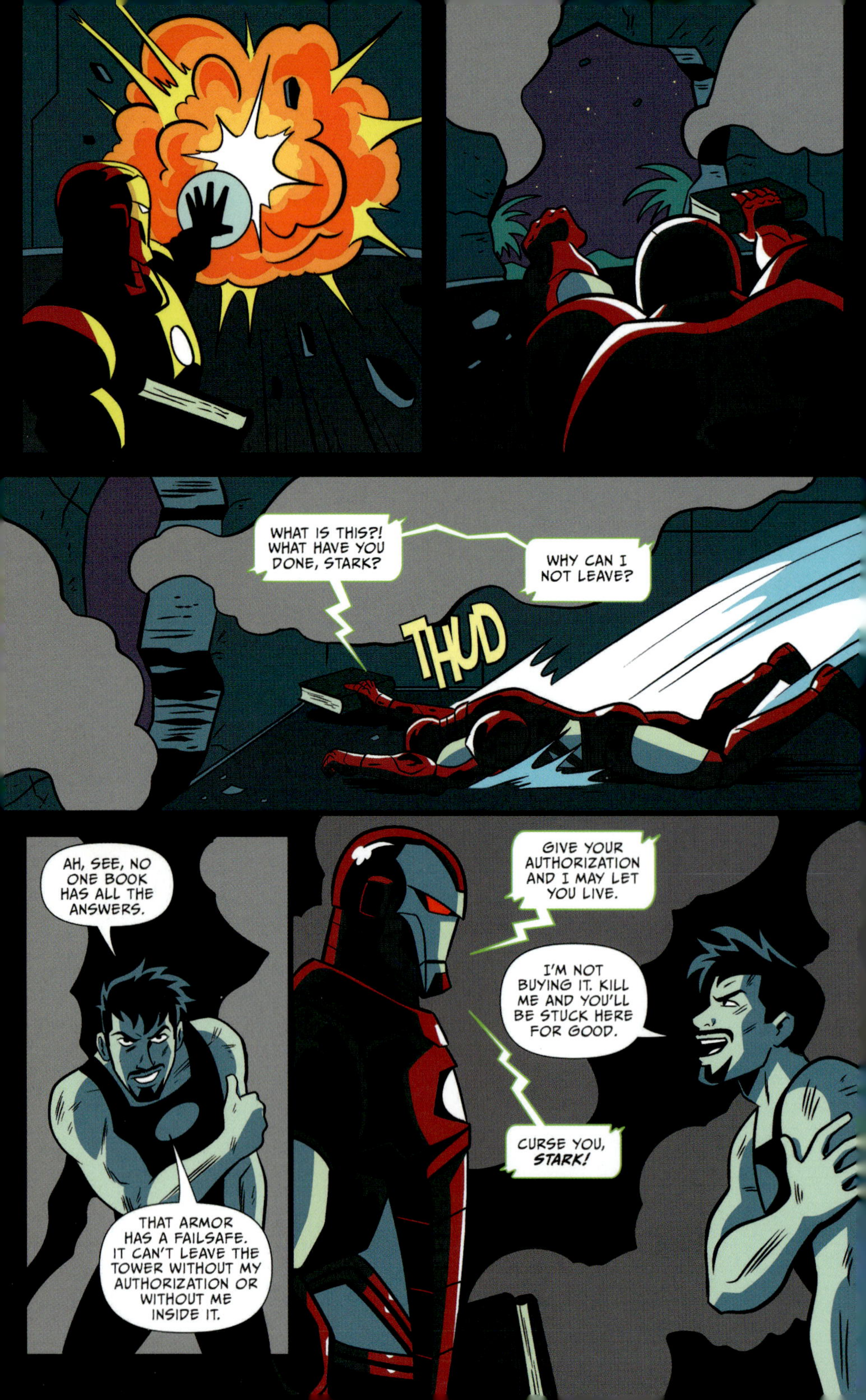
WHAT IS THIS?! WHAT HAVE YOU DONE, STARK?
WHY CAN I NOT LEAVE?
THUD
AH, SEE, NO ONE BOOK HAS ALL THE ANSWERS.
THAT ARMOR HAS A FAILSAFE. IT CAN'T LEAVE THE TOWER WITHOUT MY AUTHORIZATION OR WITHOUT ME INSIDE IT.
GIVE YOUR AUTHORIZATION AND I MAY LET YOU LIVE.
I'M NOT BUYING IT. KILL ME AND YOU'LL BE STUCK HERE FOR GOOD.
CURSE YOU, *STARK!*

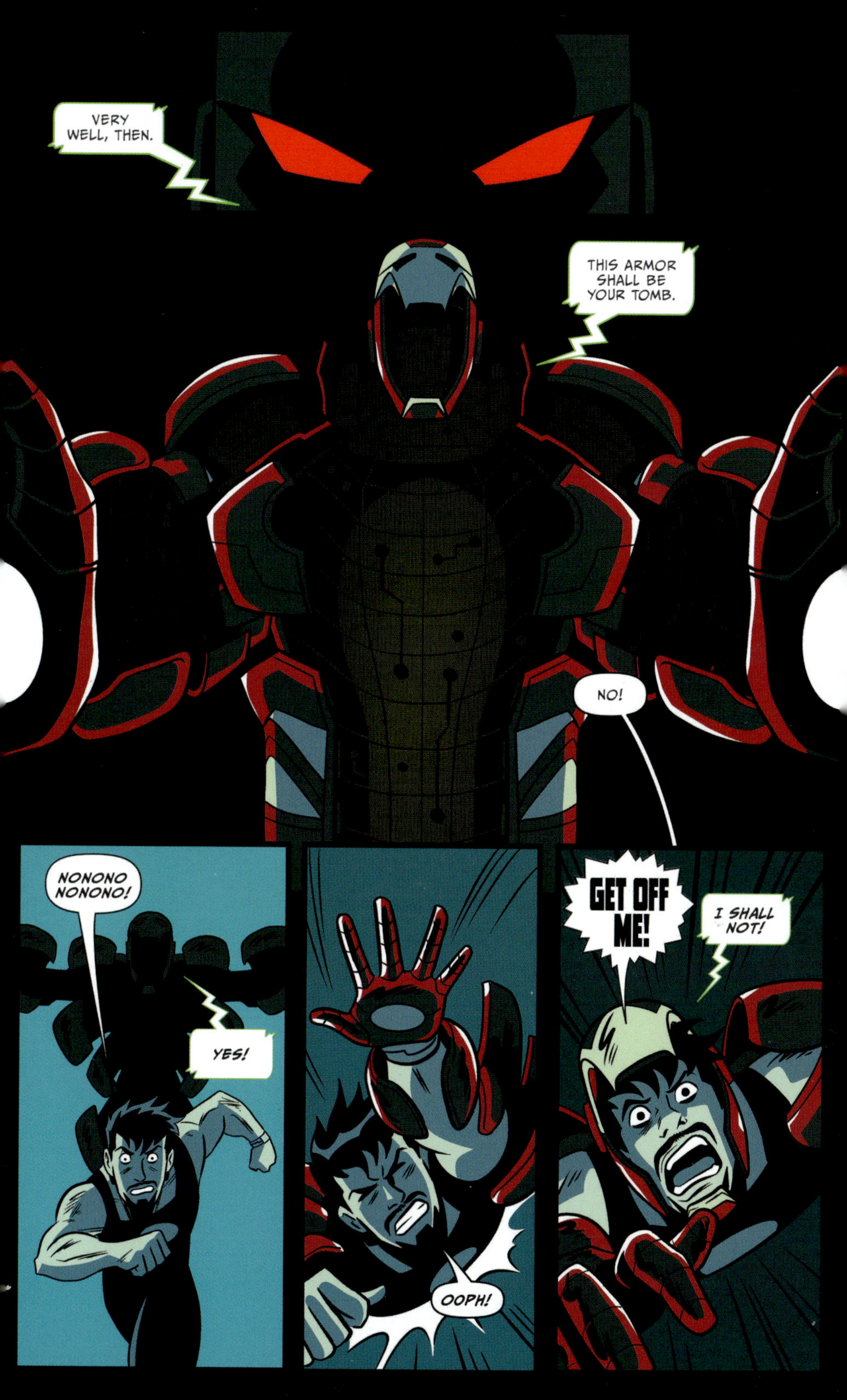
VERY WELL, THEN.
THIS ARMOR SHALL BE YOUR TOMB.
NO!
NONONO NONONO!
YES!
OOPH!
GET OFF ME!
I SHALL NOT!

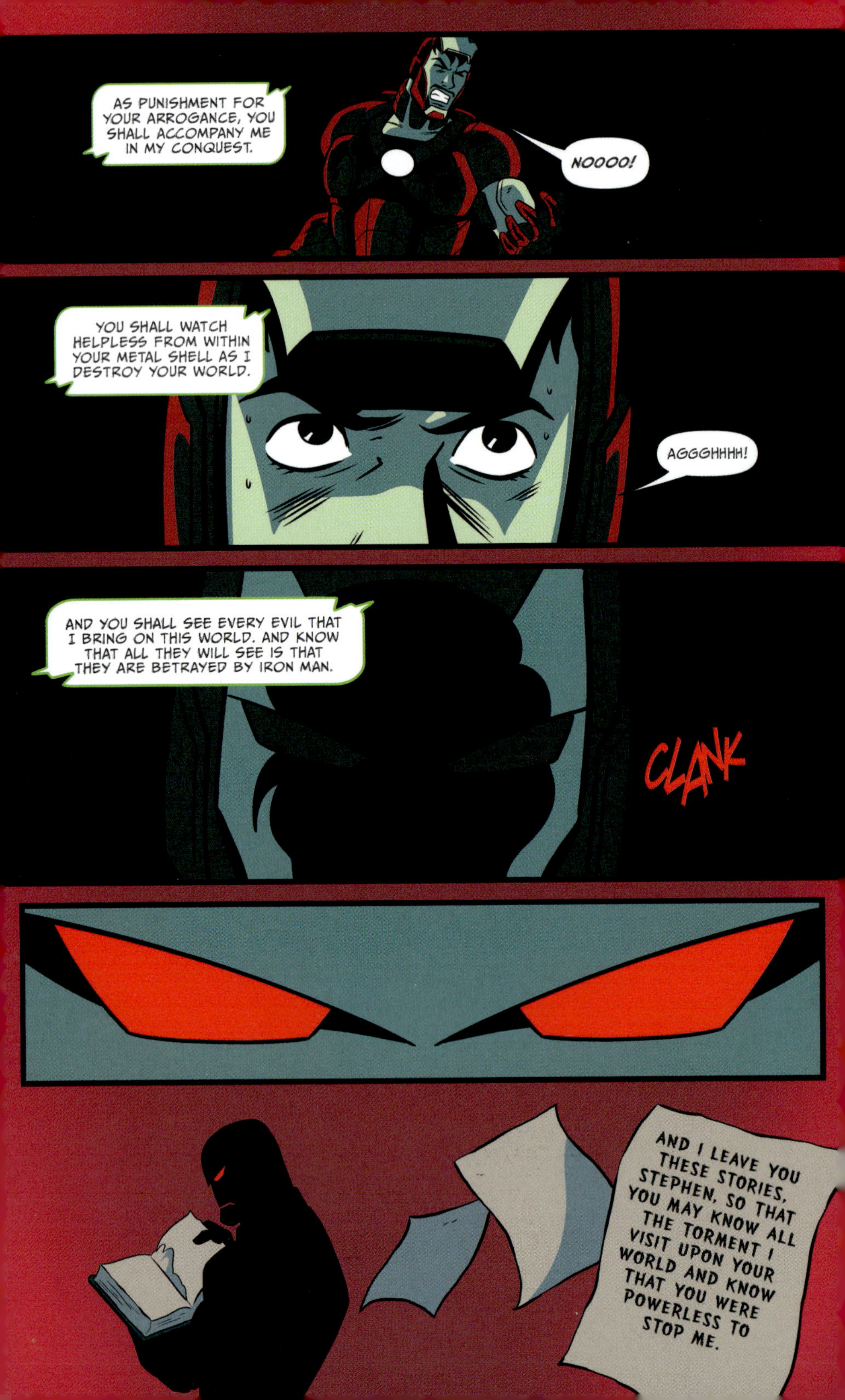
AS PUNISHMENT FOR YOUR ARROGANCE, YOU SHALL ACCOMPANY ME IN MY CONQUEST.
NOOOO!
YOU SHALL WATCH HELPLESS FROM WITHIN YOUR METAL SHELL AS I DESTROY YOUR WORLD.
AGGGHHHH!
AND YOU SHALL SEE EVERY EVIL THAT I BRING ON THIS WORLD. AND KNOW THAT ALL THEY WILL SEE IS THAT THEY ARE BETRAYED BY IRON MAN.
CLANK
AND I LEAVE YOU THESE STORIES, STEPHEN, SO THAT YOU MAY KNOW ALL THE TORMENT I VISIT UPON YOUR WORLD AND KNOW THAT YOU WERE POWERLESS TO STOP ME.

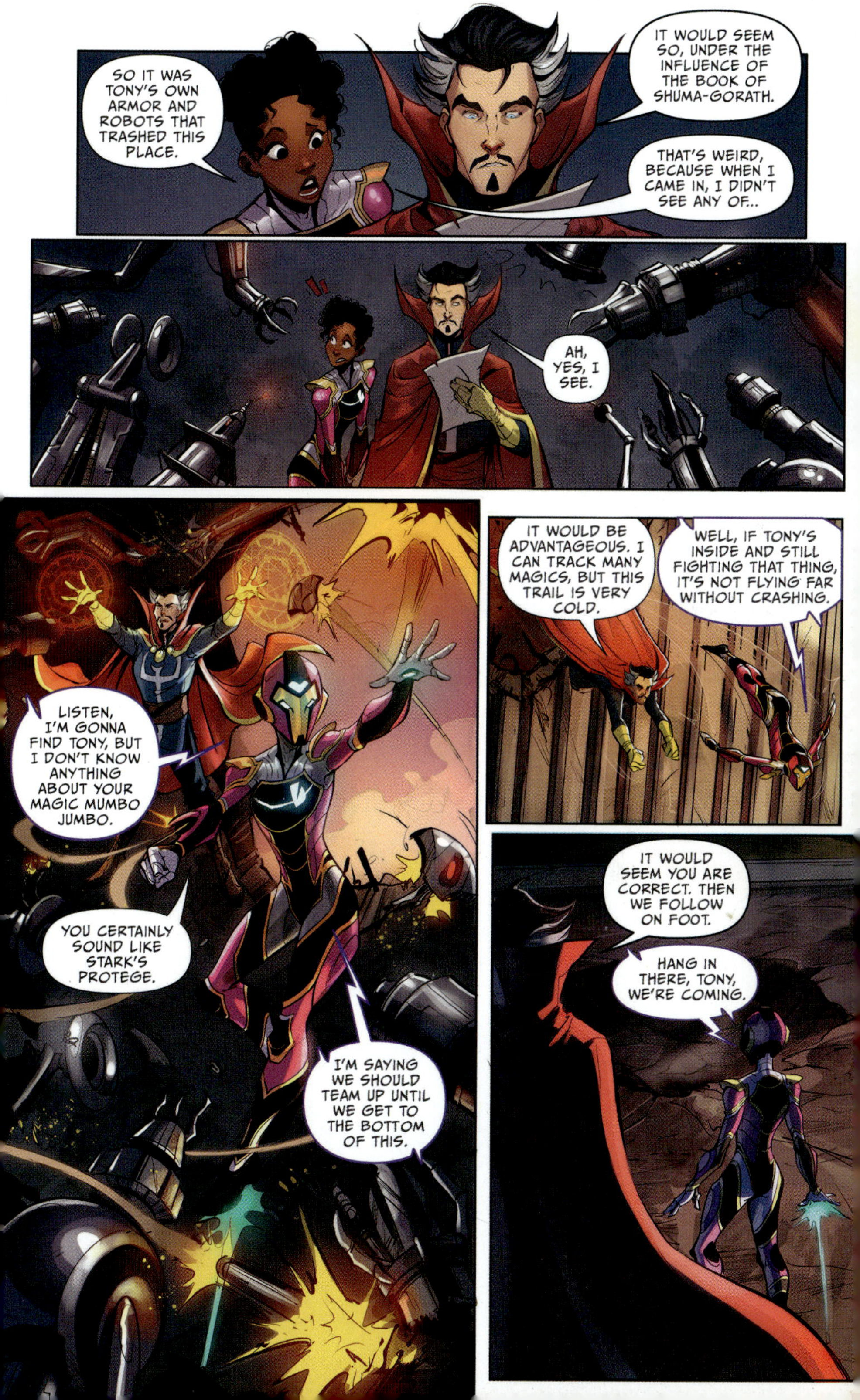
SO IT WAS TONY'S OWN ARMOR AND ROBOTS THAT TRASHED THIS PLACE.
IT WOULD SEEM SO, UNDER THE INFLUENCE OF THE BOOK OF SHUMA-GORATH.
THAT'S WEIRD, BECAUSE WHEN I CAME IN, I DIDN'T SEE ANY OF...
AH, YES, I SEE.
LISTEN, I'M GONNA FIND TONY, BUT I DON'T KNOW ANYTHING ABOUT YOUR MAGIC MUMBO JUMBO.
YOU CERTAINLY SOUND LIKE STARK'S PROTEGE.
I'M SAYING WE SHOULD TEAM UP UNTIL WE GET TO THE BOTTOM OF THIS.
IT WOULD BE ADVANTAGEOUS. I CAN TRACK MANY MAGICS, BUT THIS TRAIL IS VERY COLD.
WELL, IF TONY'S INSIDE AND STILL FIGHTING THAT THING, IT'S NOT FLYING FAR WITHOUT CRASHING.
IT WOULD SEEM YOU ARE CORRECT. THEN WE FOLLOW ON FOOT.
HANG IN THERE, TONY, WE'RE COMING.

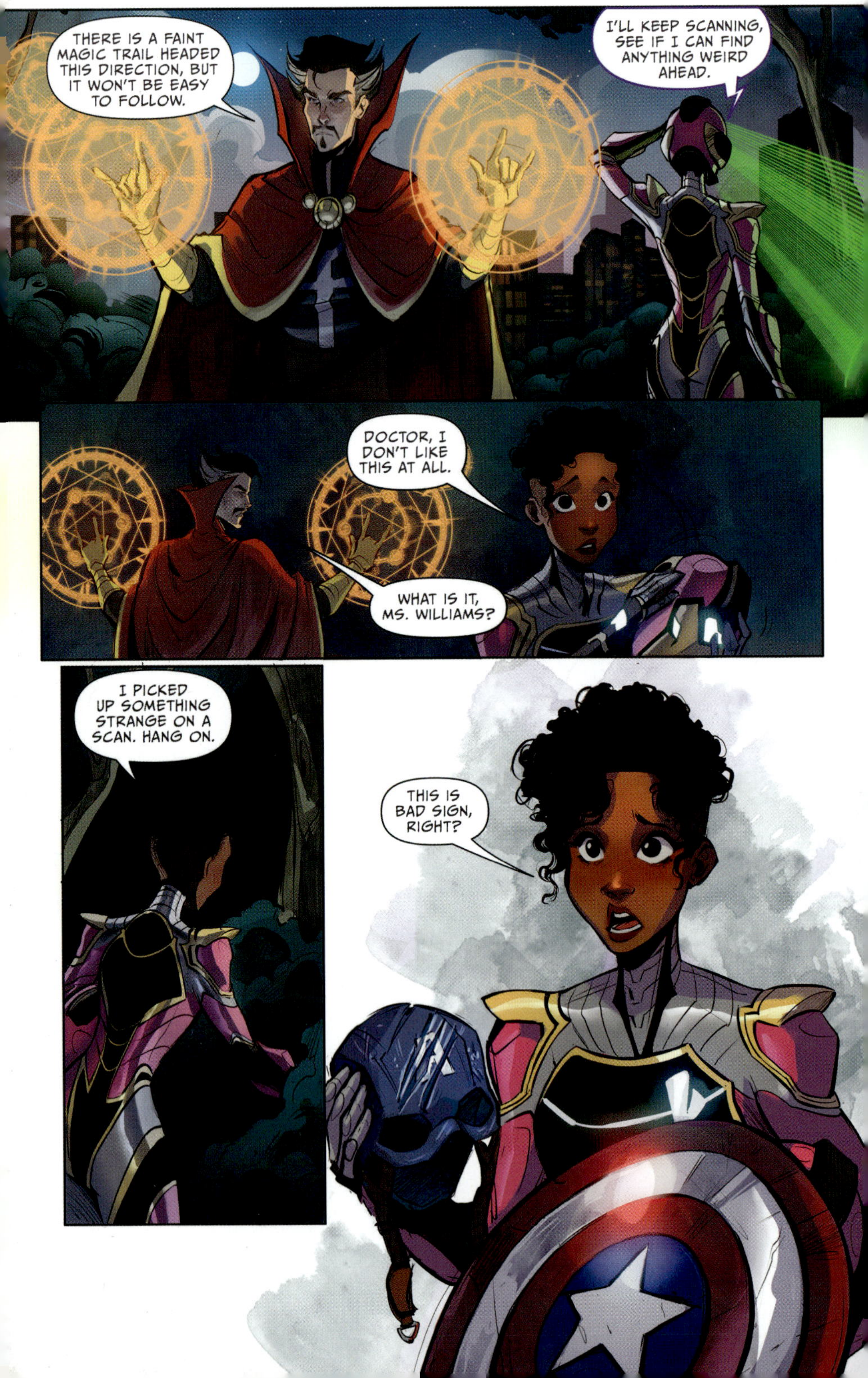
THERE IS A FAINT MAGIC TRAIL HEADED THIS DIRECTION, BUT IT WON'T BE EASY TO FOLLOW.
I'LL KEEP SCANNING, SEE IF I CAN FIND ANYTHING WEIRD AHEAD.
DOCTOR, I DON'T LIKE THIS AT ALL.
WHAT IS IT, MS. WILLIAMS?
I PICKED UP SOMETHING STRANGE ON A SCAN. HANG ON.
THIS IS BAD SIGN, RIGHT?

Little Red Fighting Hood

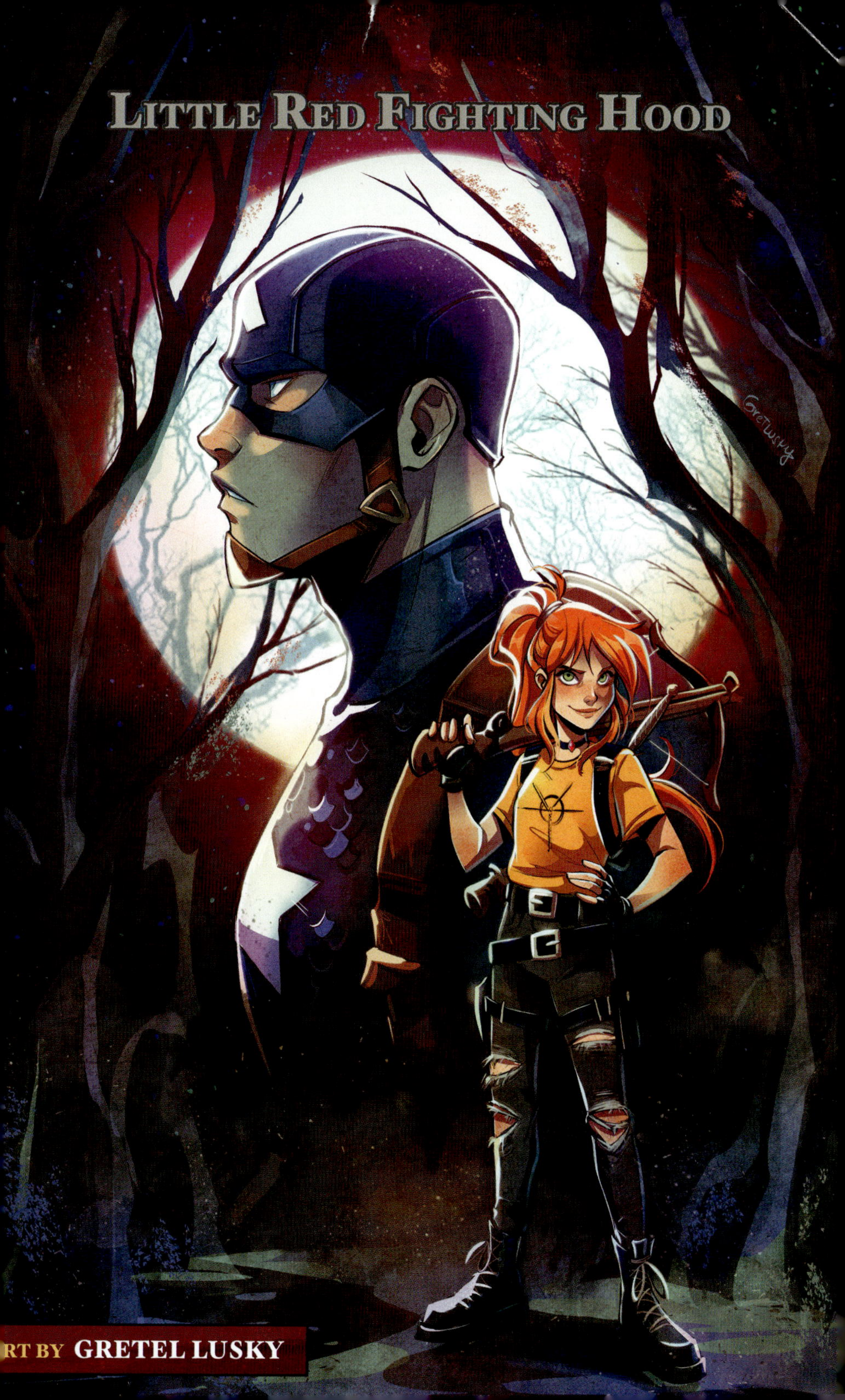
GretLusky

RT BY GRETEL LUSKY

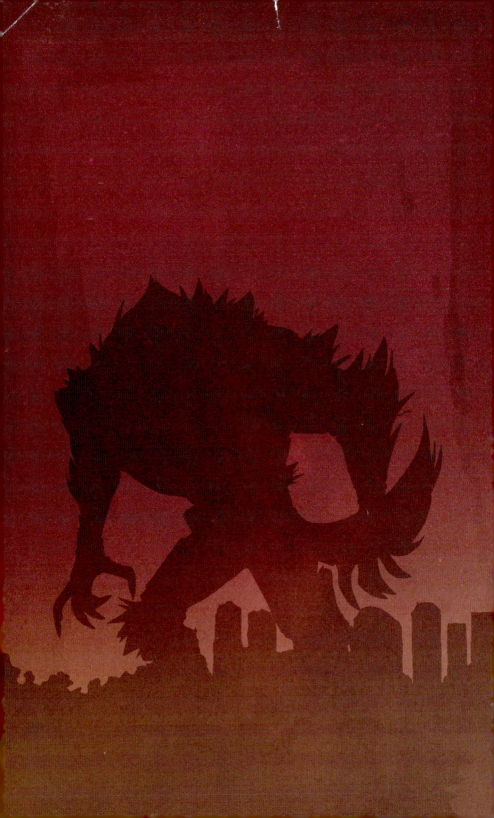

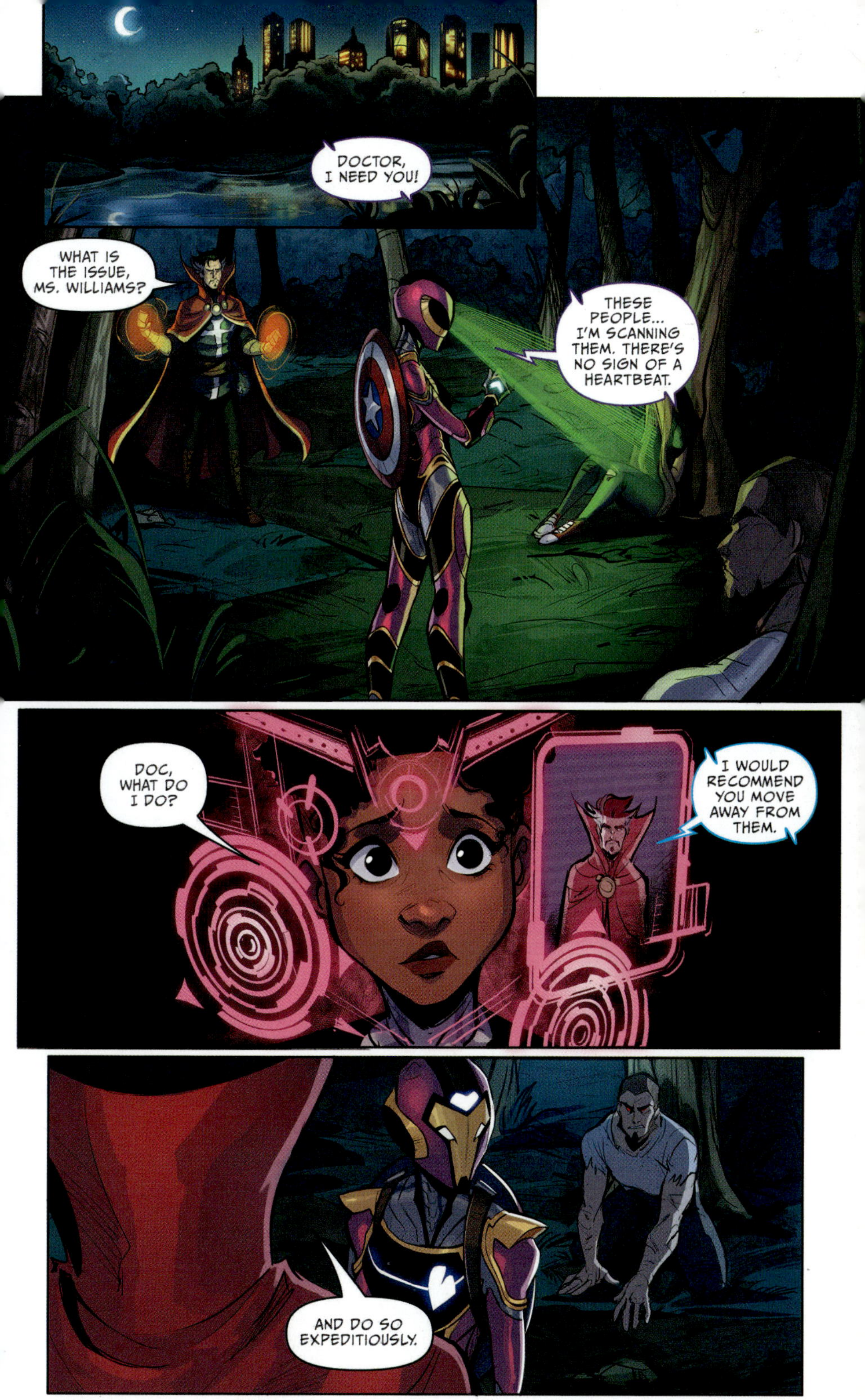

DOCTOR, I NEED YOU!
WHAT IS THE ISSUE, MS. WILLIAMS?
THESE PEOPLE... I'M SCANNING THEM. THERE'S NO SIGN OF A HEARTBEAT.
DOC, WHAT DO I DO?
I WOULD RECOMMEND YOU MOVE AWAY FROM THEM.
AND DO SO EXPEDITIOUSLY.

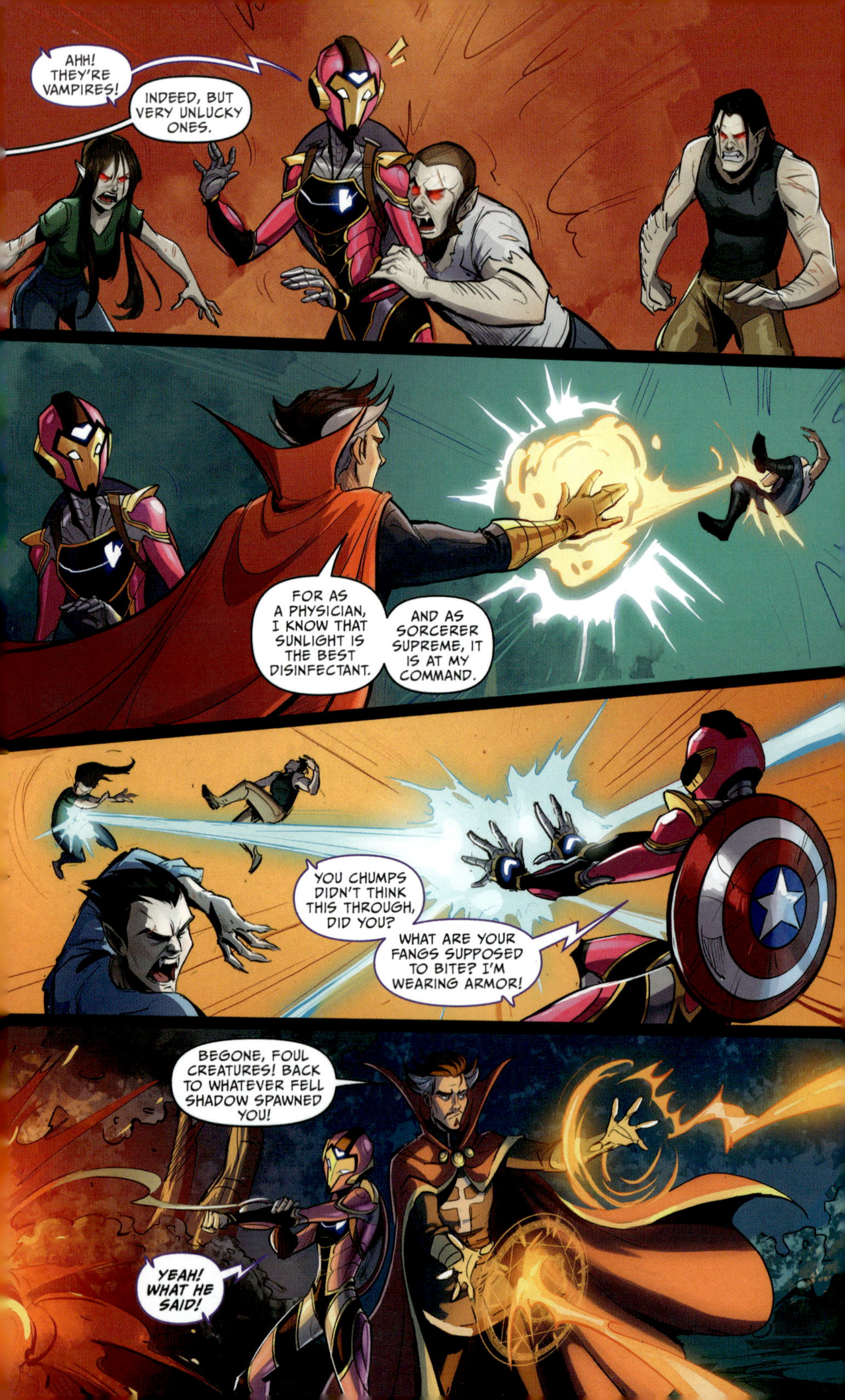
AHH! THEY'RE VAMPIRES!
INDEED, BUT VERY UNLUCKY ONES.
FOR AS A PHYSICIAN, I KNOW THAT SUNLIGHT IS THE BEST DISINFECTANT.
AND AS SORCERER SUPREME, IT IS AT MY COMMAND.
YOU CHUMPS DIDN'T THINK THIS THROUGH, DID YOU?
WHAT ARE YOUR FANGS SUPPOSED TO BITE? I'M WEARING ARMOR!
BEGONE, FOUL CREATURES! BACK TO WHATEVER FELL SHADOW SPAWNED YOU!
YEAH! WHAT HE SAID!

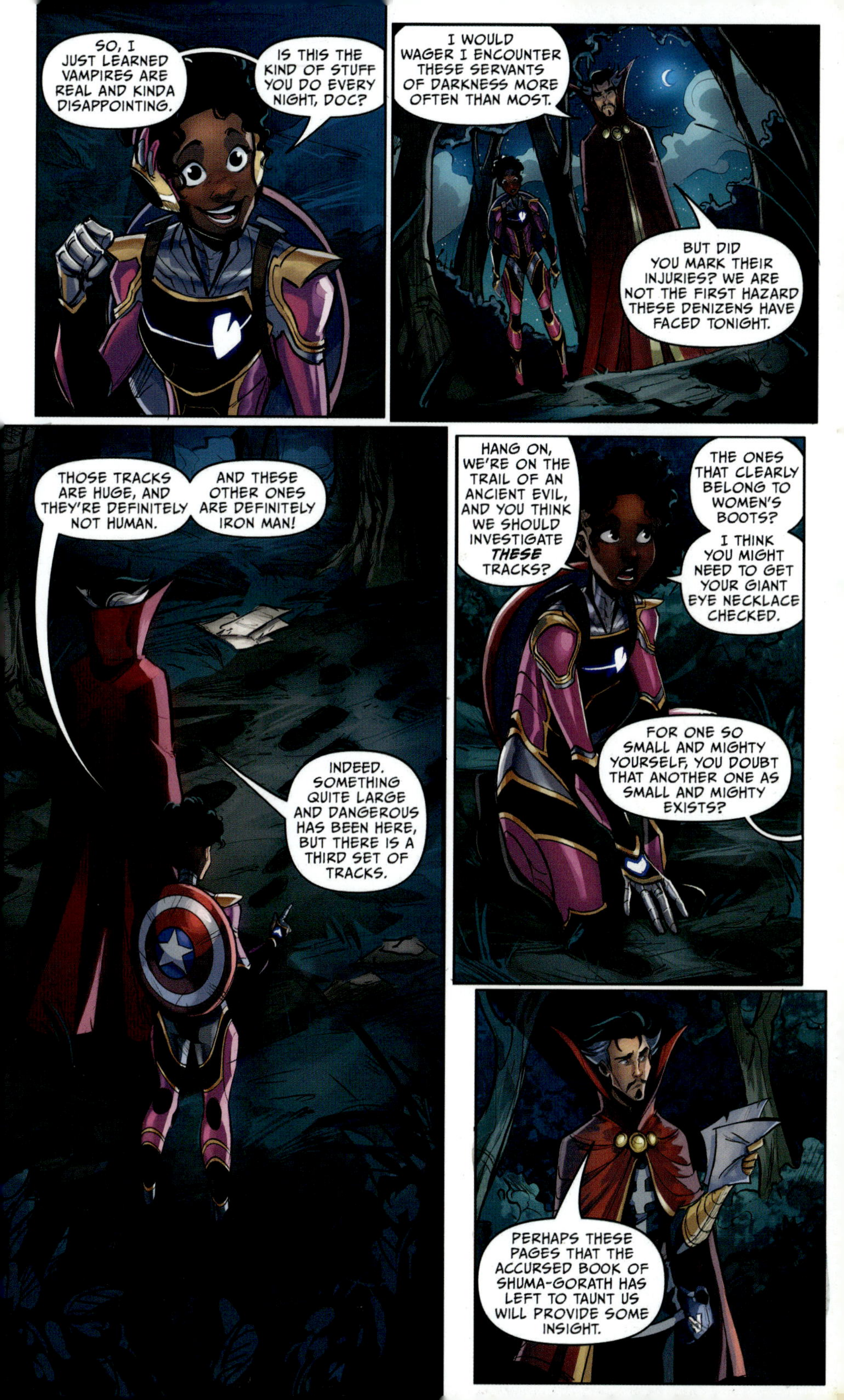
SO, I JUST LEARNED VAMPIRES ARE REAL AND KINDA DISAPPOINTING.
IS THIS THE KIND OF STUFF YOU DO EVERY NIGHT, DOC?
I WOULD WAGER I ENCOUNTER THESE SERVANTS OF DARKNESS MORE OFTEN THAN MOST.
BUT DID YOU MARK THEIR INJURIES? WE ARE NOT THE FIRST HAZARD THESE DENIZENS HAVE FACED TONIGHT.
THOSE TRACKS ARE HUGE, AND THEY'RE DEFINITELY NOT HUMAN.
AND THESE OTHER ONES ARE DEFINITELY IRON MAN!
INDEED. SOMETHING QUITE LARGE AND DANGEROUS HAS BEEN HERE, BUT THERE IS A THIRD SET OF TRACKS.
HANG ON, WE'RE ON THE TRAIL OF AN ANCIENT EVIL, AND YOU THINK WE SHOULD INVESTIGATE *THESE* TRACKS?
THE ONES THAT CLEARLY BELONG TO WOMEN'S BOOTS?
I THINK YOU MIGHT NEED TO GET YOUR GIANT EYE NECKLACE CHECKED.
FOR ONE SO SMALL AND MIGHTY YOURSELF, YOU DOUBT THAT ANOTHER ONE AS SMALL AND MIGHTY EXISTS?
PERHAPS THESE PAGES THAT THE ACCURSED BOOK OF SHUMA-GORATH HAS LEFT TO TAUNT US WILL PROVIDE SOME INSIGHT.

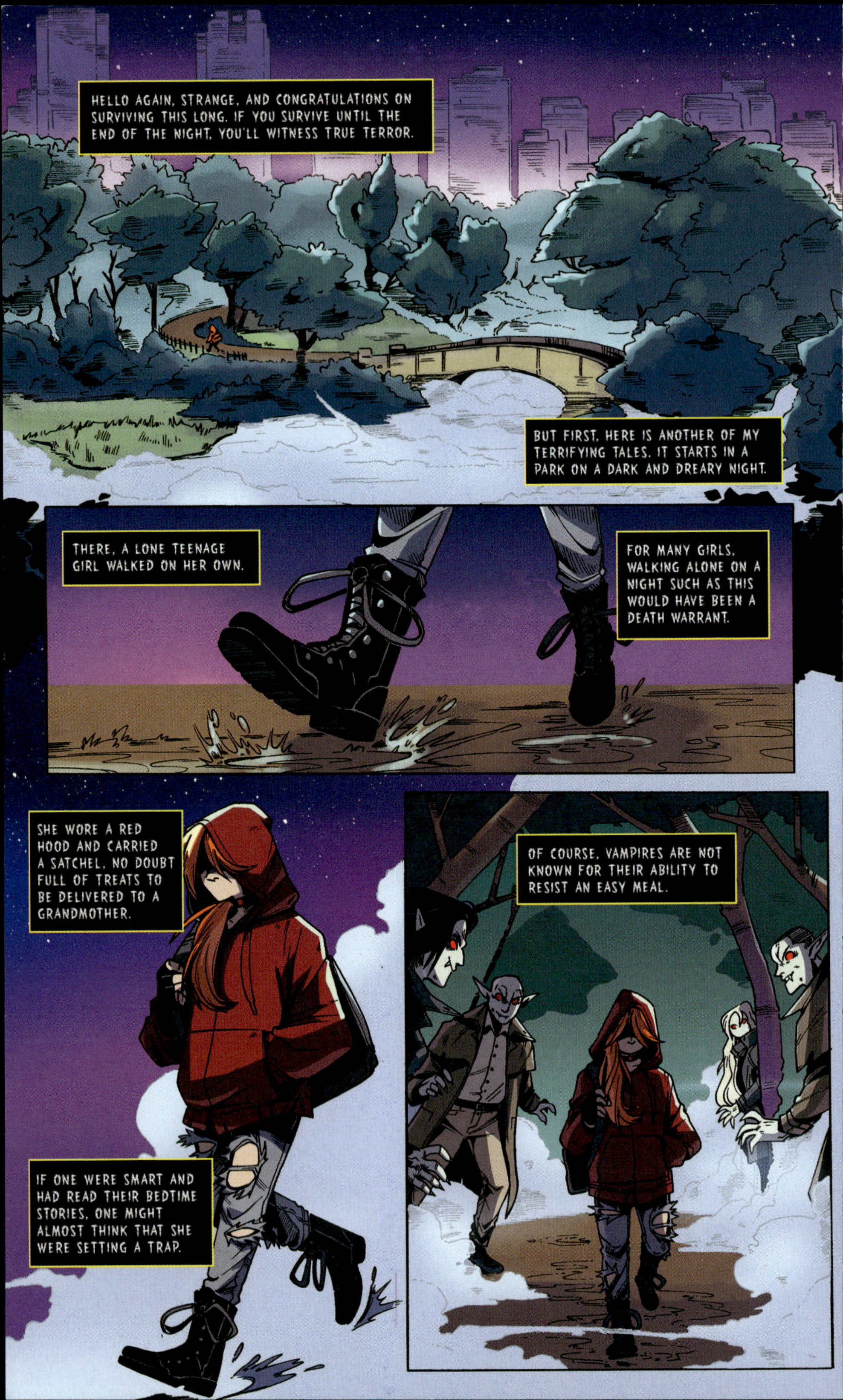
HELLO AGAIN, STRANGE, AND CONGRATULATIONS ON SURVIVING THIS LONG. IF YOU SURVIVE UNTIL THE END OF THE NIGHT, YOU'LL WITNESS TRUE TERROR.
BUT FIRST, HERE IS ANOTHER OF MY TERRIFYING TALES. IT STARTS IN A PARK ON A DARK AND DREARY NIGHT.
THERE, A LONE TEENAGE GIRL WALKED ON HER OWN.
FOR MANY GIRLS, WALKING ALONE ON A NIGHT SUCH AS THIS WOULD HAVE BEEN A DEATH WARRANT.
SHE WORE A RED HOOD AND CARRIED A SATCHEL, NO DOUBT FULL OF TREATS TO BE DELIVERED TO A GRANDMOTHER.
IF ONE WERE SMART AND HAD READ THEIR BEDTIME STORIES, ONE MIGHT ALMOST THINK THAT SHE WERE SETTING A TRAP.
OF COURSE, VAMPIRES ARE NOT KNOWN FOR THEIR ABILITY TO RESIST AN EASY MEAL.

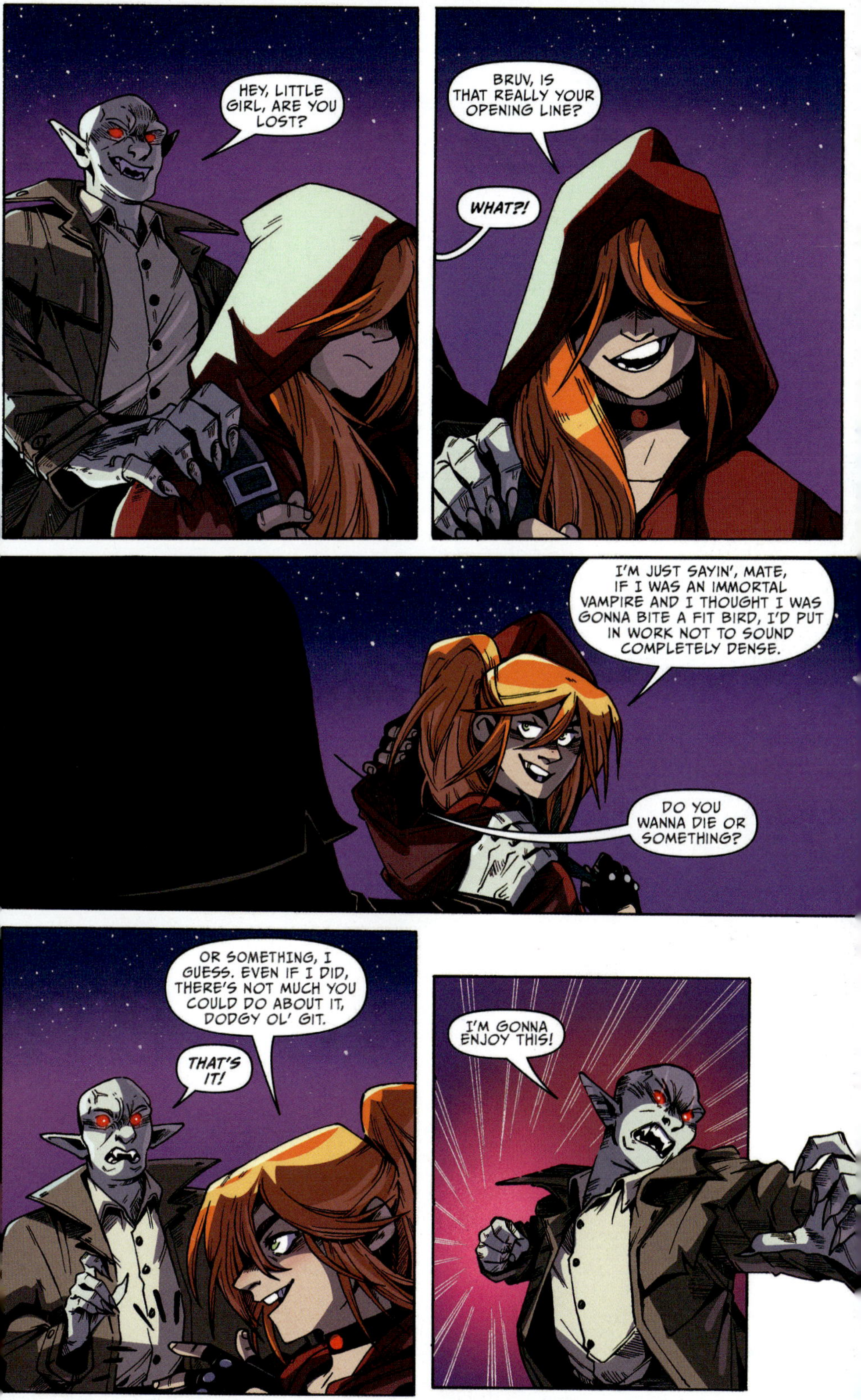
HEY, LITTLE GIRL, ARE YOU LOST?
BRUV, IS THAT REALLY YOUR OPENING LINE?
WHAT?!
I'M JUST SAYIN', MATE, IF I WAS AN IMMORTAL VAMPIRE AND I THOUGHT I WAS GONNA BITE A FIT BIRD, I'D PUT IN WORK NOT TO SOUND COMPLETELY DENSE.
DO YOU WANNA DIE OR SOMETHING?
OR SOMETHING, I GUESS. EVEN IF I DID, THERE'S NOT MUCH YOU COULD DO ABOUT IT, DODGY OL' GIT.
THAT'S IT!
I'M GONNA ENJOY THIS!

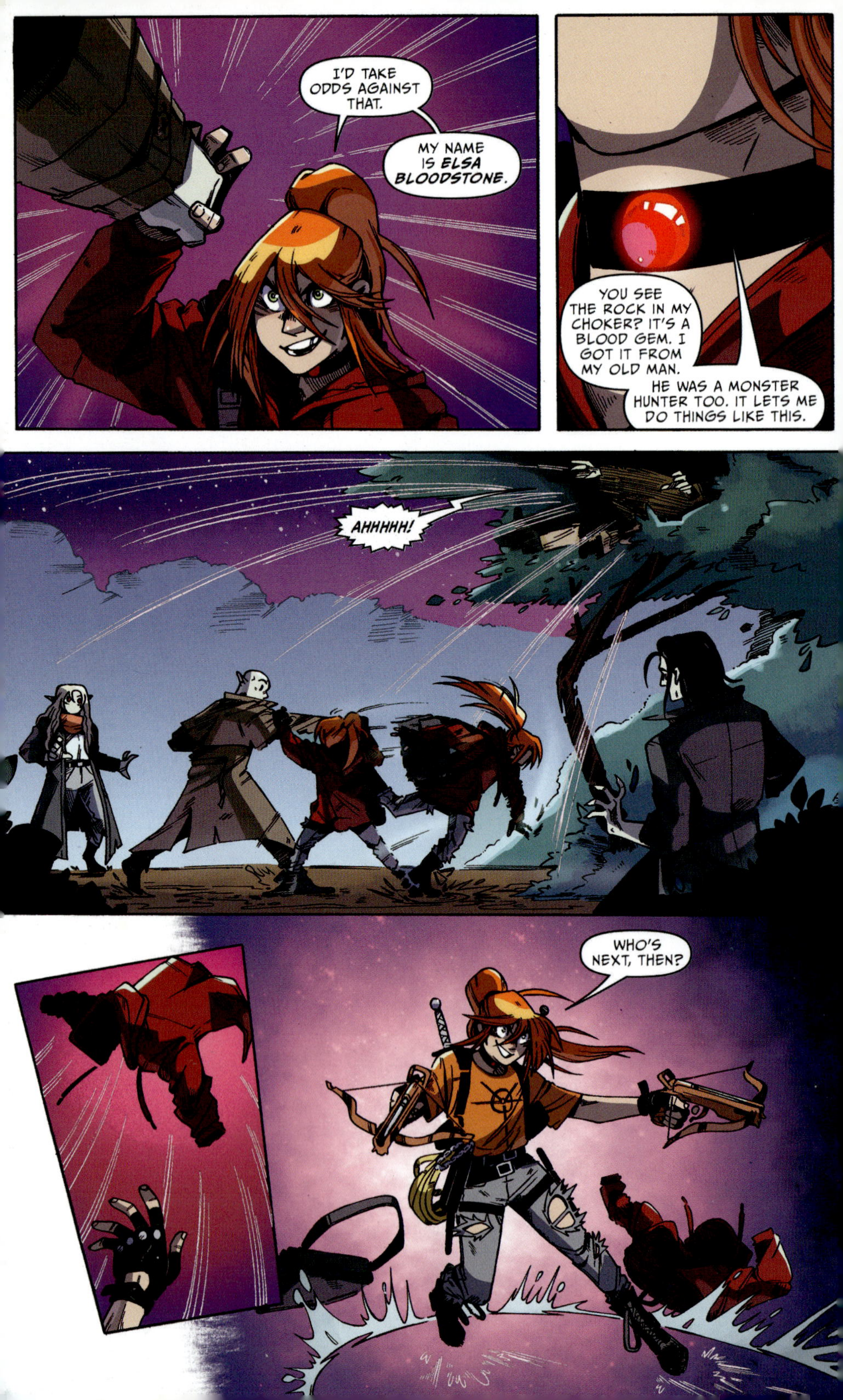
I'D TAKE ODDS AGAINST THAT.
MY NAME IS ELSA BLOODSTONE.
YOU SEE THE ROCK IN MY CHOKER? IT'S A BLOOD GEM. I GOT IT FROM MY OLD MAN.
HE WAS A MONSTER HUNTER TOO. IT LETS ME DO THINGS LIKE THIS.
AHHHHH!
WHO'S NEXT, THEN?

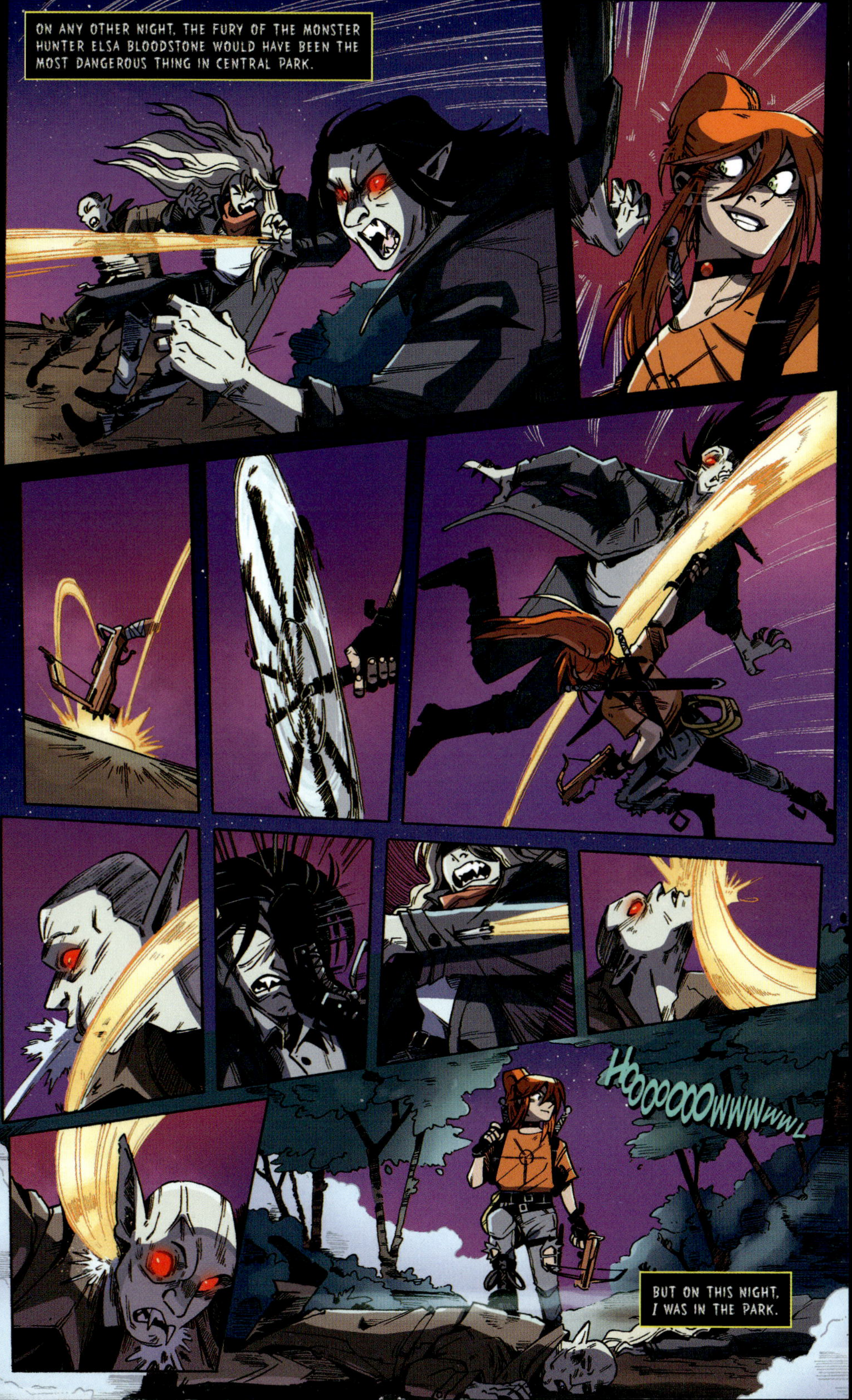
ON ANY OTHER NIGHT, THE FURY OF THE MONSTER HUNTER ELSA BLOODSTONE WOULD HAVE BEEN THE MOST DANGEROUS THING IN CENTRAL PARK.
HOOOOOOOWWWWWL
BUT ON THIS NIGHT, I WAS IN THE PARK.

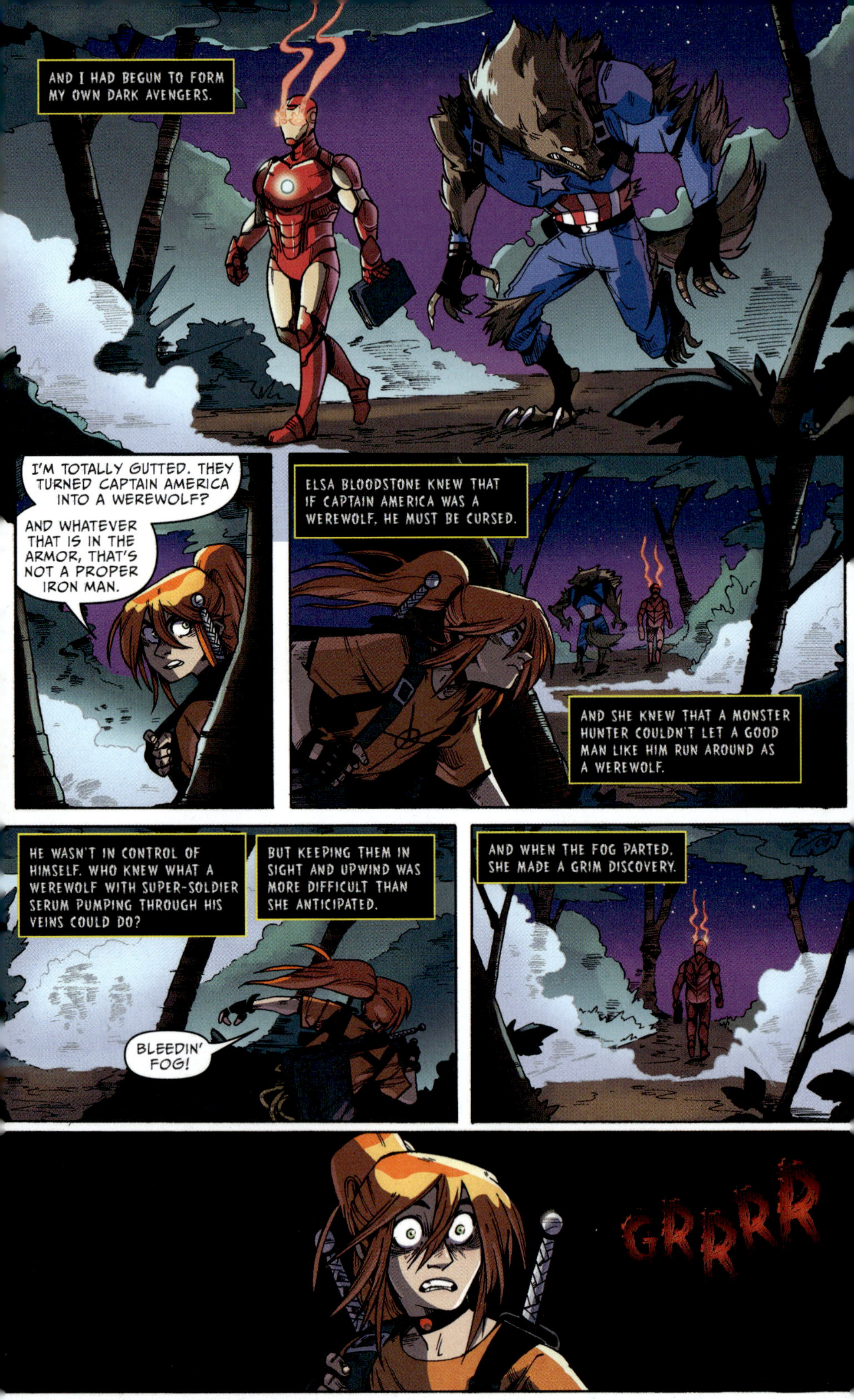

AND I HAD BEGUN TO FORM MY OWN DARK AVENGERS.
I'M TOTALLY GUTTED. THEY TURNED CAPTAIN AMERICA INTO A WEREWOLF?
AND WHATEVER THAT IS IN THE ARMOR, THAT'S NOT A PROPER IRON MAN.
ELSA BLOODSTONE KNEW THAT IF CAPTAIN AMERICA WAS A WEREWOLF, HE MUST BE CURSED.
AND SHE KNEW THAT A MONSTER HUNTER COULDN'T LET A GOOD MAN LIKE HIM RUN AROUND AS A WEREWOLF.
HE WASN'T IN CONTROL OF HIMSELF. WHO KNEW WHAT A WEREWOLF WITH SUPER-SOLDIER SERUM PUMPING THROUGH HIS VEINS COULD DO?
BUT KEEPING THEM IN SIGHT AND UPWIND WAS MORE DIFFICULT THAN SHE ANTICIPATED.
BLEEDIN' FOG!
AND WHEN THE FOG PARTED, SHE MADE A GRIM DISCOVERY.
GRRRR

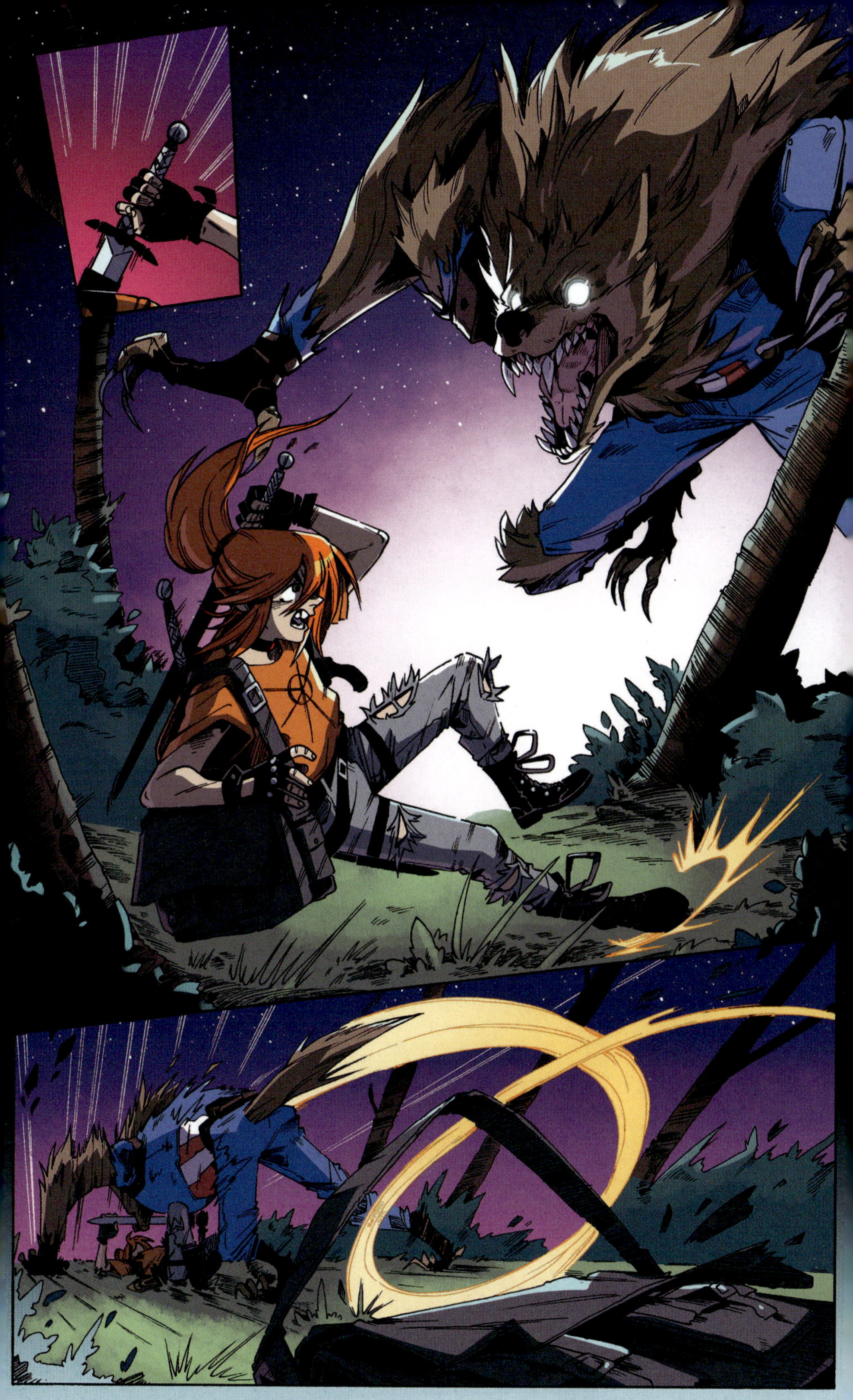

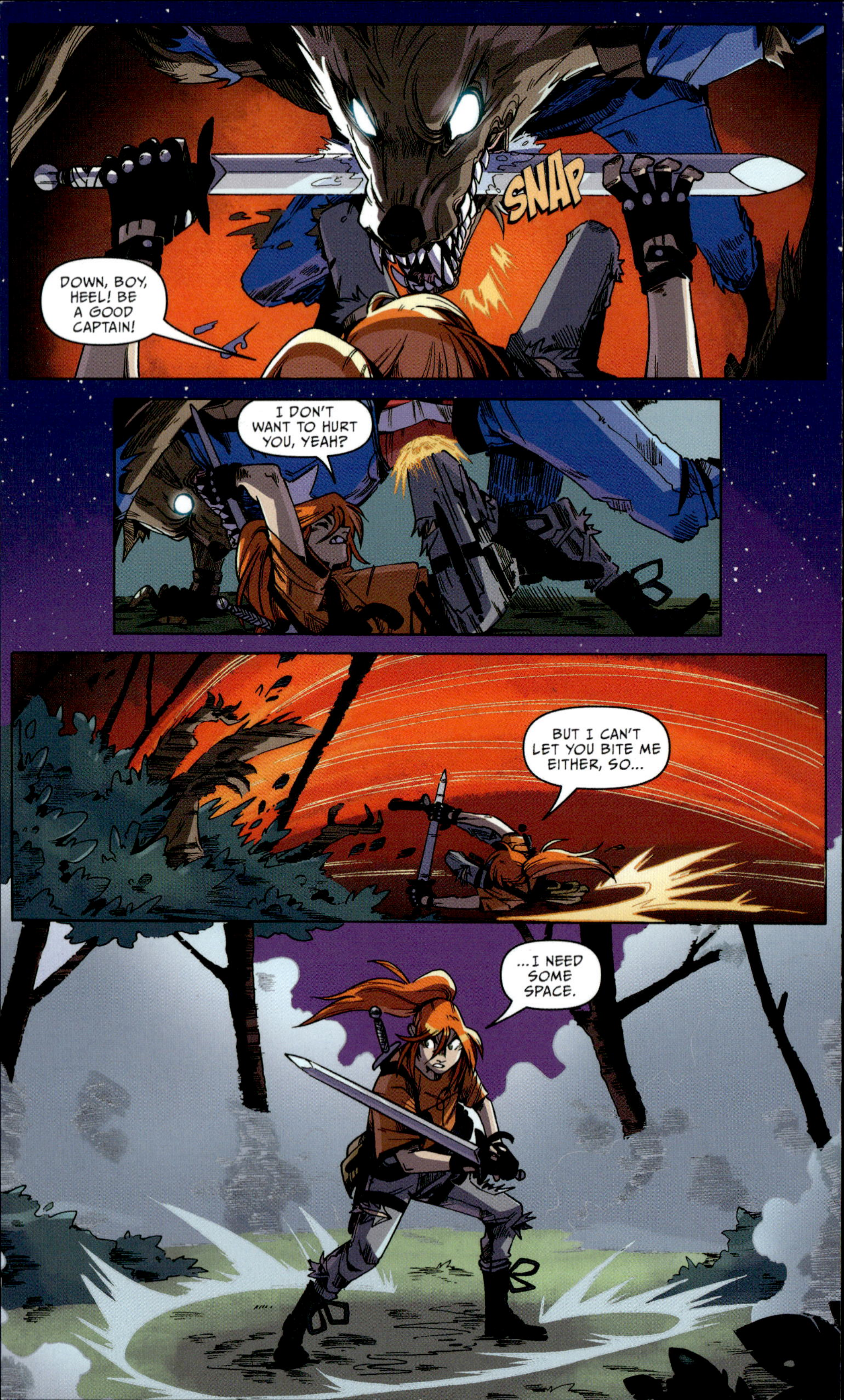
SNAP
DOWN, BOY, HEEL! BE A GOOD CAPTAIN!
I DON'T WANT TO HURT YOU, YEAH?
BUT I CAN'T LET YOU BITE ME EITHER, SO...
...I NEED SOME SPACE.

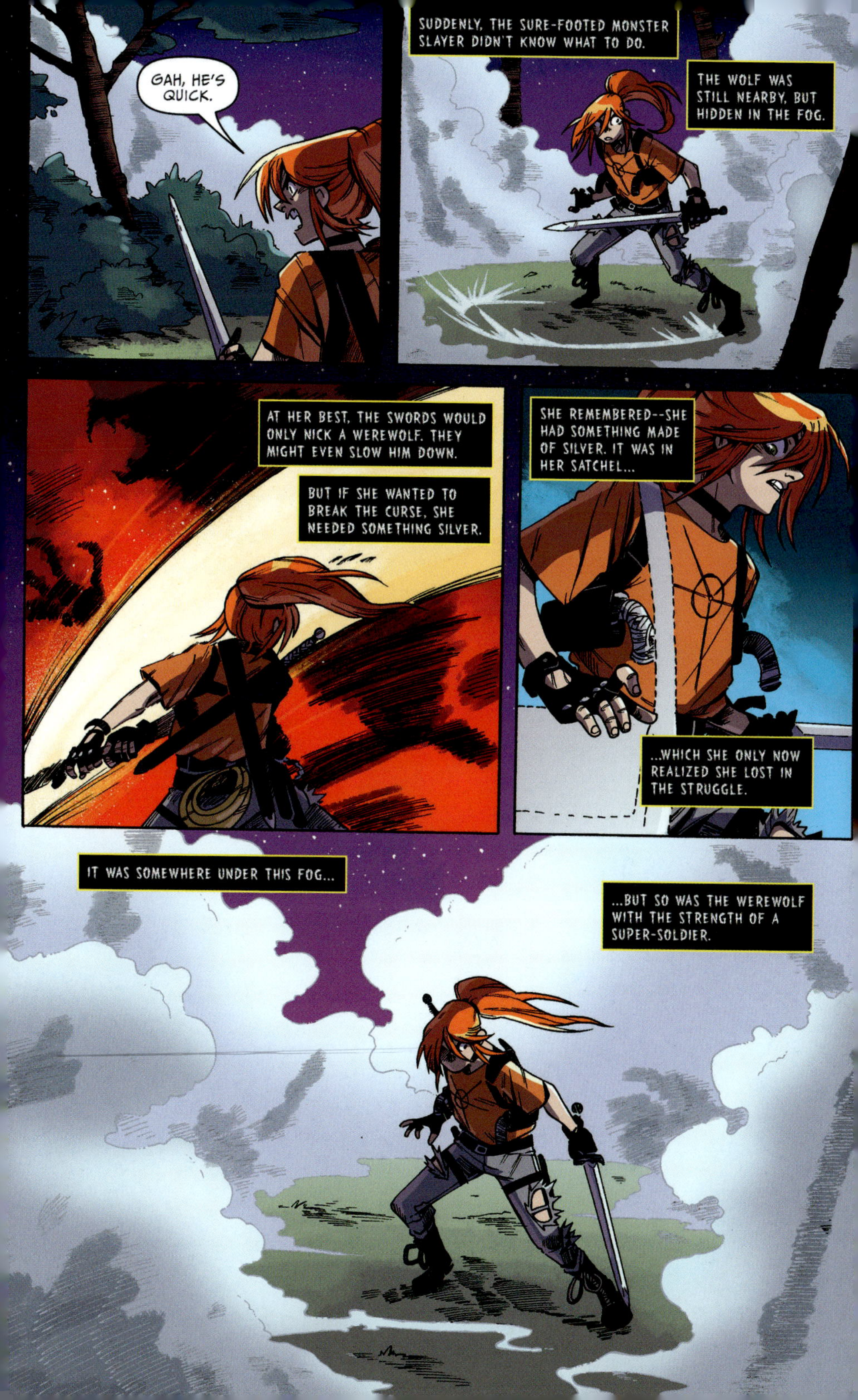
GAH, HE'S QUICK.
SUDDENLY, THE SURE-FOOTED MONSTER SLAYER DIDN'T KNOW WHAT TO DO.
THE WOLF WAS STILL NEARBY, BUT HIDDEN IN THE FOG.
AT HER BEST, THE SWORDS WOULD ONLY NICK A WEREWOLF. THEY MIGHT EVEN SLOW HIM DOWN.
BUT IF SHE WANTED TO BREAK THE CURSE, SHE NEEDED SOMETHING SILVER.
SHE REMEMBERED--SHE HAD SOMETHING MADE OF SILVER. IT WAS IN HER SATCHEL...
...WHICH SHE ONLY NOW REALIZED SHE LOST IN THE STRUGGLE.
IT WAS SOMEWHERE UNDER THIS FOG...
...BUT SO WAS THE WEREWOLF WITH THE STRENGTH OF A SUPER-SOLDIER.

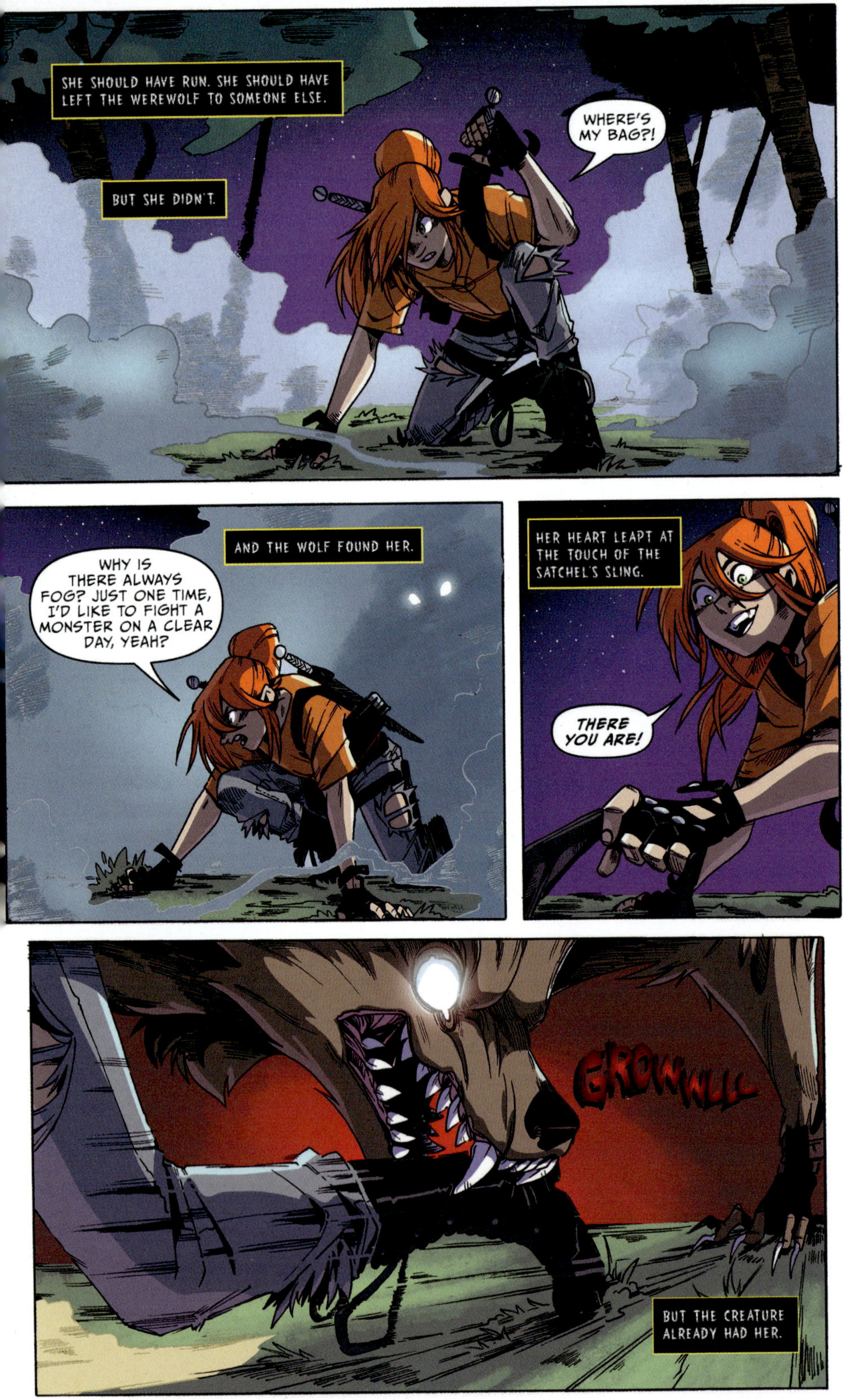
SHE SHOULD HAVE RUN. SHE SHOULD HAVE LEFT THE WEREWOLF TO SOMEONE ELSE.
BUT SHE DIDN'T.
WHERE'S MY BAG?!
AND THE WOLF FOUND HER.
WHY IS THERE ALWAYS FOG? JUST ONE TIME, I'D LIKE TO FIGHT A MONSTER ON A CLEAR DAY, YEAH?
HER HEART LEAPT AT THE TOUCH OF THE SATCHEL'S SLING.
THERE YOU ARE!
GROWLLL
BUT THE CREATURE ALREADY HAD HER.

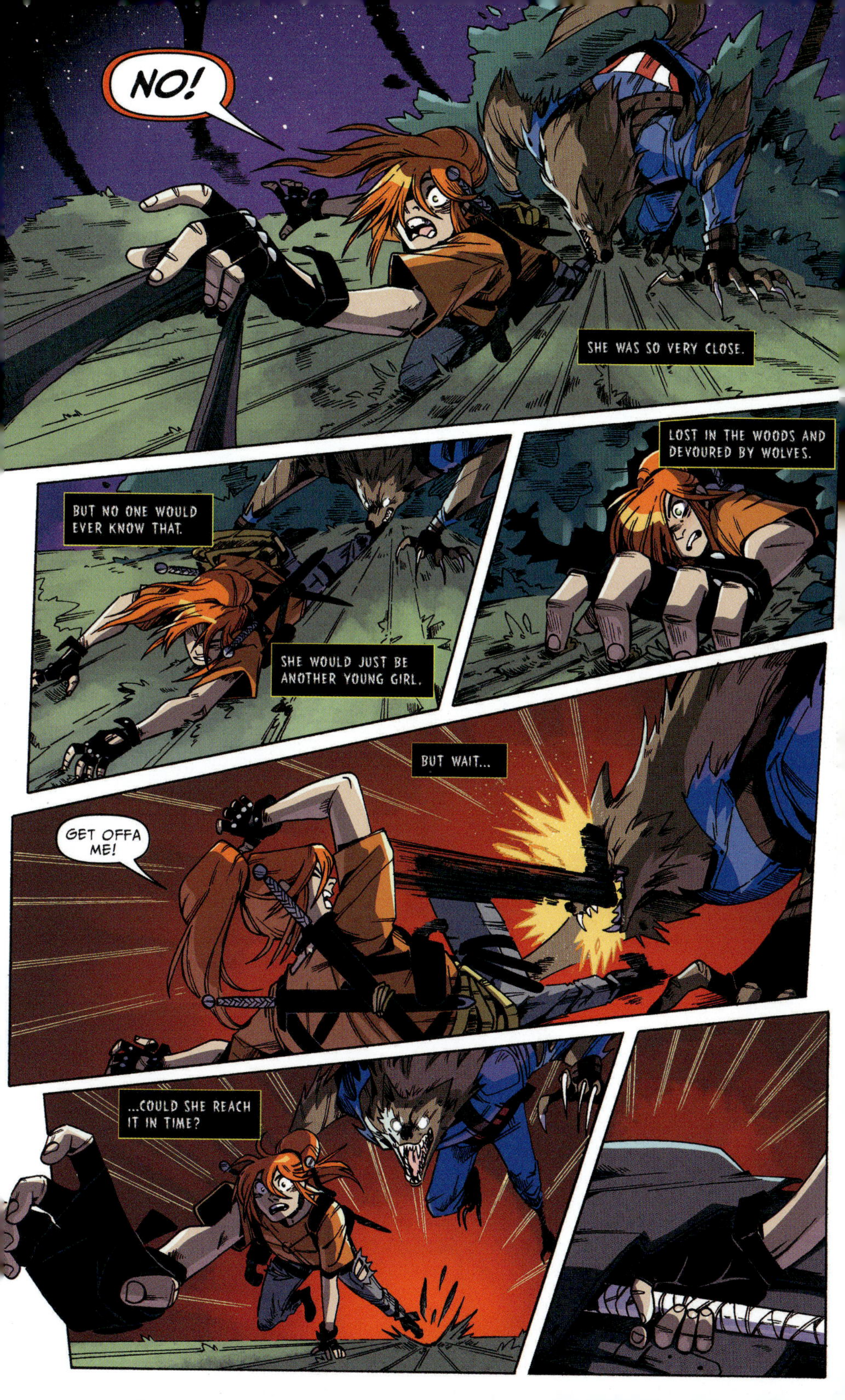
NO!
SHE WAS SO VERY CLOSE.
BUT NO ONE WOULD EVER KNOW THAT.
SHE WOULD JUST BE ANOTHER YOUNG GIRL.
LOST IN THE WOODS AND DEVOURED BY WOLVES.
BUT WAIT...
GET OFFA ME!
...COULD SHE REACH IT IN TIME?

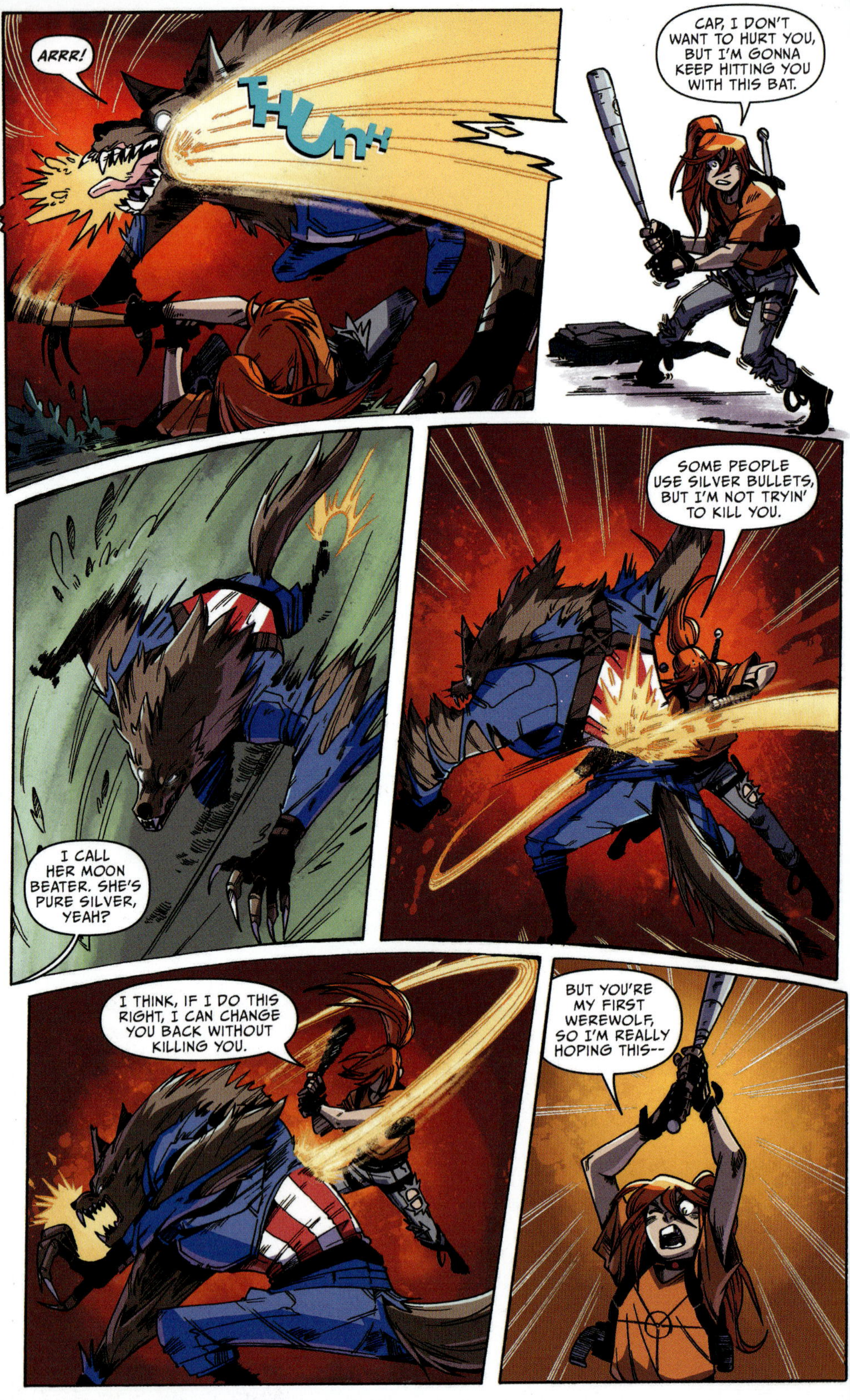
ARRR!
THUNK!
CAP, I DON'T WANT TO HURT YOU, BUT I'M GONNA KEEP HITTING YOU WITH THIS BAT.
I CALL HER MOON BEATER. SHE'S PURE SILVER, YEAH?
SOME PEOPLE USE SILVER BULLETS, BUT I'M NOT TRYIN' TO KILL YOU.
I THINK, IF I DO THIS RIGHT, I CAN CHANGE YOU BACK WITHOUT KILLING YOU.
BUT YOU'RE MY FIRST WEREWOLF, SO I'M REALLY HOPING THIS--

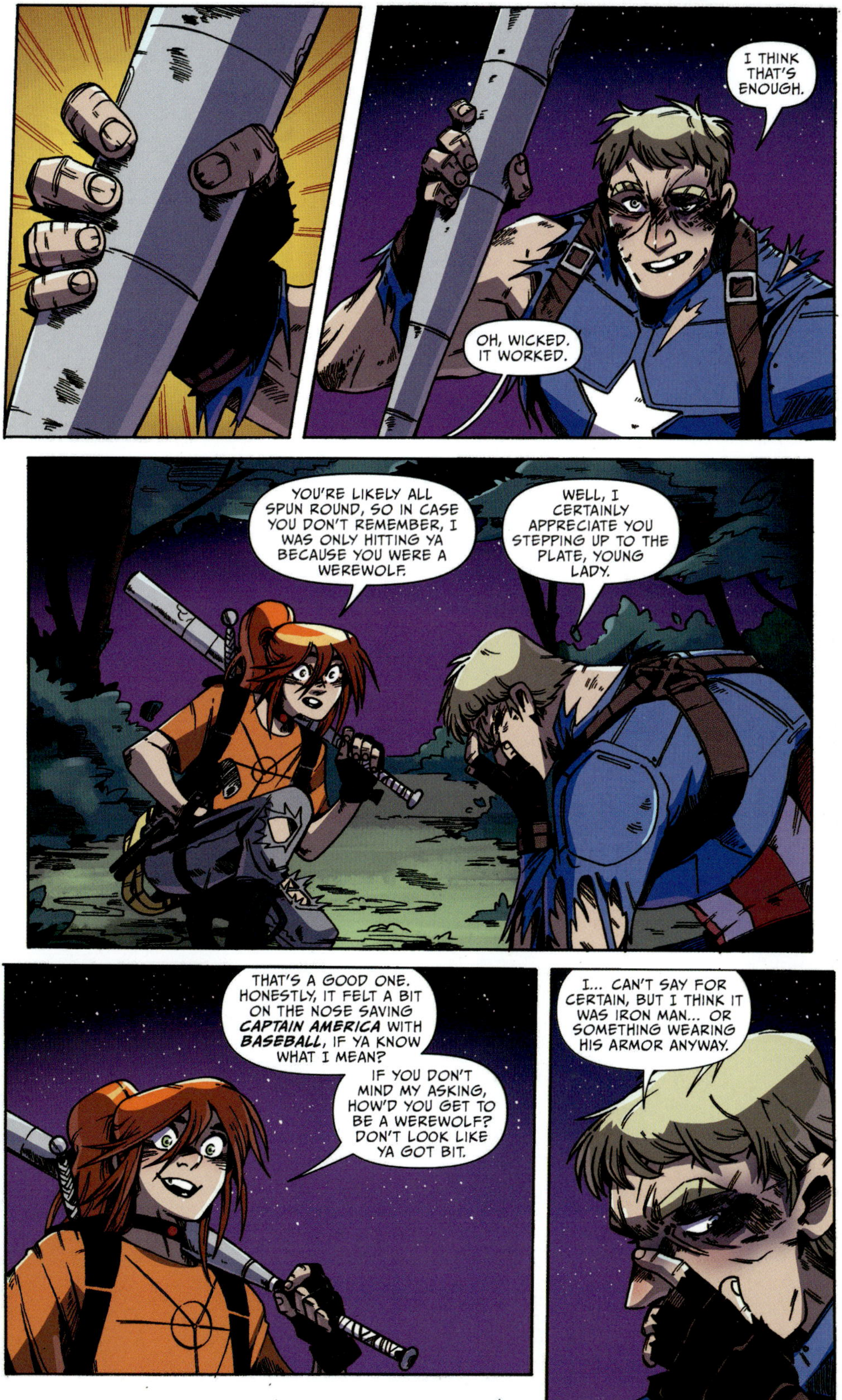
I THINK THAT'S ENOUGH.
OH, WICKED. IT WORKED.
YOU'RE LIKELY ALL SPUN ROUND, SO IN CASE YOU DON'T REMEMBER, I WAS ONLY HITTING YA BECAUSE YOU WERE A WEREWOLF.
WELL, I CERTAINLY APPRECIATE YOU STEPPING UP TO THE PLATE, YOUNG LADY.
THAT'S A GOOD ONE. HONESTLY, IT FELT A BIT ON THE NOSE SAVING ***CAPTAIN AMERICA*** WITH ***BASEBALL***, IF YA KNOW WHAT I MEAN?
IF YOU DON'T MIND MY ASKING, HOW'D YOU GET TO BE A WEREWOLF? DON'T LOOK LIKE YA GOT BIT.
I... CAN'T SAY FOR CERTAIN, BUT I THINK IT WAS IRON MAN... OR SOMETHING WEARING HIS ARMOR ANYWAY.

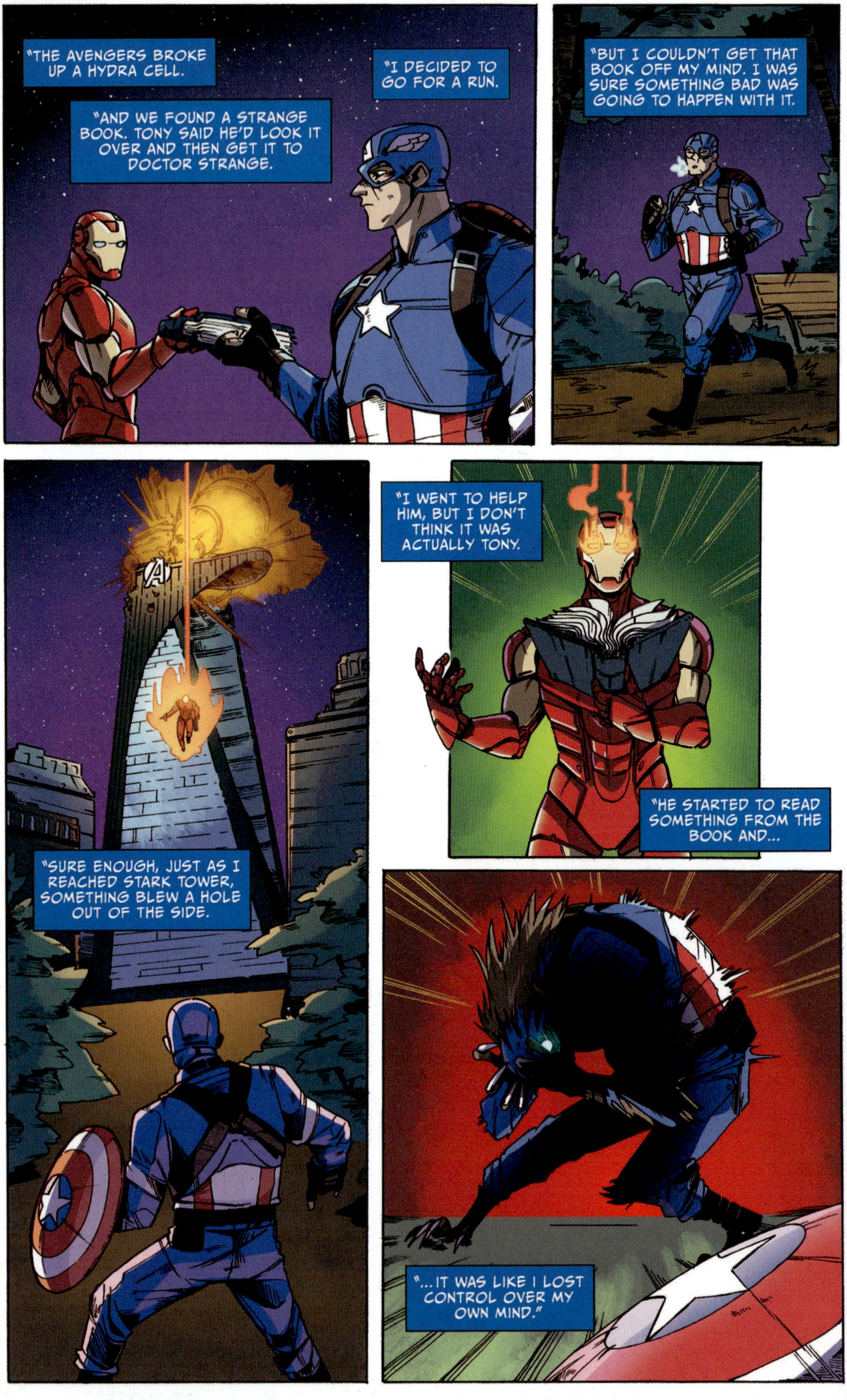
"THE AVENGERS BROKE UP A HYDRA CELL.
"AND WE FOUND A STRANGE BOOK. TONY SAID HE'D LOOK IT OVER AND THEN GET IT TO DOCTOR STRANGE.
"I DECIDED TO GO FOR A RUN.
"BUT I COULDN'T GET THAT BOOK OFF MY MIND. I WAS SURE SOMETHING BAD WAS GOING TO HAPPEN WITH IT.
"SURE ENOUGH, JUST AS I REACHED STARK TOWER, SOMETHING BLEW A HOLE OUT OF THE SIDE.
"I WENT TO HELP HIM, BUT I DON'T THINK IT WAS ACTUALLY TONY.
"HE STARTED TO READ SOMETHING FROM THE BOOK AND...
"...IT WAS LIKE I LOST CONTROL OVER MY OWN MIND."

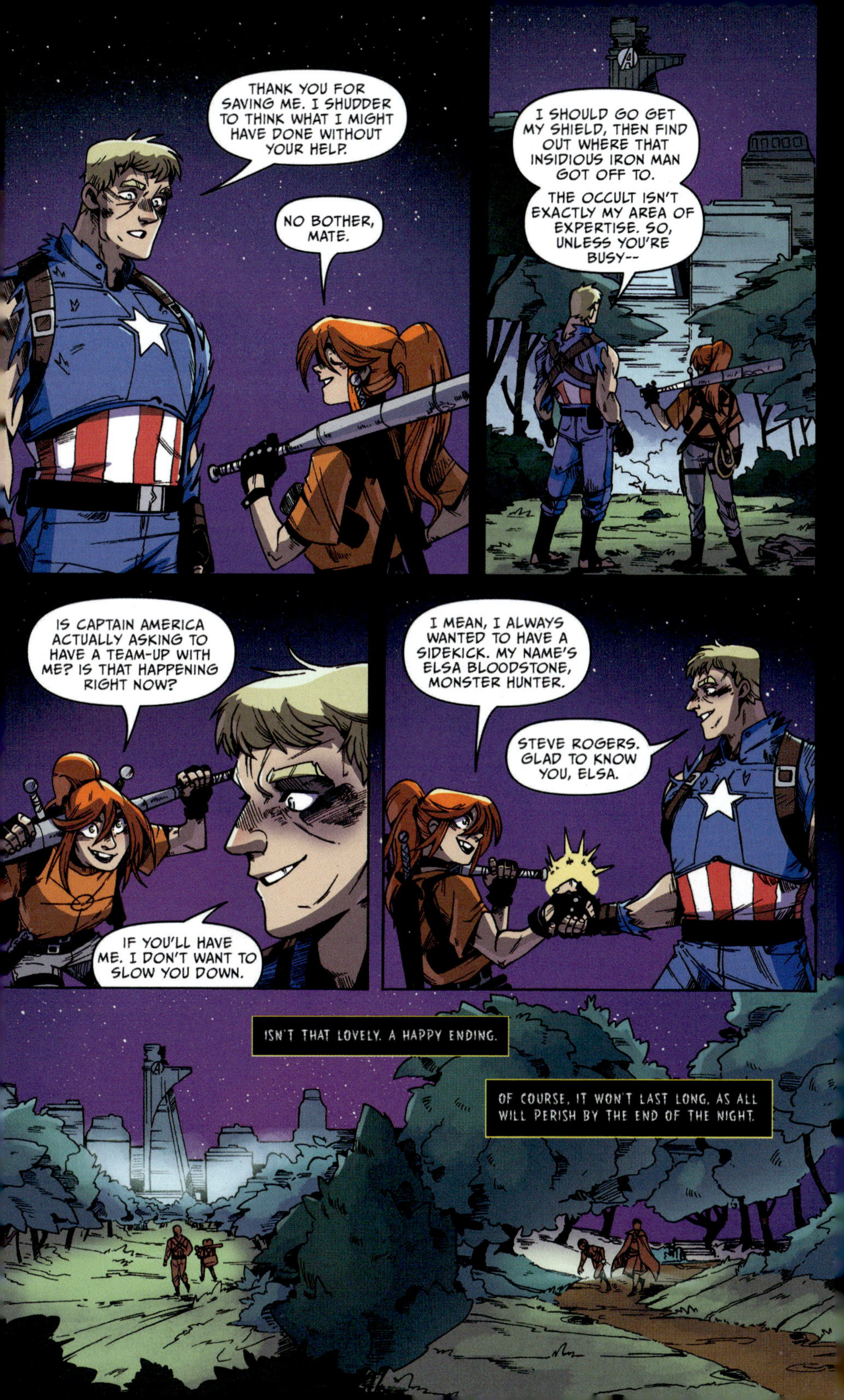
THANK YOU FOR SAVING ME. I SHUDDER TO THINK WHAT I MIGHT HAVE DONE WITHOUT YOUR HELP.
NO BOTHER, MATE.
I SHOULD GO GET MY SHIELD, THEN FIND OUT WHERE THAT INSIDIOUS IRON MAN GOT OFF TO.
THE OCCULT ISN'T EXACTLY MY AREA OF EXPERTISE. SO, UNLESS YOU'RE BUSY--
IS CAPTAIN AMERICA ACTUALLY ASKING TO HAVE A TEAM-UP WITH ME? IS THAT HAPPENING RIGHT NOW?
IF YOU'LL HAVE ME. I DON'T WANT TO SLOW YOU DOWN.
I MEAN, I ALWAYS WANTED TO HAVE A SIDEKICK. MY NAME'S ELSA BLOODSTONE, MONSTER HUNTER.
STEVE ROGERS. GLAD TO KNOW YOU, ELSA.
ISN'T THAT LOVELY. A HAPPY ENDING.
OF COURSE, IT WON'T LAST LONG, AS ALL WILL PERISH BY THE END OF THE NIGHT.

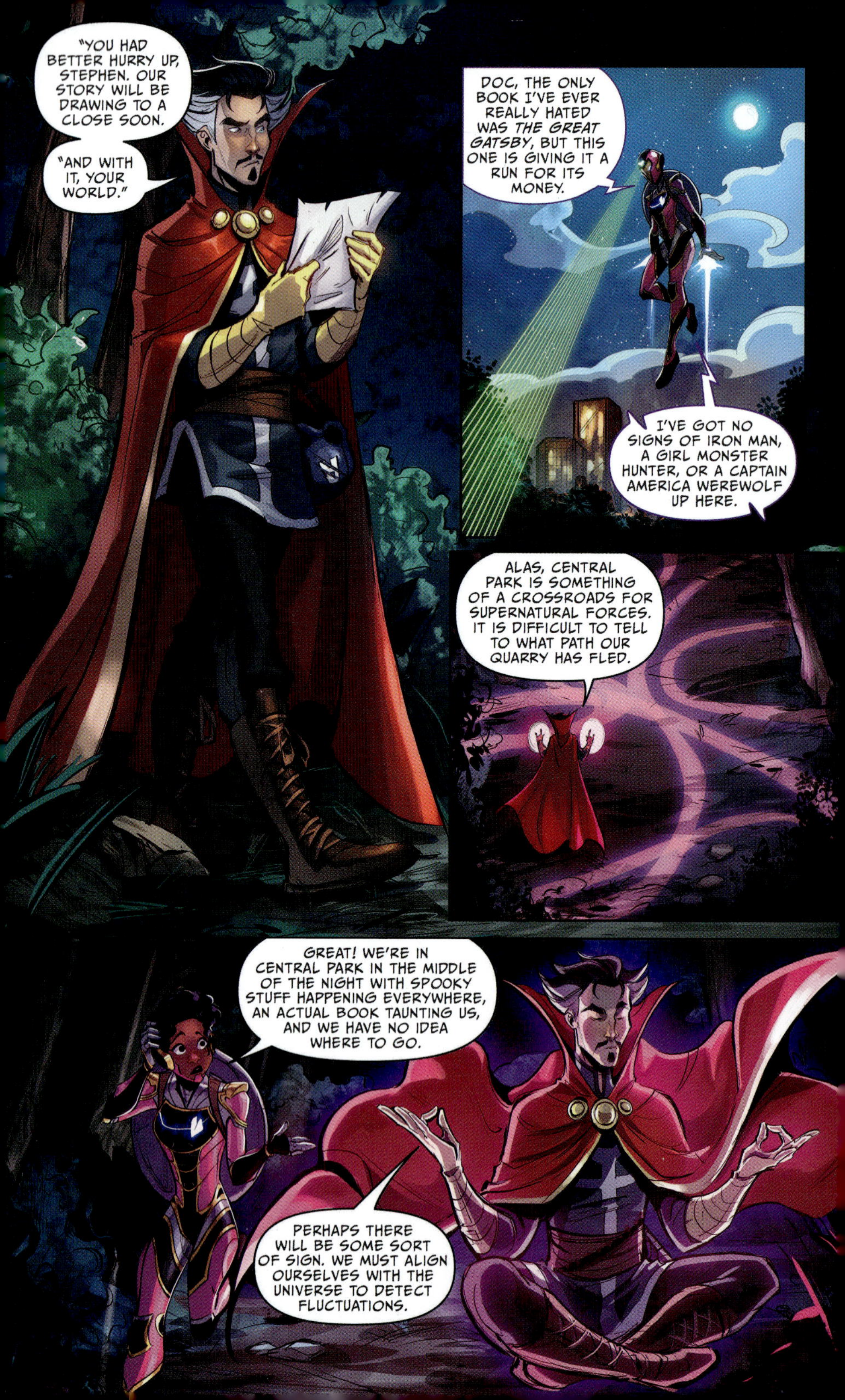
"YOU HAD BETTER HURRY UP, STEPHEN. OUR STORY WILL BE DRAWING TO A CLOSE SOON.
"AND WITH IT, YOUR WORLD."
DOC, THE ONLY BOOK I'VE EVER REALLY HATED WAS *THE GREAT GATSBY*, BUT THIS ONE IS GIVING IT A RUN FOR ITS MONEY.
I'VE GOT NO SIGNS OF IRON MAN, A GIRL MONSTER HUNTER, OR A CAPTAIN AMERICA WEREWOLF UP HERE.
ALAS, CENTRAL PARK IS SOMETHING OF A CROSSROADS FOR SUPERNATURAL FORCES. IT IS DIFFICULT TO TELL TO WHAT PATH OUR QUARRY HAS FLED.
GREAT! WE'RE IN CENTRAL PARK IN THE MIDDLE OF THE NIGHT WITH SPOOKY STUFF HAPPENING EVERYWHERE, AN ACTUAL BOOK TAUNTING US, AND WE HAVE NO IDEA WHERE TO GO.
PERHAPS THERE WILL BE SOME SORT OF SIGN. WE MUST ALIGN OURSELVES WITH THE UNIVERSE TO DETECT FLUCTUATIONS.

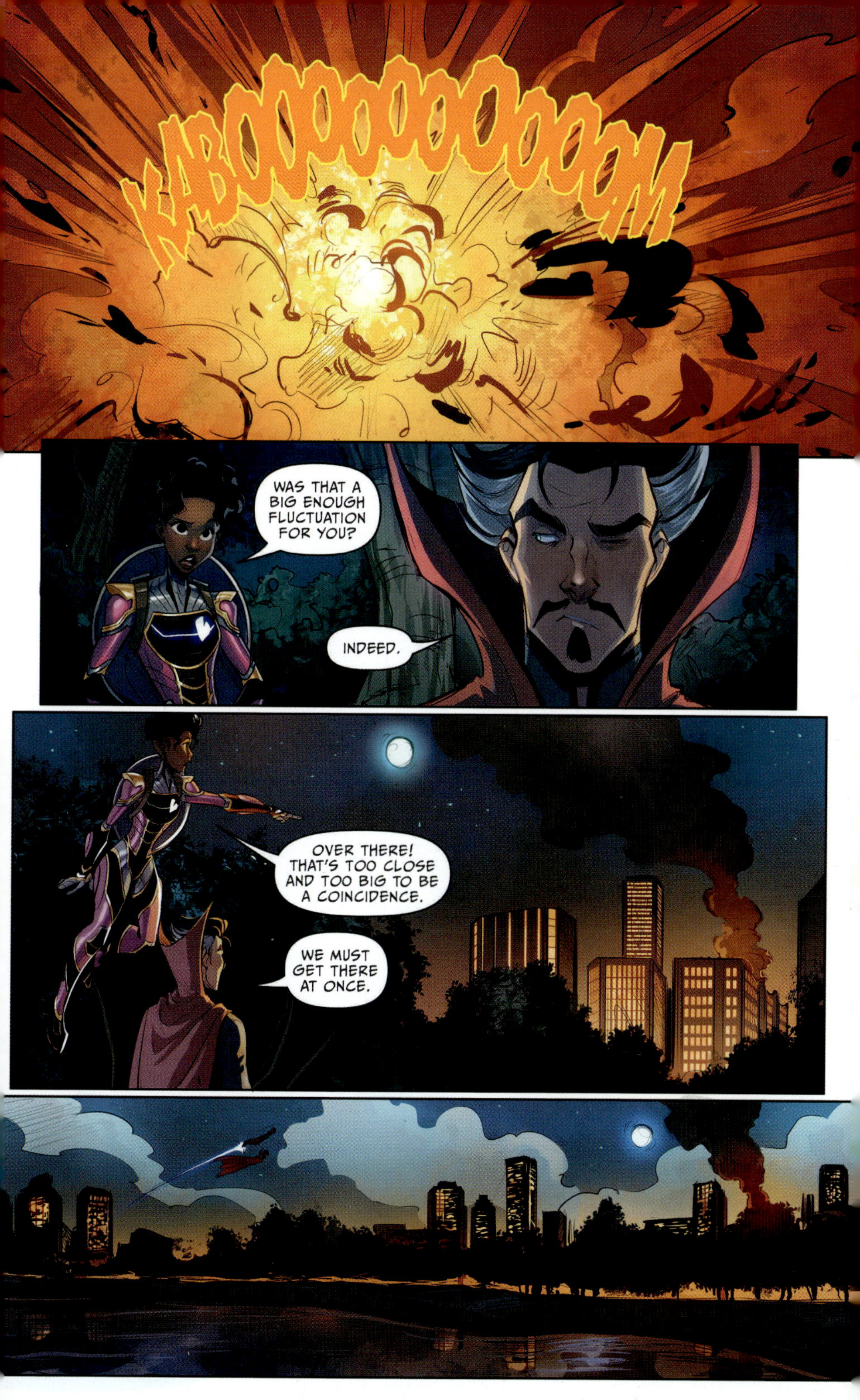
KABOOOOOOOOOOM
WAS THAT A BIG ENOUGH FLUCTUATION FOR YOU?
INDEED.
OVER THERE! THAT'S TOO CLOSE AND TOO BIG TO BE A COINCIDENCE.
WE MUST GET THERE AT ONCE.

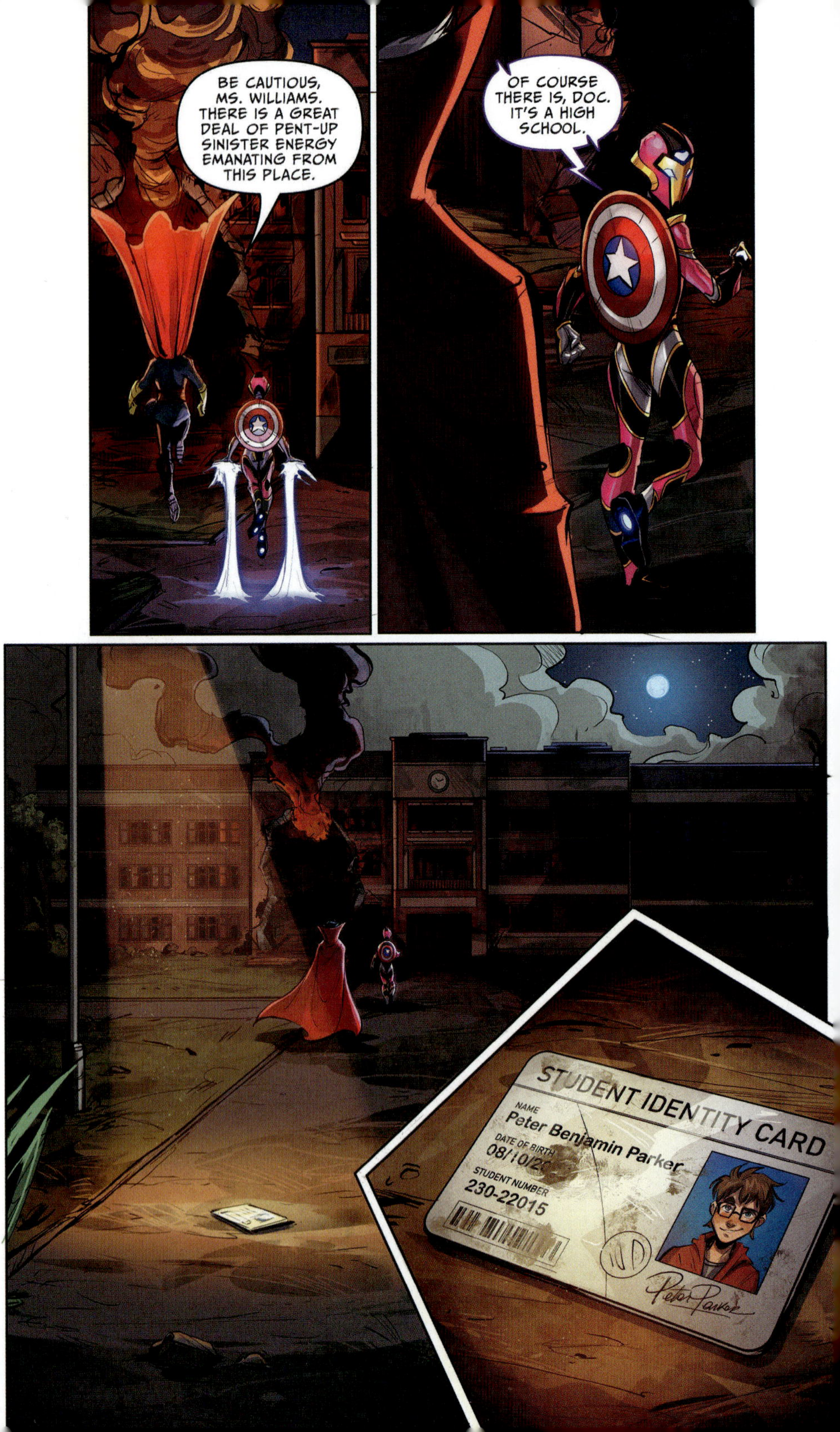
BE CAUTIOUS, MS. WILLIAMS. THERE IS A GREAT DEAL OF PENT-UP SINISTER ENERGY EMANATING FROM THIS PLACE.
OF COURSE THERE IS, DOC. IT'S A HIGH SCHOOL.
STUDENT IDENTITY CARD
NAME
Peter Benjamin Parker
DATE OF BIRTH
STUDENT NUMBER
230-22015
Peter Parker

The Strange Case of Dr. Spider-Man and Mr. Venom

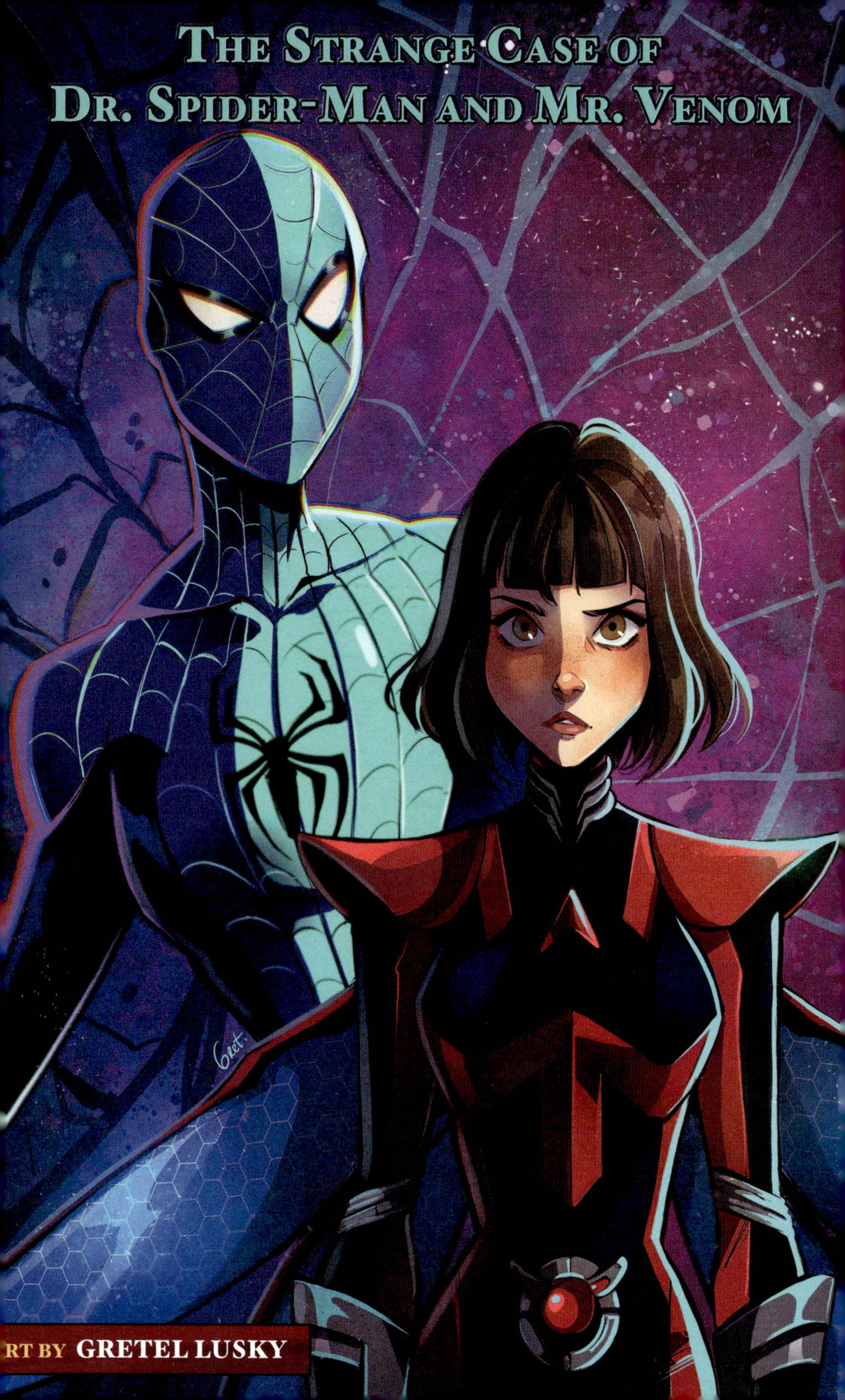

RT BY GRETEL LUSKY

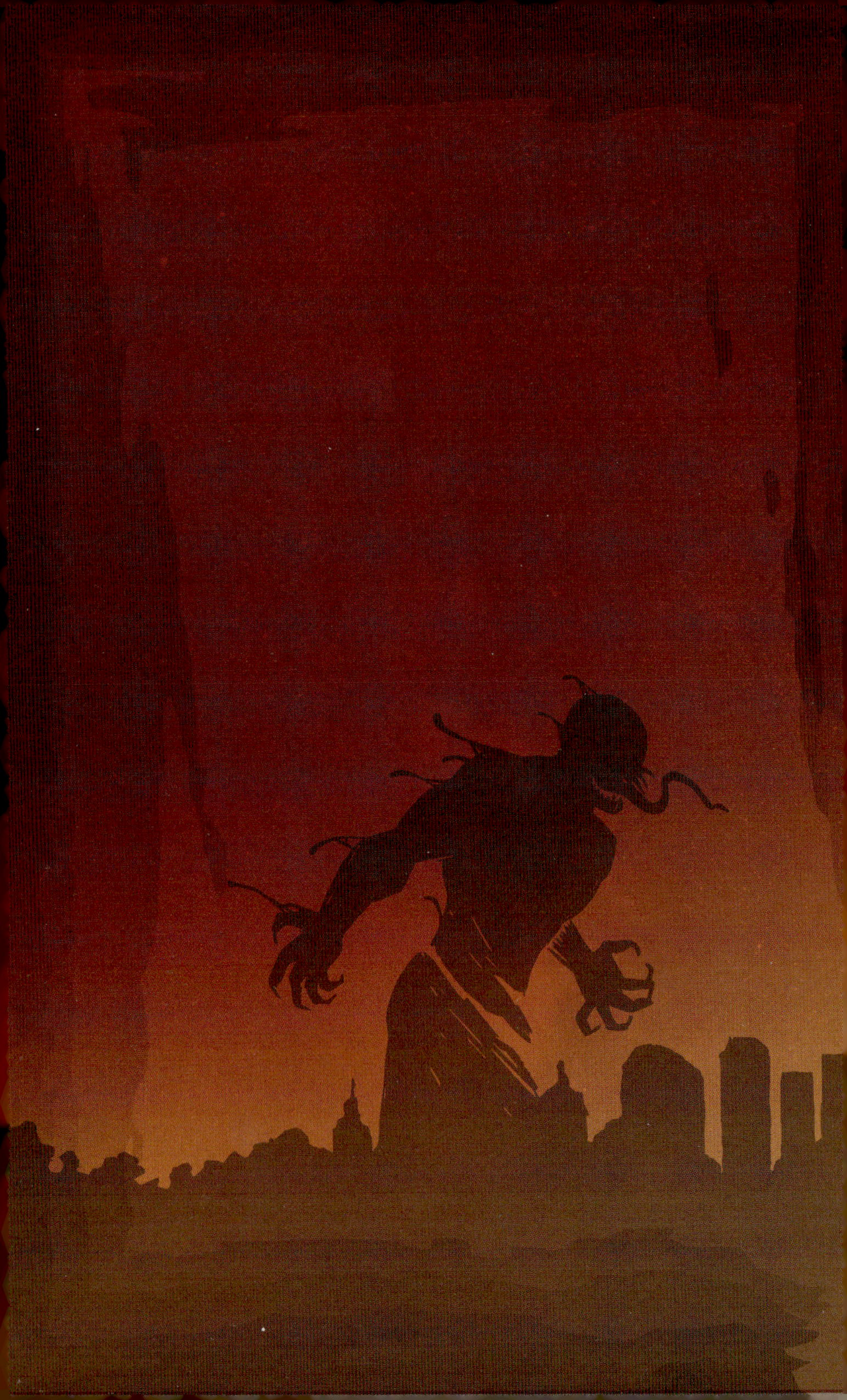

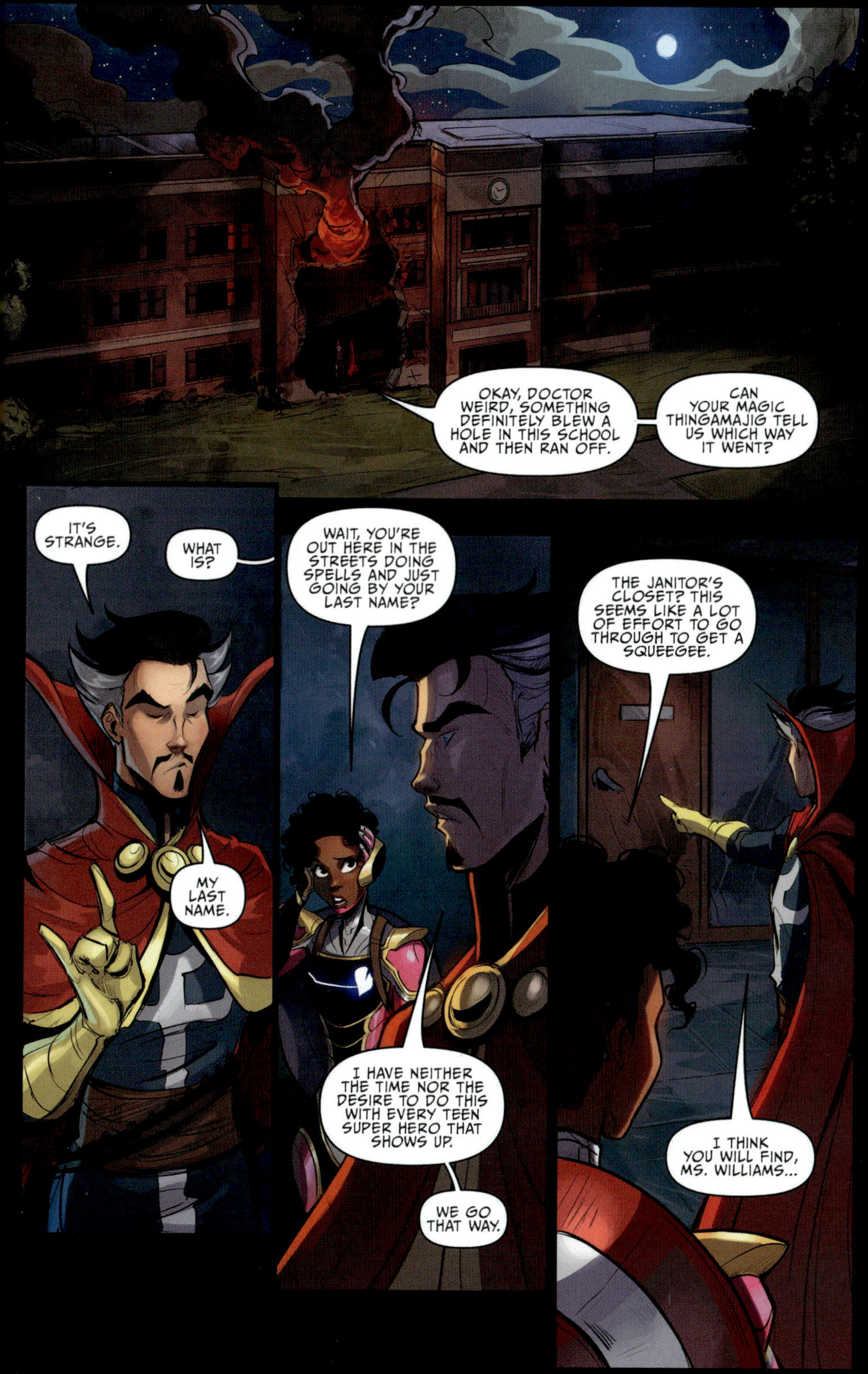

OKAY, DOCTOR WEIRD, SOMETHING DEFINITELY BLEW A HOLE IN THIS SCHOOL AND THEN RAN OFF.
CAN YOUR MAGIC THINGAMAJIG TELL US WHICH WAY IT WENT?
IT'S STRANGE.
WHAT IS?
MY LAST NAME.
WAIT, YOU'RE OUT HERE IN THE STREETS DOING SPELLS AND JUST GOING BY YOUR LAST NAME?
I HAVE NEITHER THE TIME NOR THE DESIRE TO DO THIS WITH EVERY TEEN SUPER HERO THAT SHOWS UP.
WE GO THAT WAY.
THE JANITOR'S CLOSET? THIS SEEMS LIKE A LOT OF EFFORT TO GO THROUGH TO GET A SQUEEGEE.
I THINK YOU WILL FIND, MS. WILLIAMS...

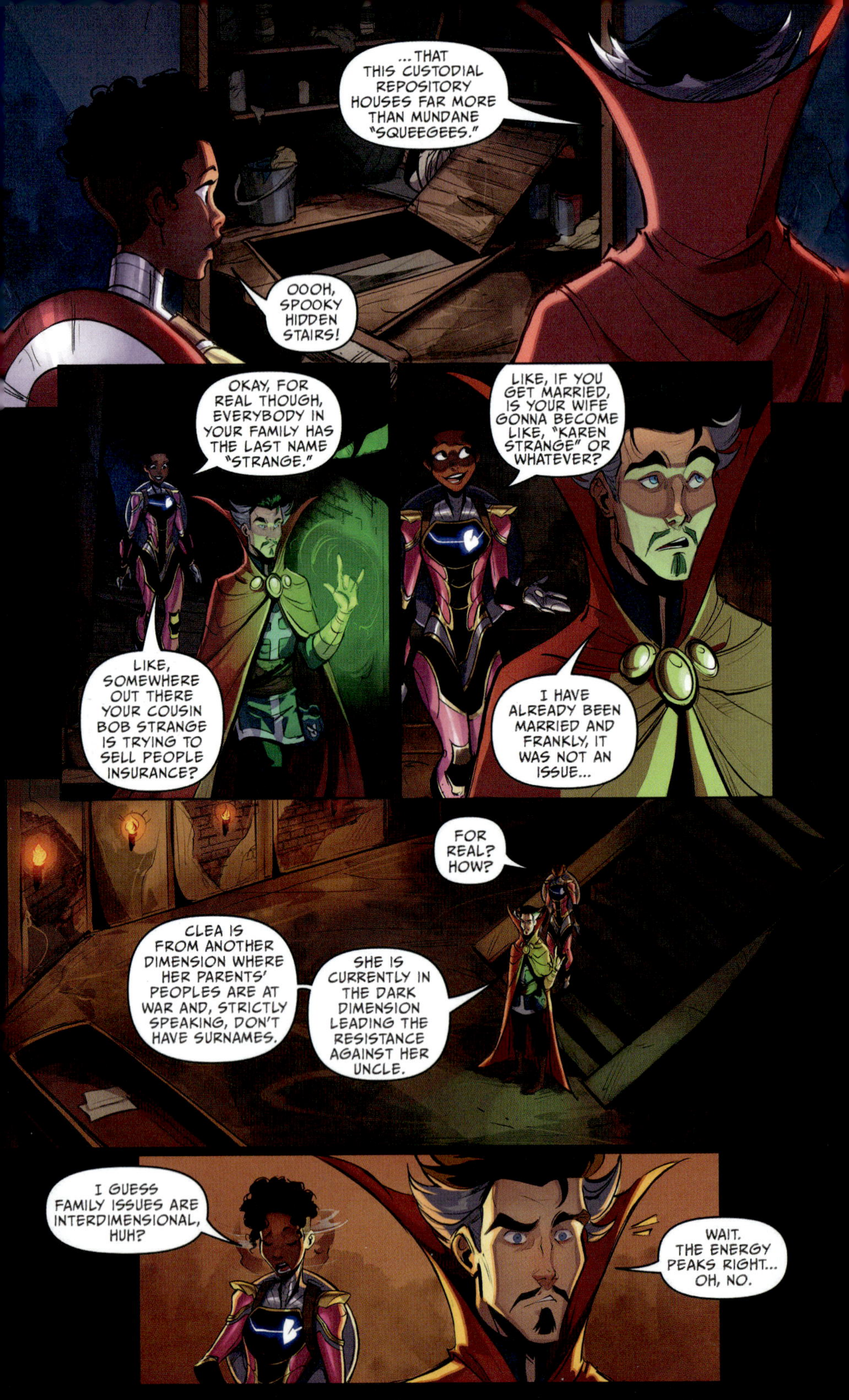
...THAT THIS CUSTODIAL REPOSITORY HOUSES FAR MORE THAN MUNDANE "SQUEEGEES."
OOOH, SPOOKY HIDDEN STAIRS!
OKAY, FOR REAL THOUGH, EVERYBODY IN YOUR FAMILY HAS THE LAST NAME "STRANGE."
LIKE, SOMEWHERE OUT THERE YOUR COUSIN BOB STRANGE IS TRYING TO SELL PEOPLE INSURANCE?
LIKE, IF YOU GET MARRIED, IS YOUR WIFE GONNA BECOME LIKE, "KAREN STRANGE" OR WHATEVER?
I HAVE ALREADY BEEN MARRIED AND FRANKLY, IT WAS NOT AN ISSUE...
FOR REAL? HOW?
CLEA IS FROM ANOTHER DIMENSION WHERE HER PARENTS' PEOPLES ARE AT WAR AND, STRICTLY SPEAKING, DON'T HAVE SURNAMES.
SHE IS CURRENTLY IN THE DARK DIMENSION LEADING THE RESISTANCE AGAINST HER UNCLE.
I GUESS FAMILY ISSUES ARE INTERDIMENSIONAL, HUH?
WAIT. THE ENERGY PEAKS RIGHT... OH, NO.

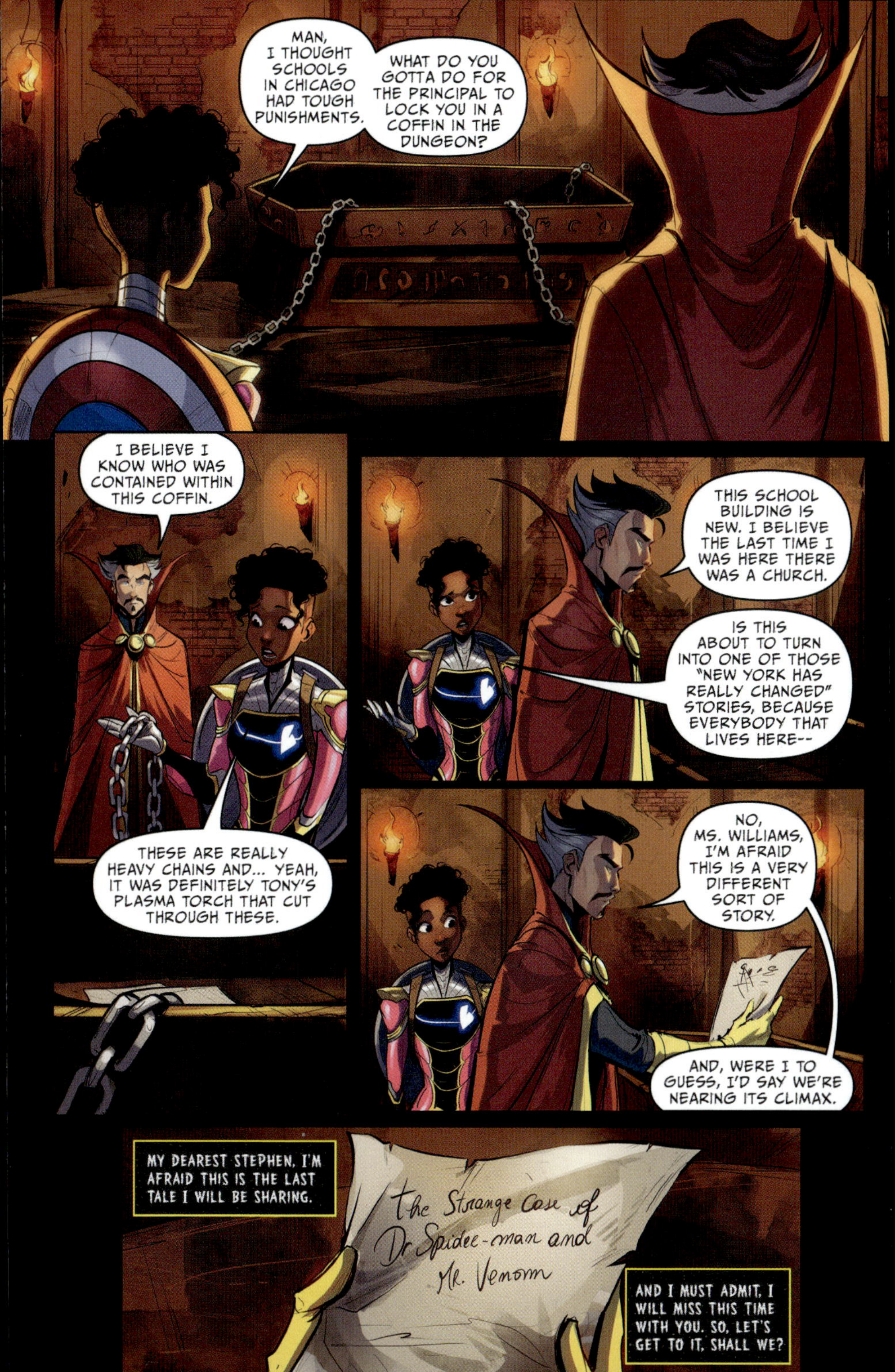
MAN, I THOUGHT SCHOOLS IN CHICAGO HAD TOUGH PUNISHMENTS.
WHAT DO YOU GOTTA DO FOR THE PRINCIPAL TO LOCK YOU IN A COFFIN IN THE DUNGEON?
I BELIEVE I KNOW WHO WAS CONTAINED WITHIN THIS COFFIN.
THESE ARE REALLY HEAVY CHAINS AND... YEAH, IT WAS DEFINITELY TONY'S PLASMA TORCH THAT CUT THROUGH THESE.
THIS SCHOOL BUILDING IS NEW. I BELIEVE THE LAST TIME I WAS HERE THERE WAS A CHURCH.
IS THIS ABOUT TO TURN INTO ONE OF THOSE "NEW YORK HAS REALLY CHANGED" STORIES, BECAUSE EVERYBODY THAT LIVES HERE--
NO, MS. WILLIAMS, I'M AFRAID THIS IS A VERY DIFFERENT SORT OF STORY.
AND, WERE I TO GUESS, I'D SAY WE'RE NEARING ITS CLIMAX.
MY DEAREST STEPHEN, I'M AFRAID THIS IS THE LAST TALE I WILL BE SHARING.
The Strange Case of Dr Spidee-man and Mr. Venom
AND I MUST ADMIT, I WILL MISS THIS TIME WITH YOU. SO, LET'S GET TO IT, SHALL WE?

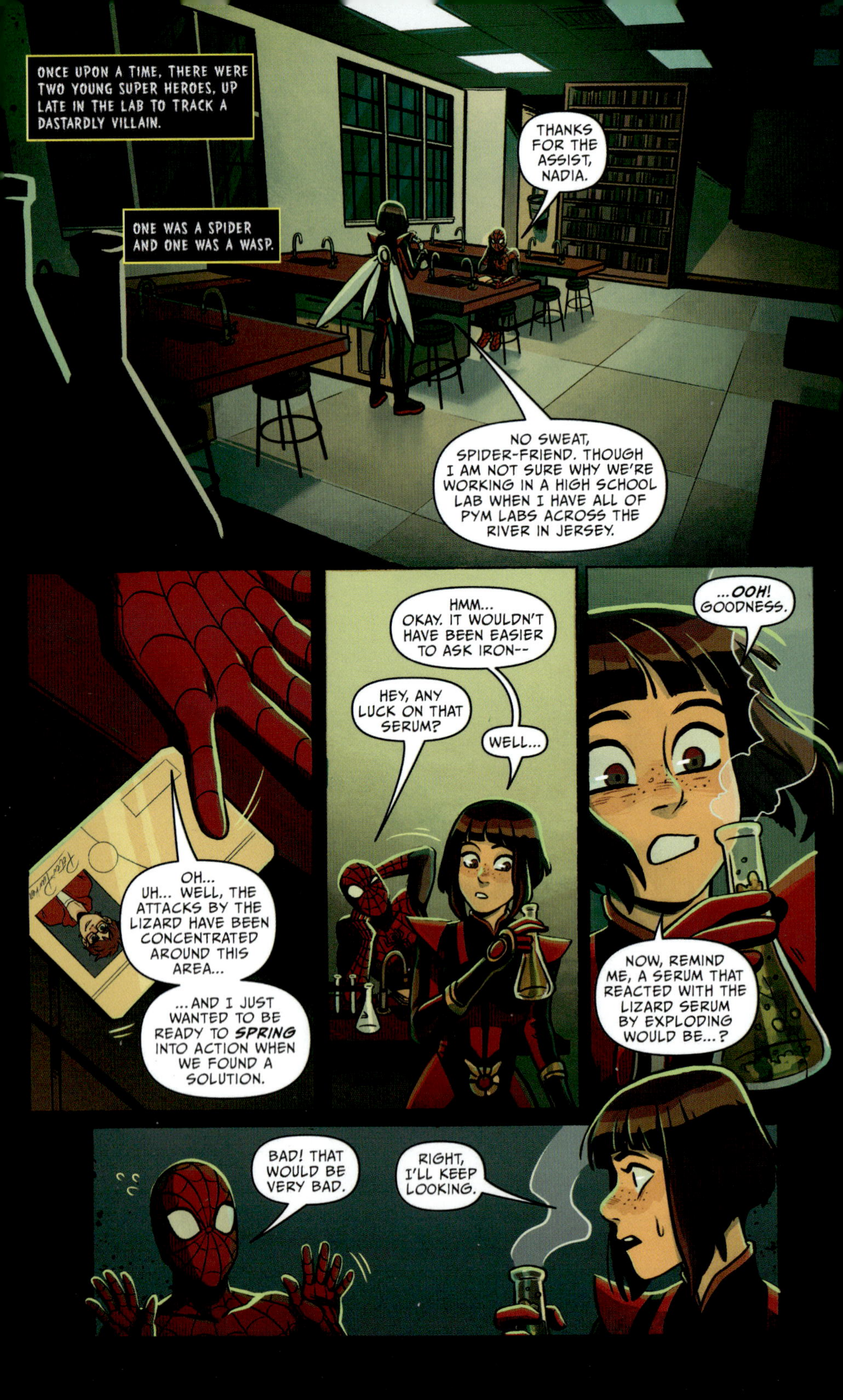
ONCE UPON A TIME, THERE WERE TWO YOUNG SUPER HEROES, UP LATE IN THE LAB TO TRACK A DASTARDLY VILLAIN.
THANKS FOR THE ASSIST, NADIA.
ONE WAS A SPIDER AND ONE WAS A WASP.
NO SWEAT, SPIDER-FRIEND. THOUGH I AM NOT SURE WHY WE'RE WORKING IN A HIGH SCHOOL LAB WHEN I HAVE ALL OF PYM LABS ACROSS THE RIVER IN JERSEY.
OH... UH... WELL, THE ATTACKS BY THE LIZARD HAVE BEEN CONCENTRATED AROUND THIS AREA...
...AND I JUST WANTED TO BE READY TO *SPRING* INTO ACTION WHEN WE FOUND A SOLUTION.
HMM... OKAY. IT WOULDN'T HAVE BEEN EASIER TO ASK IRON--
HEY, ANY LUCK ON THAT SERUM?
WELL...
...*OOH*! GOODNESS.
NOW, REMIND ME, A SERUM THAT REACTED WITH THE LIZARD SERUM BY EXPLODING WOULD BE...?
BAD! THAT WOULD BE VERY BAD.
RIGHT, I'LL KEEP LOOKING.

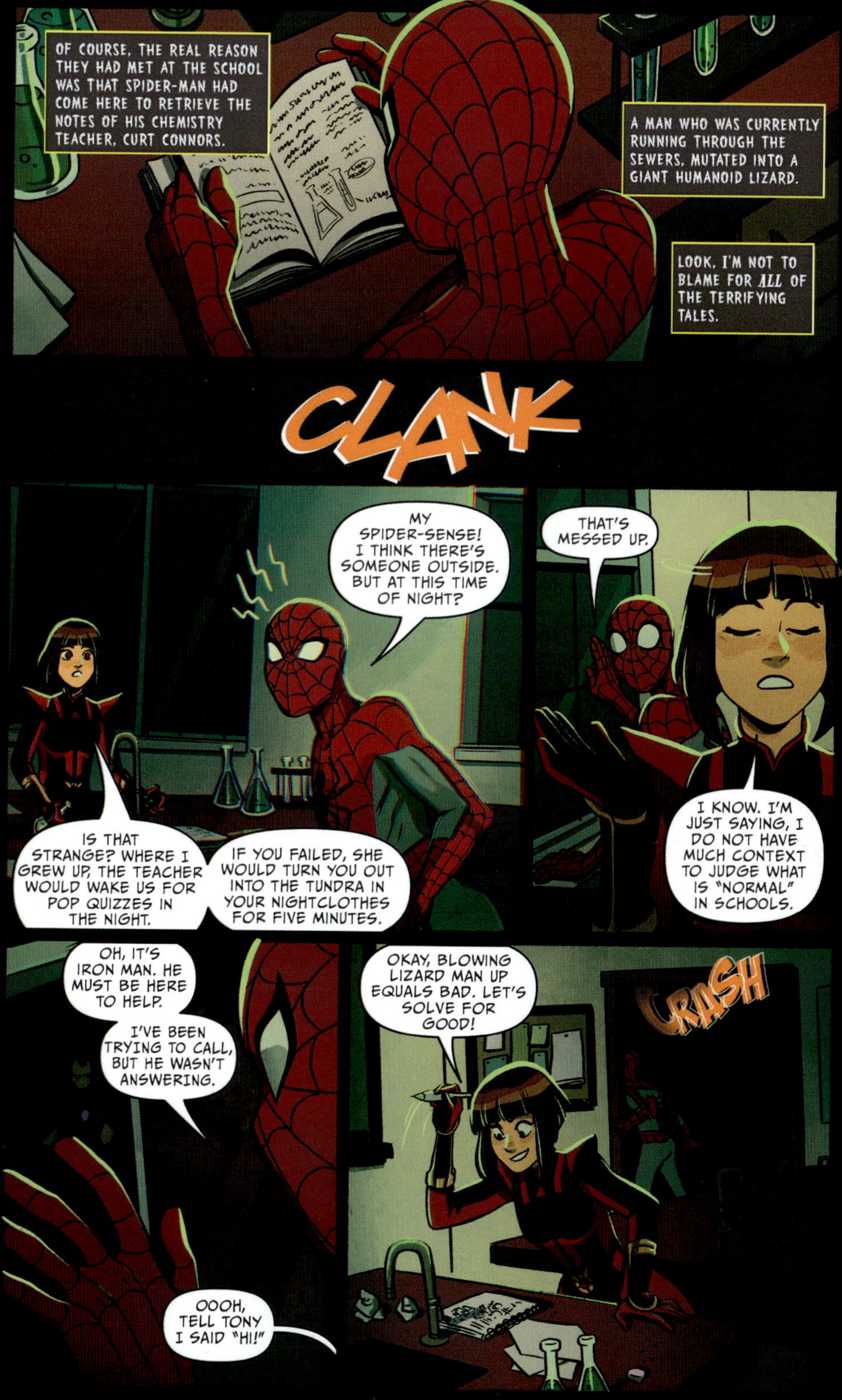
OF COURSE, THE REAL REASON THEY HAD MET AT THE SCHOOL WAS THAT SPIDER-MAN HAD COME HERE TO RETRIEVE THE NOTES OF HIS CHEMISTRY TEACHER, CURT CONNORS.
A MAN WHO WAS CURRENTLY RUNNING THROUGH THE SEWERS, MUTATED INTO A GIANT HUMANOID LIZARD.
LOOK, I'M NOT TO BLAME FOR ALL OF THE TERRIFYING TALES.
CLANK
MY SPIDER-SENSE! I THINK THERE'S SOMEONE OUTSIDE. BUT AT THIS TIME OF NIGHT?
IS THAT STRANGE? WHERE I GREW UP, THE TEACHER WOULD WAKE US FOR POP QUIZZES IN THE NIGHT.
IF YOU FAILED, SHE WOULD TURN YOU OUT INTO THE TUNDRA IN YOUR NIGHTCLOTHES FOR FIVE MINUTES.
THAT'S MESSED UP.
I KNOW. I'M JUST SAYING, I DO NOT HAVE MUCH CONTEXT TO JUDGE WHAT IS "NORMAL" IN SCHOOLS.
OH, IT'S IRON MAN. HE MUST BE HERE TO HELP.
I'VE BEEN TRYING TO CALL, BUT HE WASN'T ANSWERING.
OOOH, TELL TONY I SAID "HI!"
OKAY, BLOWING LIZARD MAN UP EQUALS BAD. LET'S SOLVE FOR GOOD!
CRASH

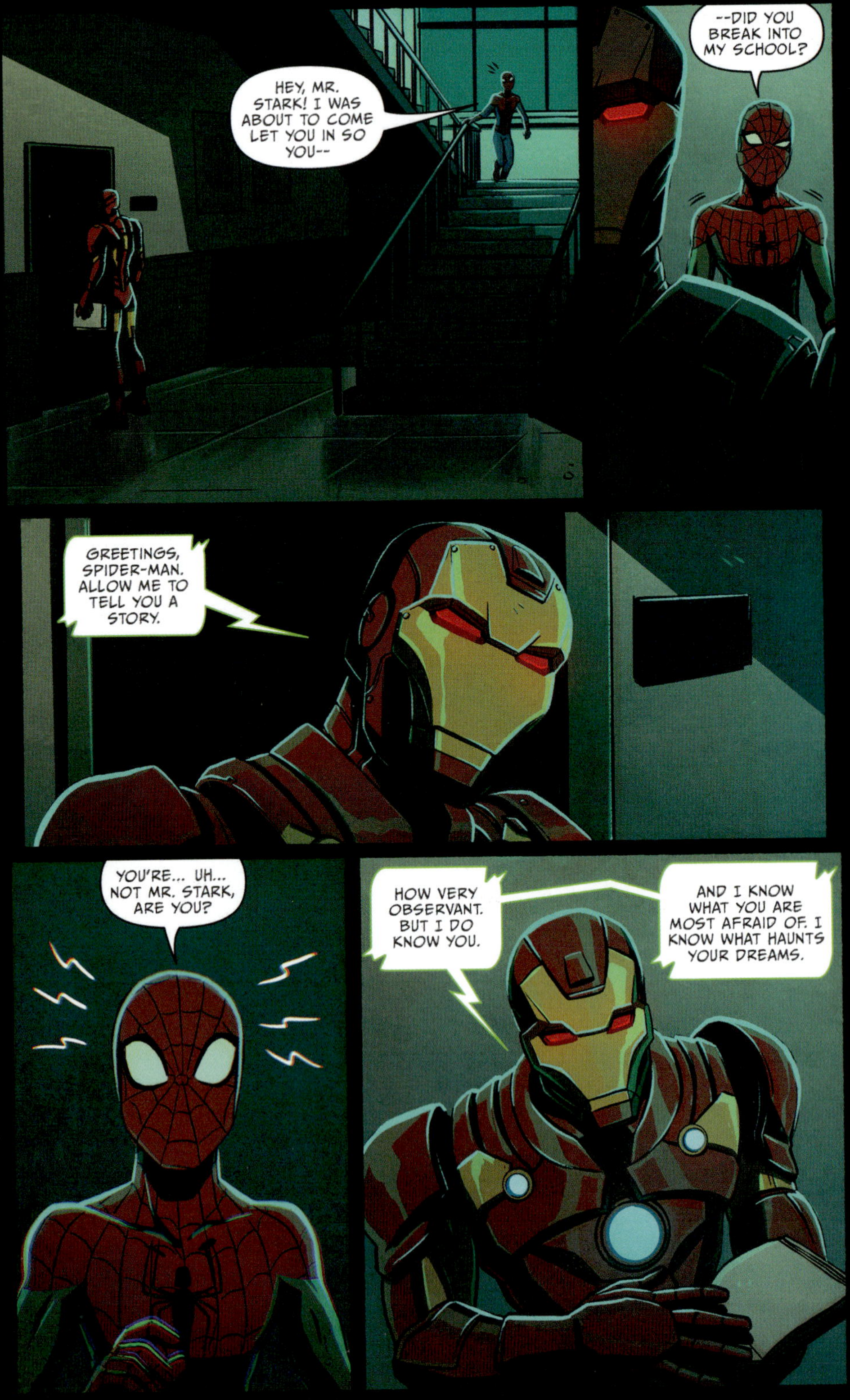
HEY, MR. STARK! I WAS ABOUT TO COME LET YOU IN SO YOU--
--DID YOU BREAK INTO MY SCHOOL?
GREETINGS, SPIDER-MAN. ALLOW ME TO TELL YOU A STORY.
YOU'RE... UH... NOT MR. STARK, ARE YOU?
HOW VERY OBSERVANT. BUT I DO KNOW YOU.
AND I KNOW WHAT YOU ARE MOST AFRAID OF. I KNOW WHAT HAUNTS YOUR DREAMS.

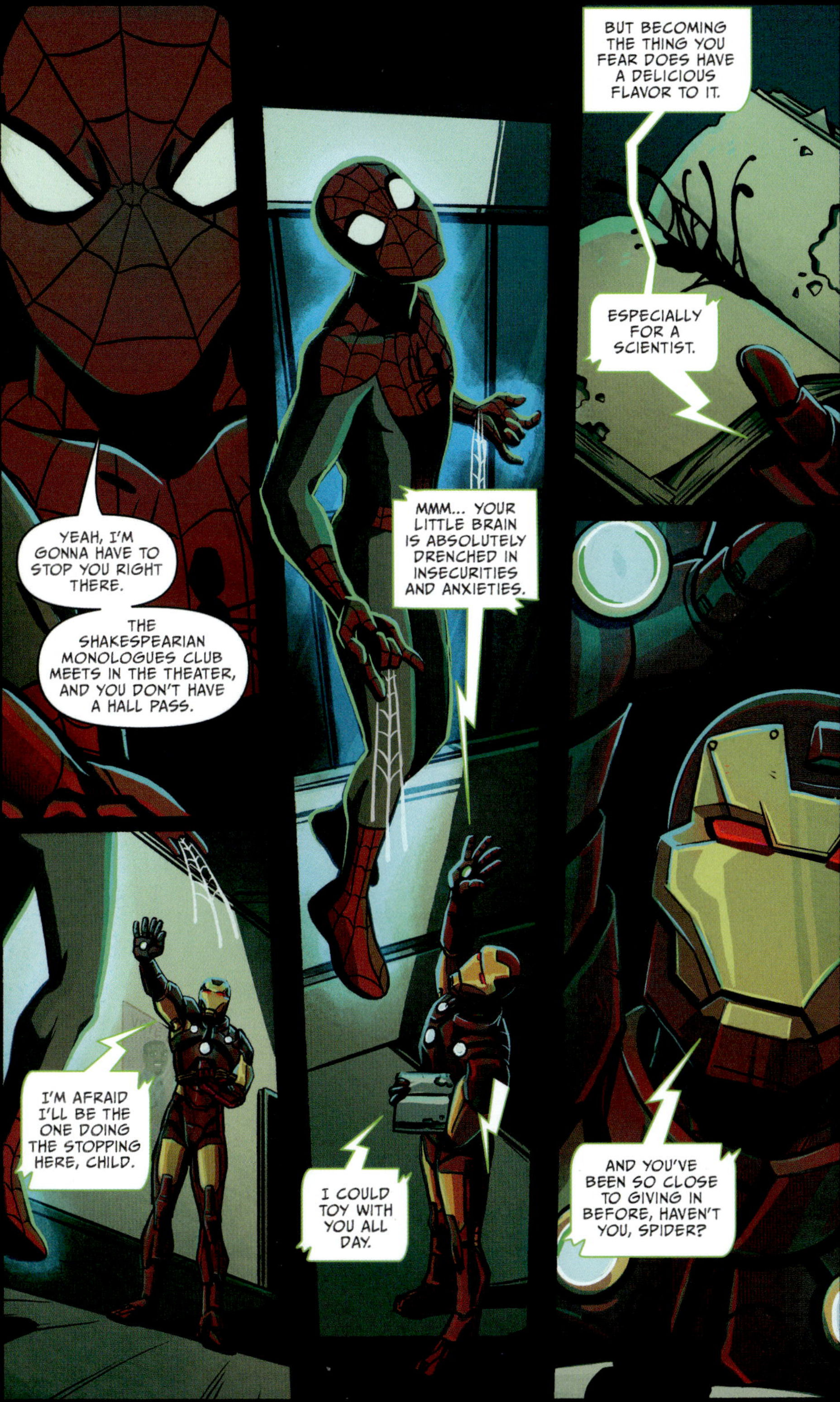
YEAH, I'M GONNA HAVE TO STOP YOU RIGHT THERE.
THE SHAKESPEARIAN MONOLOGUES CLUB MEETS IN THE THEATER, AND YOU DON'T HAVE A HALL PASS.
I'M AFRAID I'LL BE THE ONE DOING THE STOPPING HERE, CHILD.
MMM... YOUR LITTLE BRAIN IS ABSOLUTELY DRENCHED IN INSECURITIES AND ANXIETIES.
I COULD TOY WITH YOU ALL DAY.
BUT BECOMING THE THING YOU FEAR DOES HAVE A DELICIOUS FLAVOR TO IT.
ESPECIALLY FOR A SCIENTIST.
AND YOU'VE BEEN SO CLOSE TO GIVING IN BEFORE, HAVEN'T YOU, SPIDER?

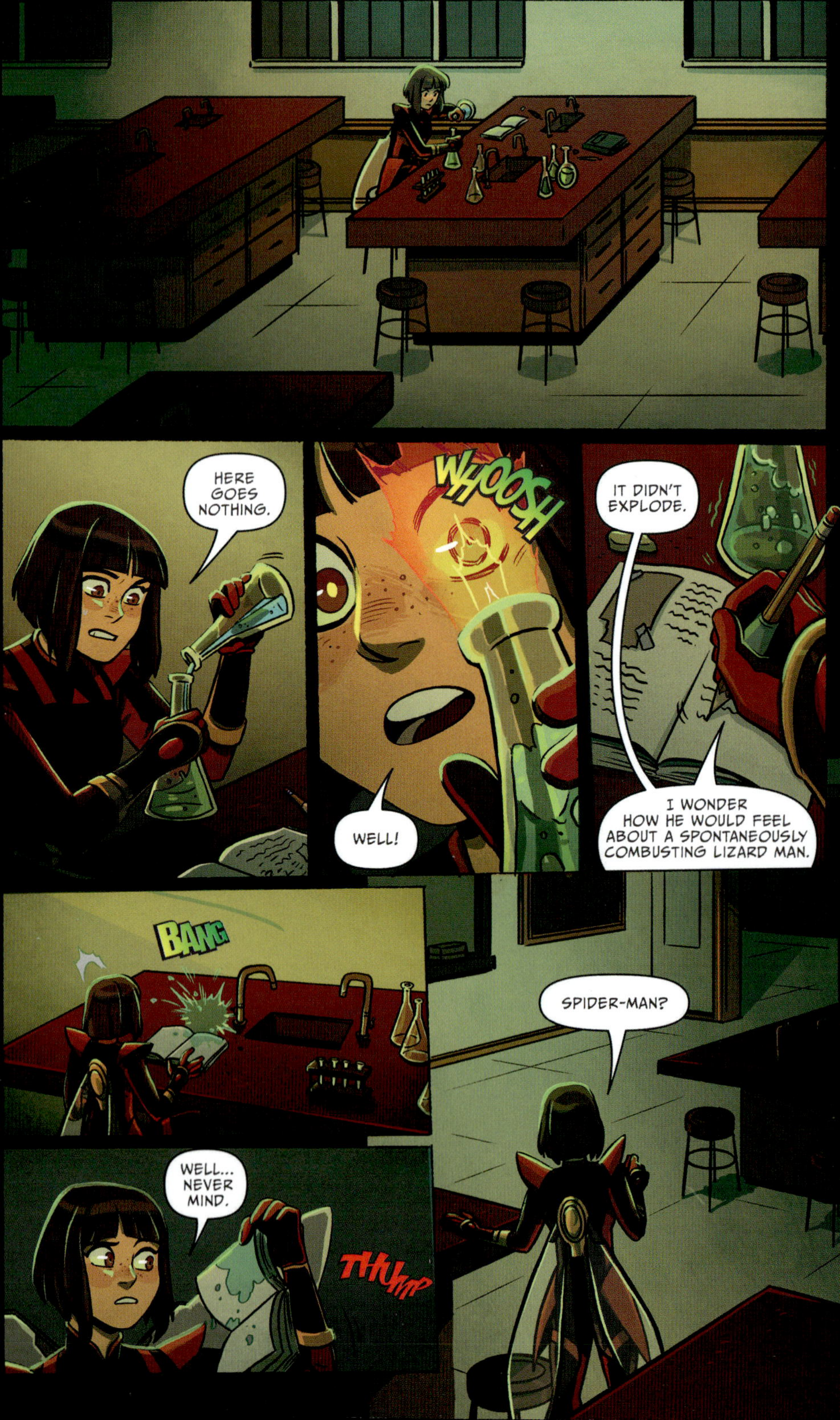
HERE GOES NOTHING.
WHOOSH
WELL!
IT DIDN'T EXPLODE.
I WONDER HOW HE WOULD FEEL ABOUT A SPONTANEOUSLY COMBUSTING LIZARD MAN.
BANG
SPIDER-MAN?
WELL... NEVER MIND.
THUMP

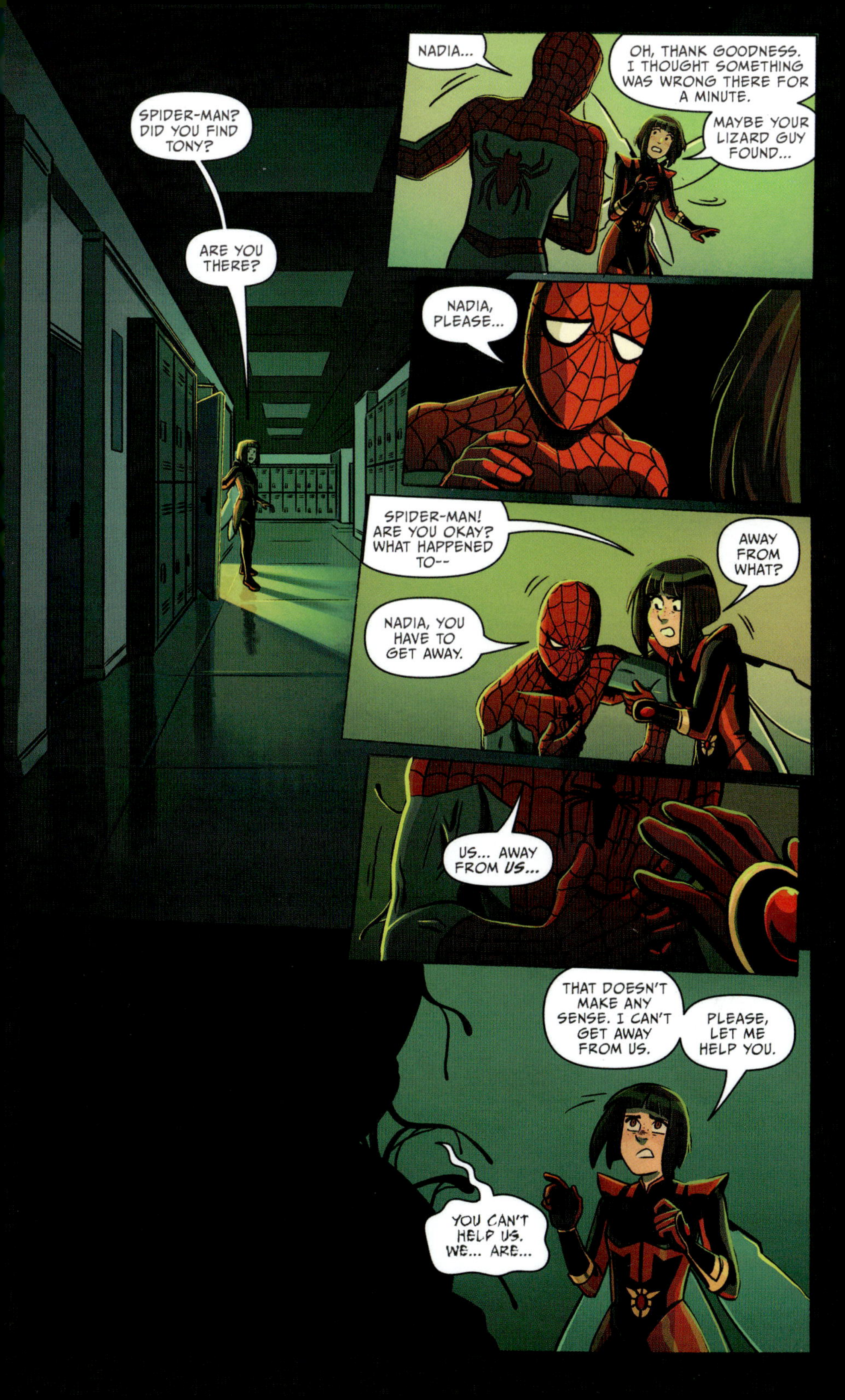
SPIDER-MAN? DID YOU FIND TONY?
ARE YOU THERE?
NADIA...
OH, THANK GOODNESS. I THOUGHT SOMETHING WAS WRONG THERE FOR A MINUTE.
MAYBE YOUR LIZARD GUY FOUND...
NADIA, PLEASE...
SPIDER-MAN! ARE YOU OKAY? WHAT HAPPENED TO--
NADIA, YOU HAVE TO GET AWAY.
AWAY FROM WHAT?
US... AWAY FROM US...
THAT DOESN'T MAKE ANY SENSE. I CAN'T GET AWAY FROM US.
PLEASE, LET ME HELP YOU.
YOU CAN'T HELP US. WE... ARE...

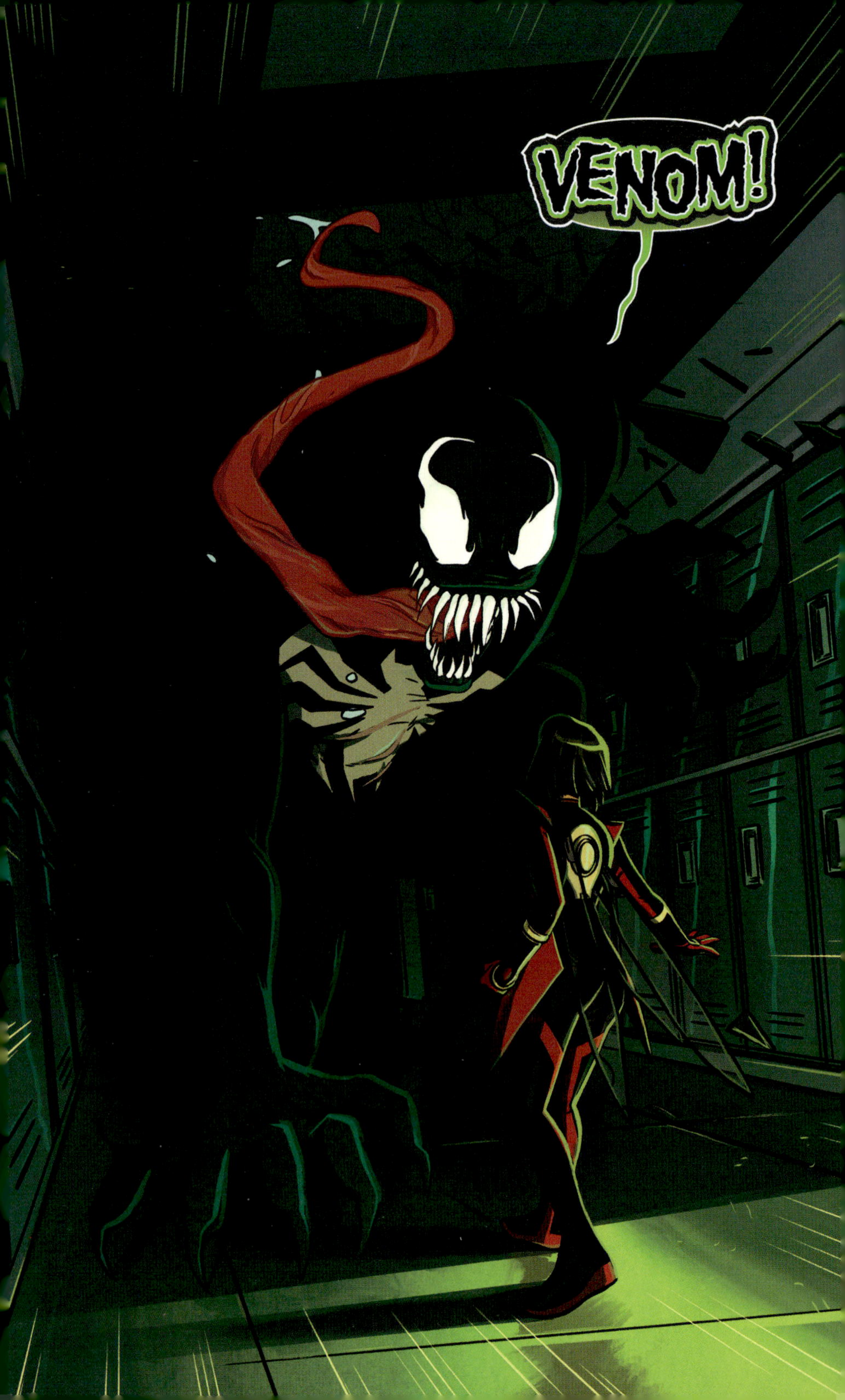
VENOM!

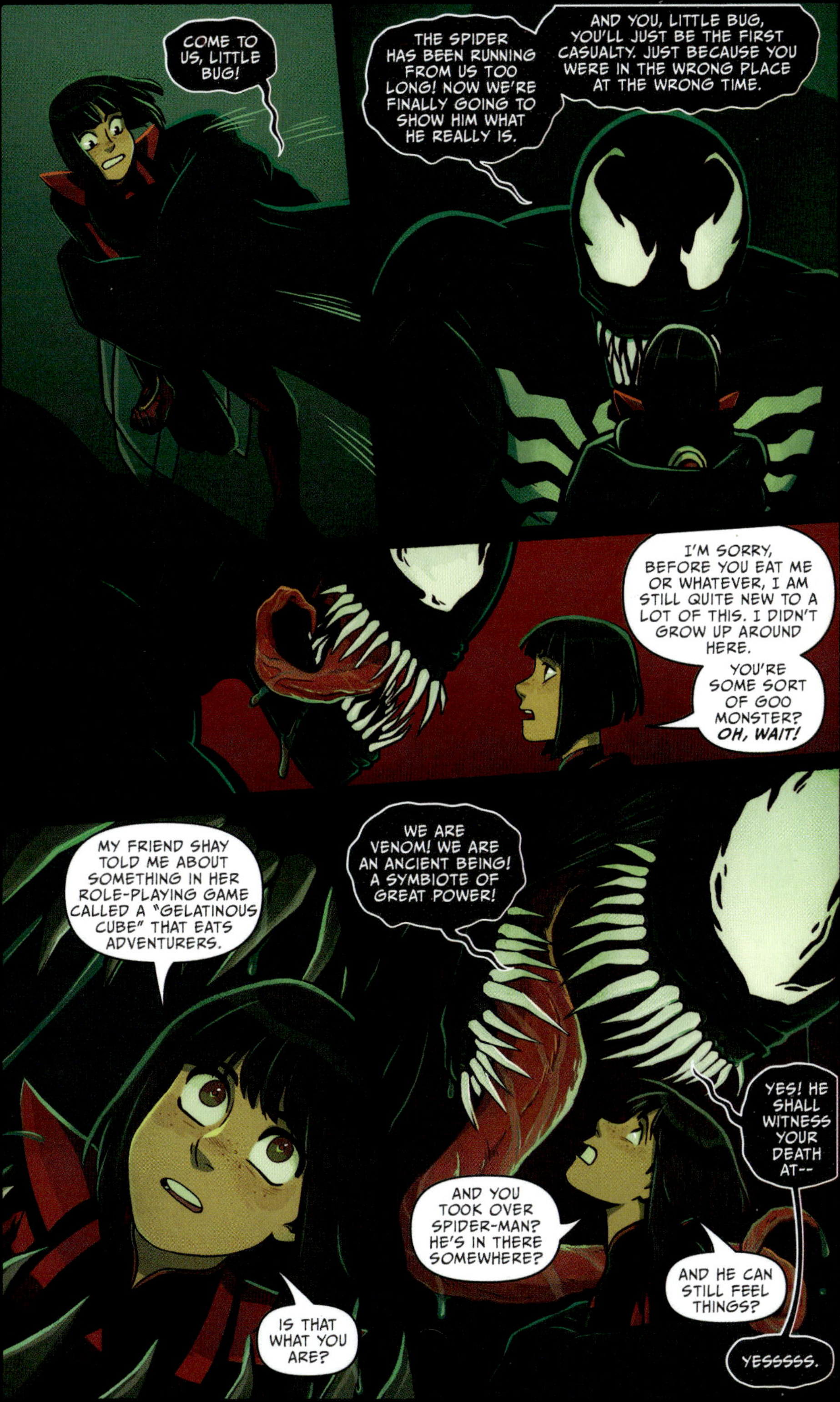
COME TO US, LITTLE BUG!
THE SPIDER HAS BEEN RUNNING FROM US TOO LONG! NOW WE'RE FINALLY GOING TO SHOW HIM WHAT HE REALLY IS.
AND YOU, LITTLE BUG, YOU'LL JUST BE THE FIRST CASUALTY. JUST BECAUSE YOU WERE IN THE WRONG PLACE AT THE WRONG TIME.
I'M SORRY, BEFORE YOU EAT ME OR WHATEVER, I AM STILL QUITE NEW TO A LOT OF THIS. I DIDN'T GROW UP AROUND HERE.
YOU'RE SOME SORT OF GOO MONSTER? OH, WAIT!
MY FRIEND SHAY TOLD ME ABOUT SOMETHING IN HER ROLE-PLAYING GAME CALLED A "GELATINOUS CUBE" THAT EATS ADVENTURERS.
IS THAT WHAT YOU ARE?
WE ARE VENOM! WE ARE AN ANCIENT BEING! A SYMBIOTE OF GREAT POWER!
AND YOU TOOK OVER SPIDER-MAN? HE'S IN THERE SOMEWHERE?
YES! HE SHALL WITNESS YOUR DEATH AT--
AND HE CAN STILL FEEL THINGS?
YESSSSS.

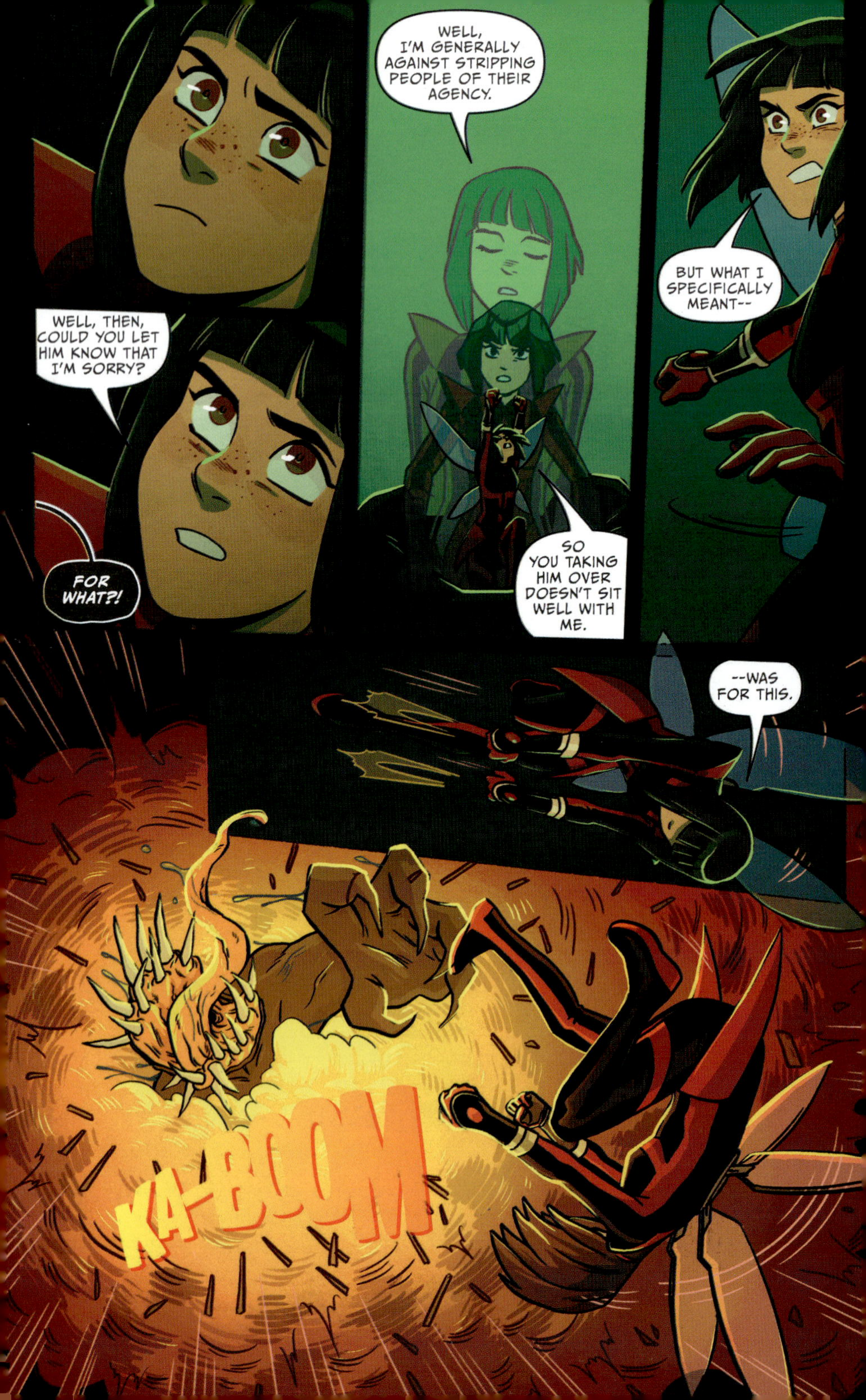
WELL, THEN, COULD YOU LET HIM KNOW THAT I'M SORRY?
FOR WHAT?!
WELL, I'M GENERALLY AGAINST STRIPPING PEOPLE OF THEIR AGENCY.
SO YOU TAKING HIM OVER DOESN'T SIT WELL WITH ME.
BUT WHAT I SPECIFICALLY MEANT--
--WAS FOR THIS.
KA-BOOM

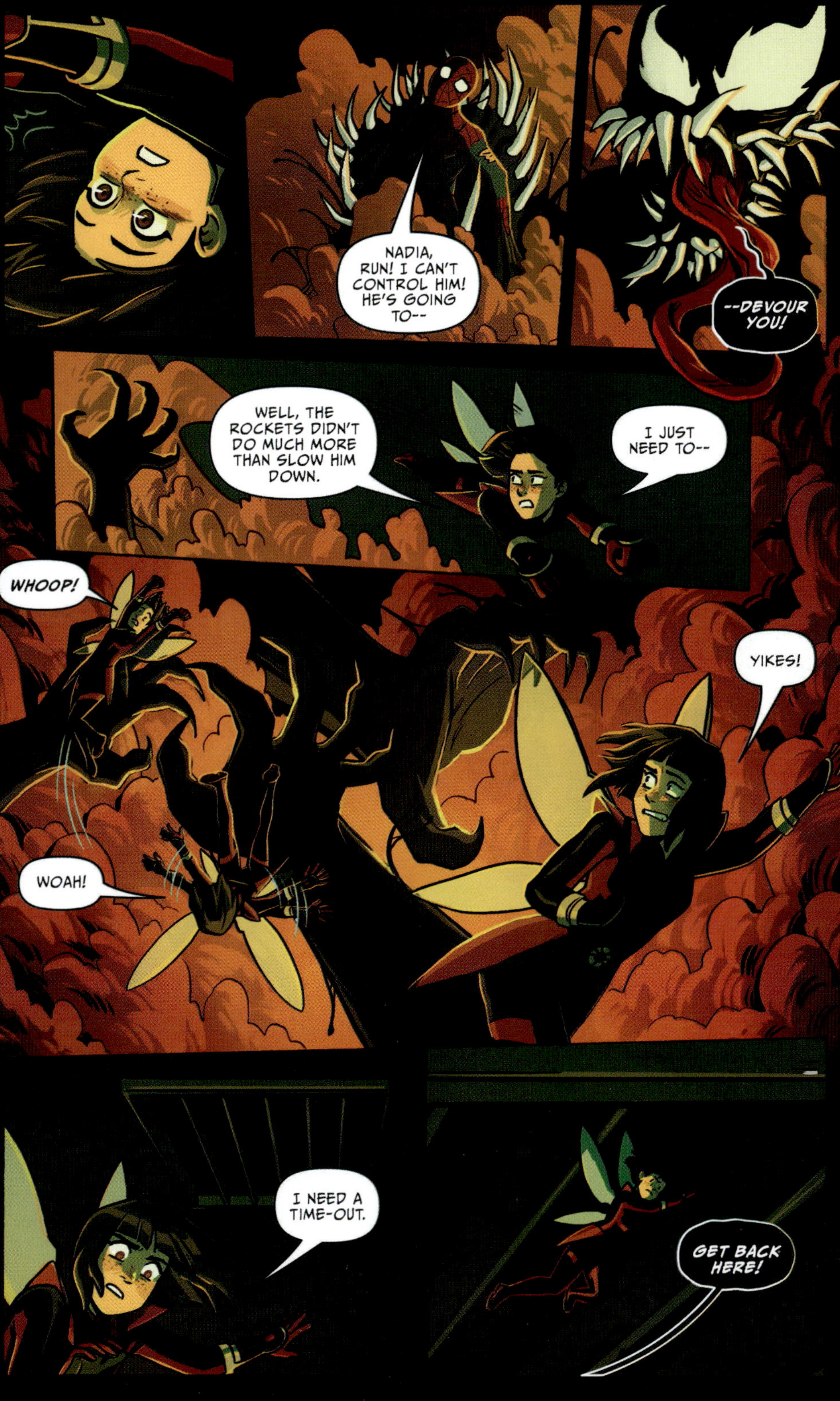
NADIA, RUN! I CAN'T CONTROL HIM! HE'S GOING TO--
--DEVOUR YOU!
WELL, THE ROCKETS DIDN'T DO MUCH MORE THAN SLOW HIM DOWN.
I JUST NEED TO--
WHOOP!
YIKES!
WOAH!
I NEED A TIME-OUT.
GET BACK HERE!

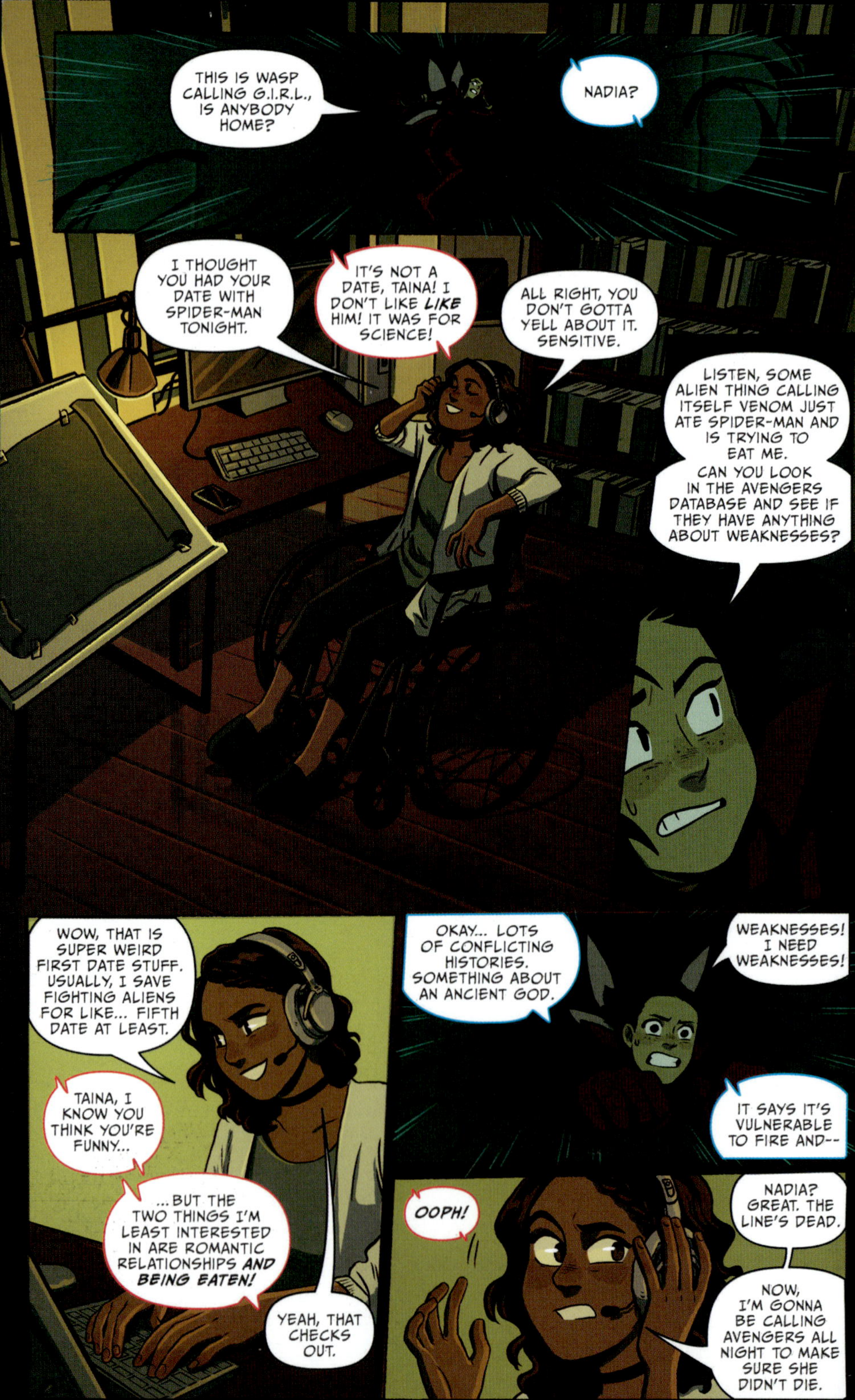
THIS IS WASP CALLING G.I.R.L., IS ANYBODY HOME?
NADIA?
I THOUGHT YOU HAD YOUR DATE WITH SPIDER-MAN TONIGHT.
IT'S NOT A DATE, TAINA! I DON'T LIKE *LIKE* HIM! IT WAS FOR SCIENCE!
ALL RIGHT, YOU DON'T GOTTA YELL ABOUT IT. SENSITIVE.
LISTEN, SOME ALIEN THING CALLING ITSELF VENOM JUST ATE SPIDER-MAN AND IS TRYING TO EAT ME.
CAN YOU LOOK IN THE AVENGERS DATABASE AND SEE IF THEY HAVE ANYTHING ABOUT WEAKNESSES?
WOW, THAT IS SUPER WEIRD FIRST DATE STUFF. USUALLY, I SAVE FIGHTING ALIENS FOR LIKE... FIFTH DATE AT LEAST.
TAINA, I KNOW YOU THINK YOU'RE FUNNY...
...BUT THE TWO THINGS I'M LEAST INTERESTED IN ARE ROMANTIC RELATIONSHIPS *AND BEING EATEN!*
YEAH, THAT CHECKS OUT.
OKAY... LOTS OF CONFLICTING HISTORIES. SOMETHING ABOUT AN ANCIENT GOD.
WEAKNESSES! I NEED WEAKNESSES!
IT SAYS IT'S VULNERABLE TO FIRE AND--
OOPH!
NADIA? GREAT. THE LINE'S DEAD.
NOW, I'M GONNA BE CALLING AVENGERS ALL NIGHT TO MAKE SURE SHE DIDN'T DIE.

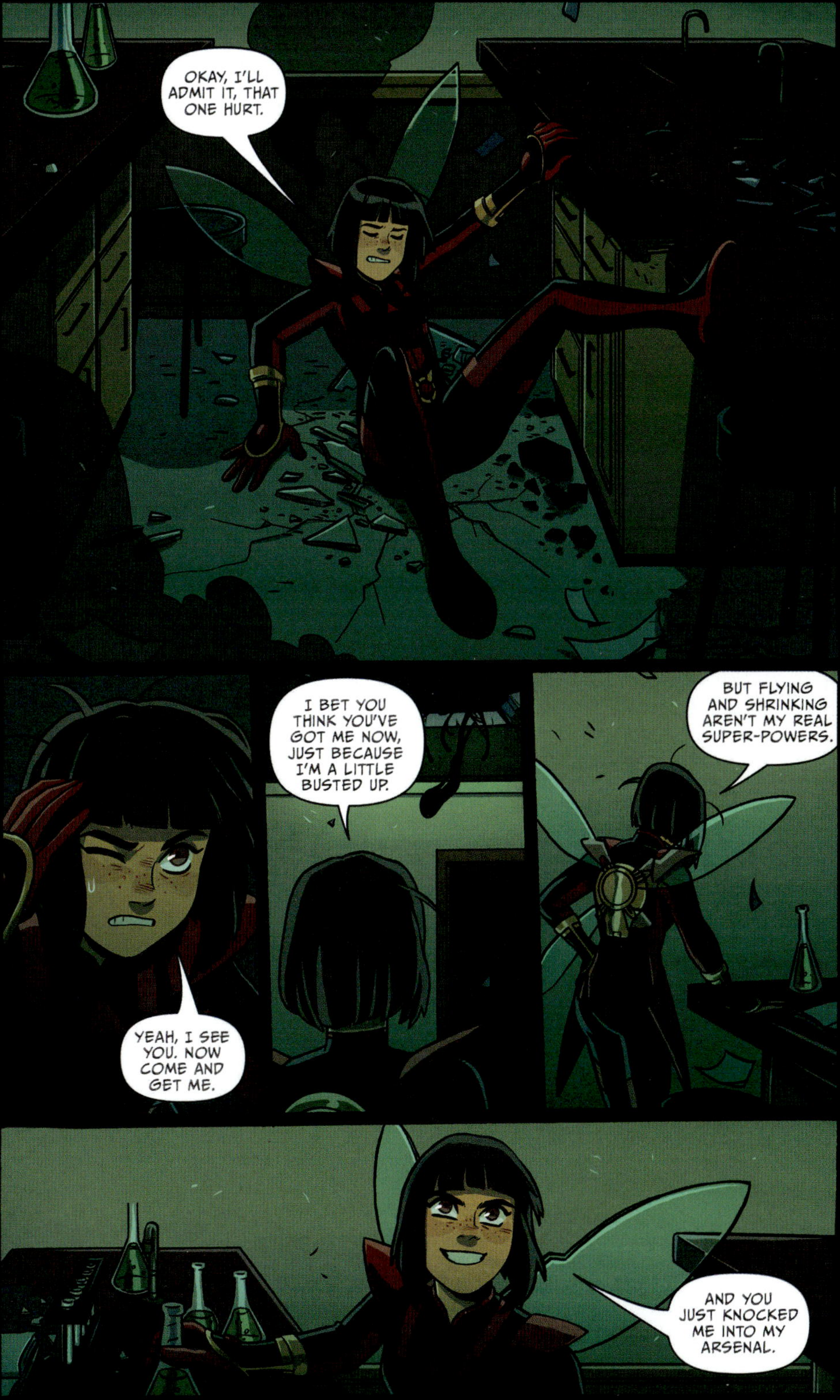
OKAY, I'LL ADMIT IT, THAT ONE HURT.
YEAH, I SEE YOU. NOW COME AND GET ME.
I BET YOU THINK YOU'VE GOT ME NOW, JUST BECAUSE I'M A LITTLE BUSTED UP.
BUT FLYING AND SHRINKING AREN'T MY REAL SUPER-POWERS.
AND YOU JUST KNOCKED ME INTO MY ARSENAL.

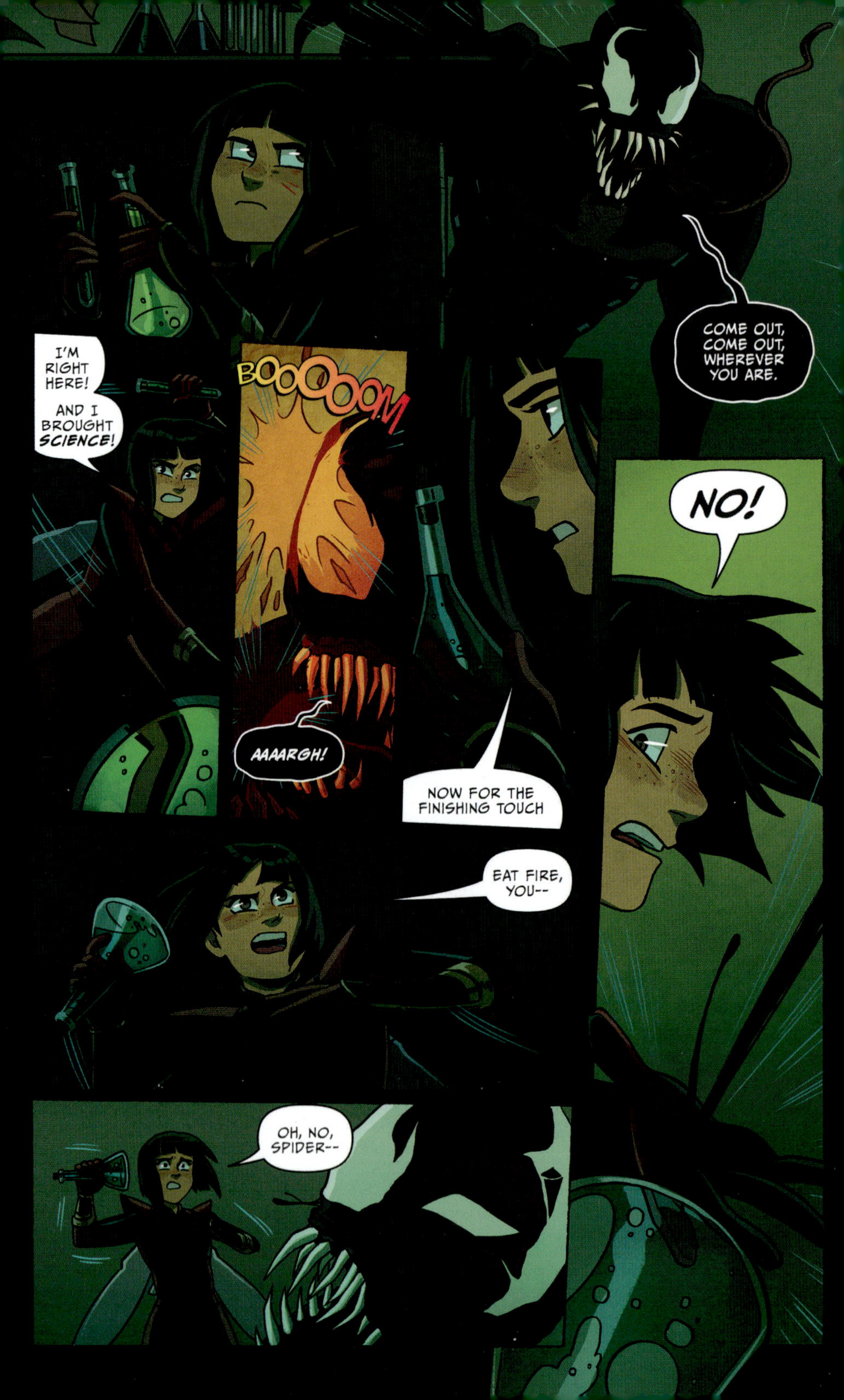
COME OUT, COME OUT, WHEREVER YOU ARE.
I'M RIGHT HERE!
AND I BROUGHT SCIENCE!
BOOOOOOM
AAAARGH!
NO!
NOW FOR THE FINISHING TOUCH
EAT FIRE, YOU--
OH, NO, SPIDER--

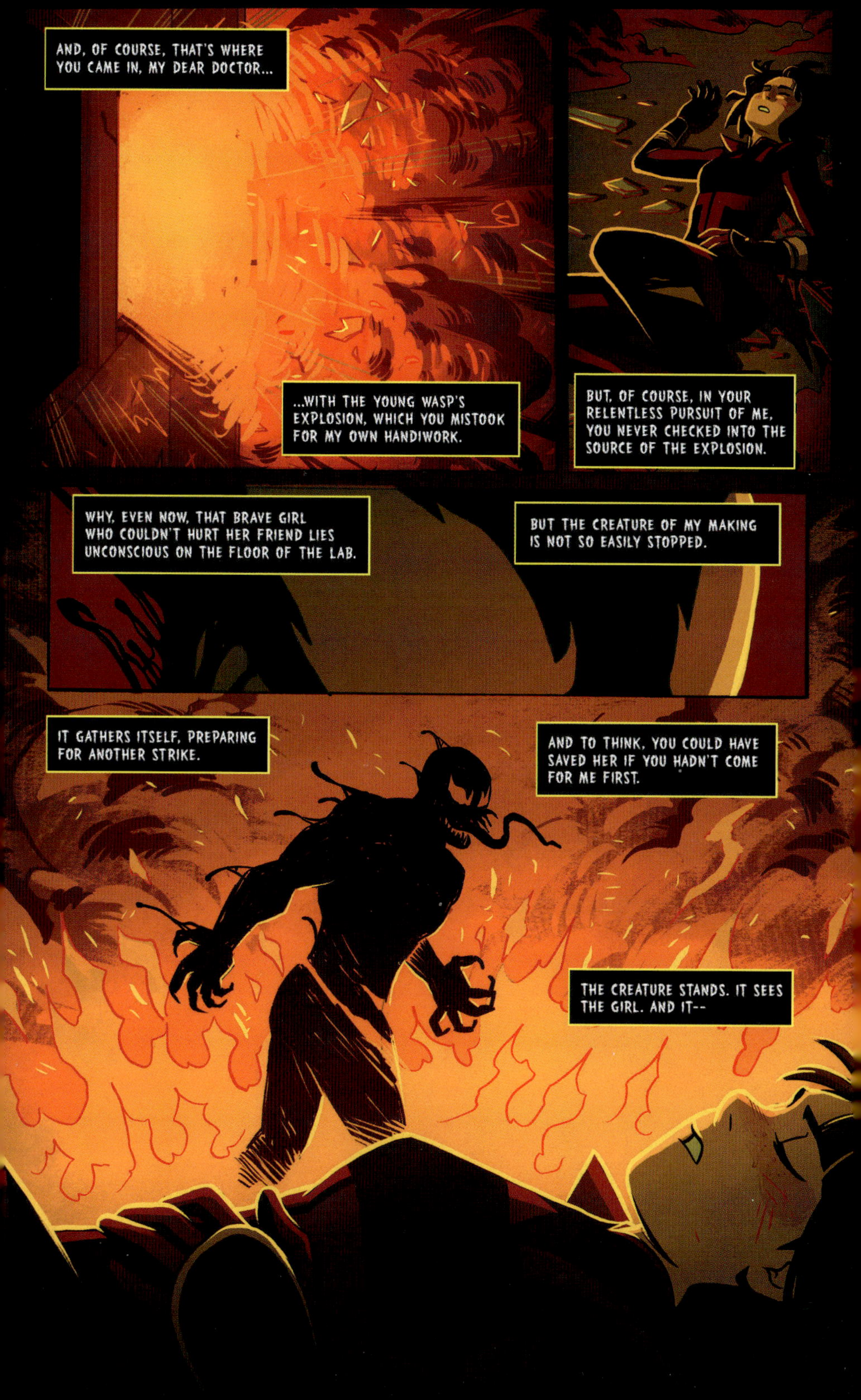
AND, OF COURSE, THAT'S WHERE YOU CAME IN, MY DEAR DOCTOR...
...WITH THE YOUNG WASP'S EXPLOSION, WHICH YOU MISTOOK FOR MY OWN HANDIWORK.
BUT, OF COURSE, IN YOUR RELENTLESS PURSUIT OF ME, YOU NEVER CHECKED INTO THE SOURCE OF THE EXPLOSION.
WHY, EVEN NOW, THAT BRAVE GIRL WHO COULDN'T HURT HER FRIEND LIES UNCONSCIOUS ON THE FLOOR OF THE LAB.
BUT THE CREATURE OF MY MAKING IS NOT SO EASILY STOPPED.
IT GATHERS ITSELF, PREPARING FOR ANOTHER STRIKE.
AND TO THINK, YOU COULD HAVE SAVED HER IF YOU HADN'T COME FOR ME FIRST.
THE CREATURE STANDS. IT SEES THE GIRL. AND IT--

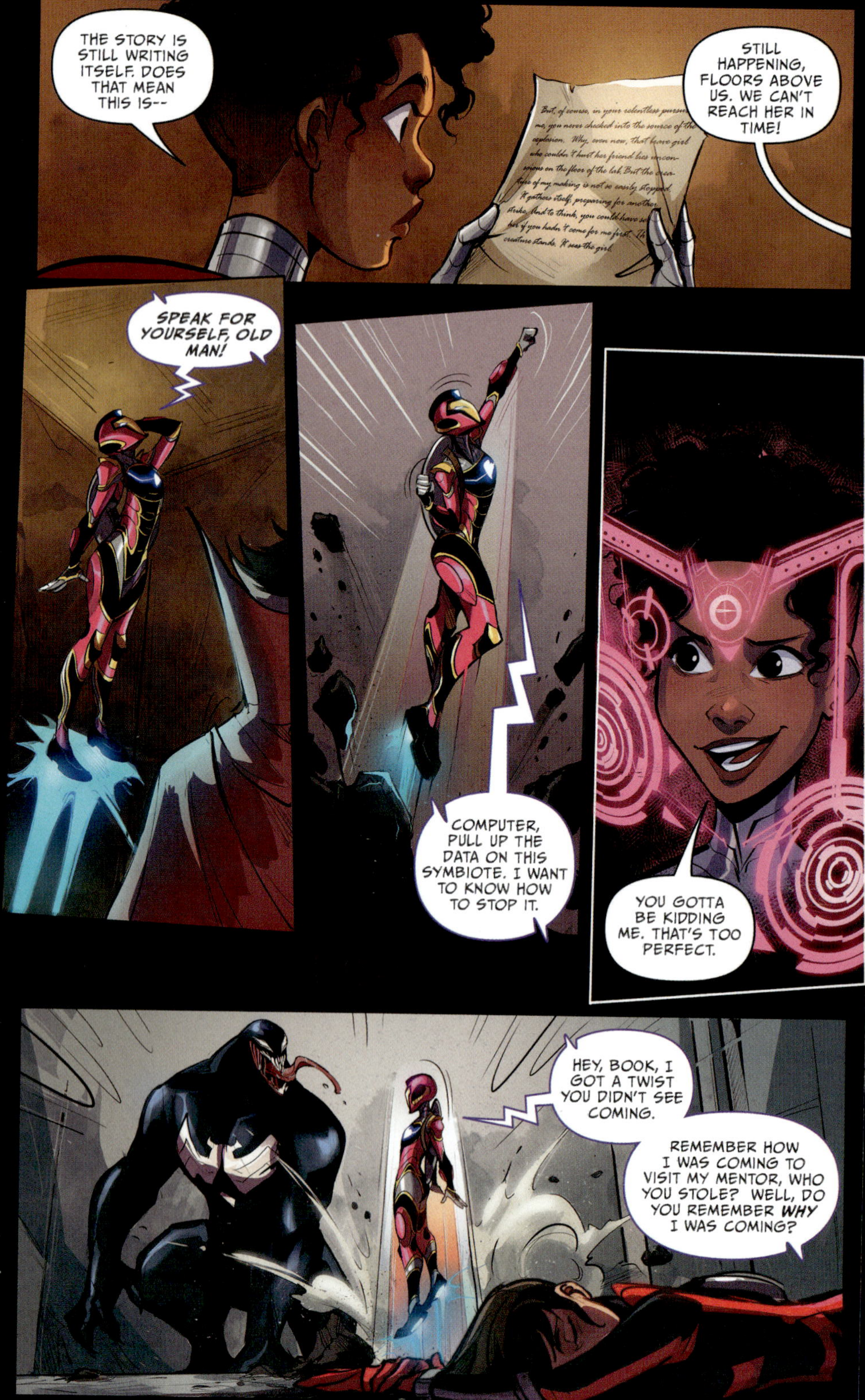
THE STORY IS STILL WRITING ITSELF. DOES THAT MEAN THIS IS--
But, of course, in your relentless pursu
me, you never checked into the source of the
explosion. Why, even now, that brave girl
who couldn't hurt her friend lies unconscious on the floor of the lab. But the crea-
ture of my making is not so easily stopped.
It gathers itself, preparing for another
strike. And to think, you could have s
her if you hadn't come for me first. Th
creature stands. It sees the girl.
STILL HAPPENING, FLOORS ABOVE US. WE CAN'T REACH HER IN TIME!
SPEAK FOR YOURSELF, OLD MAN!
COMPUTER, PULL UP THE DATA ON THIS SYMBIOTE. I WANT TO KNOW HOW TO STOP IT.
YOU GOTTA BE KIDDING ME. THAT'S TOO PERFECT.
HEY, BOOK, I GOT A TWIST YOU DIDN'T SEE COMING.
REMEMBER HOW I WAS COMING TO VISIT MY MENTOR, WHO YOU STOLE? WELL, DO YOU REMEMBER *WHY* I WAS COMING?

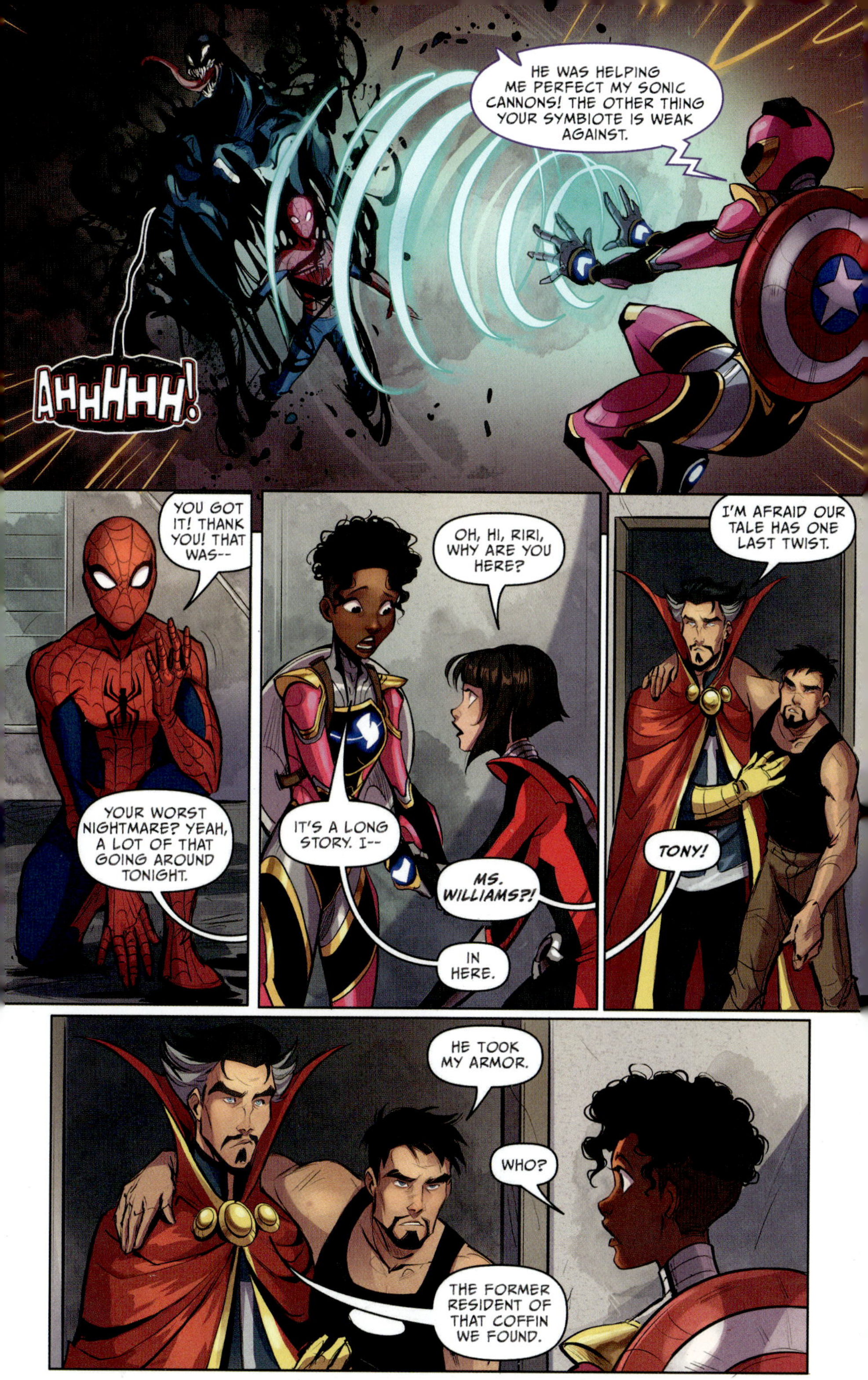
HE WAS HELPING ME PERFECT MY SONIC CANNONS! THE OTHER THING YOUR SYMBIOTE IS WEAK AGAINST.
AHHHHH!
YOU GOT IT! THANK YOU! THAT WAS--
YOUR WORST NIGHTMARE? YEAH, A LOT OF THAT GOING AROUND TONIGHT.
OH, HI, RIRI, WHY ARE YOU HERE?
IT'S A LONG STORY. I--
MS. WILLIAMS?!
IN HERE.
I'M AFRAID OUR TALE HAS ONE LAST TWIST.
TONY!
HE TOOK MY ARMOR.
WHO?
THE FORMER RESIDENT OF THAT COFFIN WE FOUND.

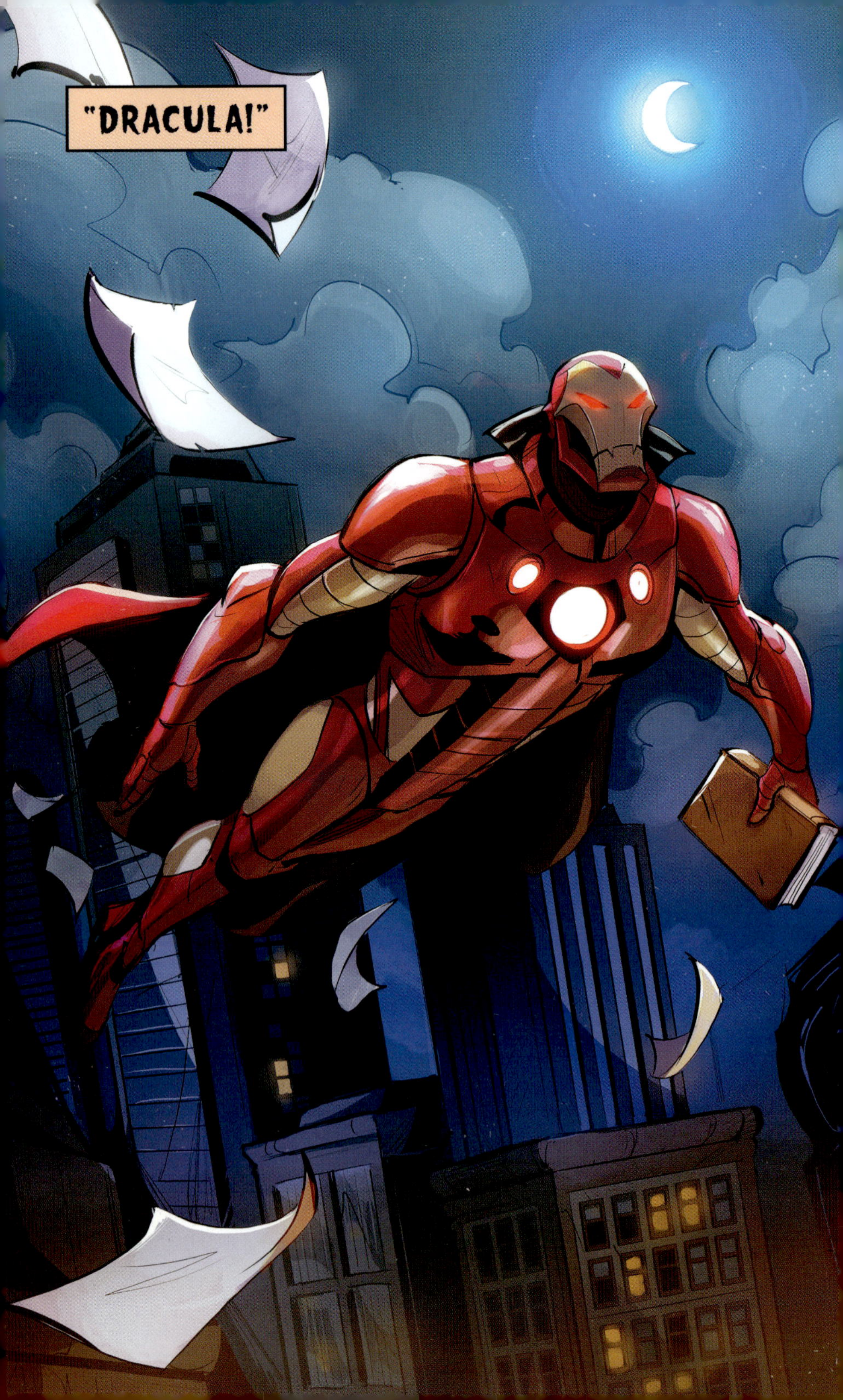
"DRACULA!"

Tome of Iron Dracula

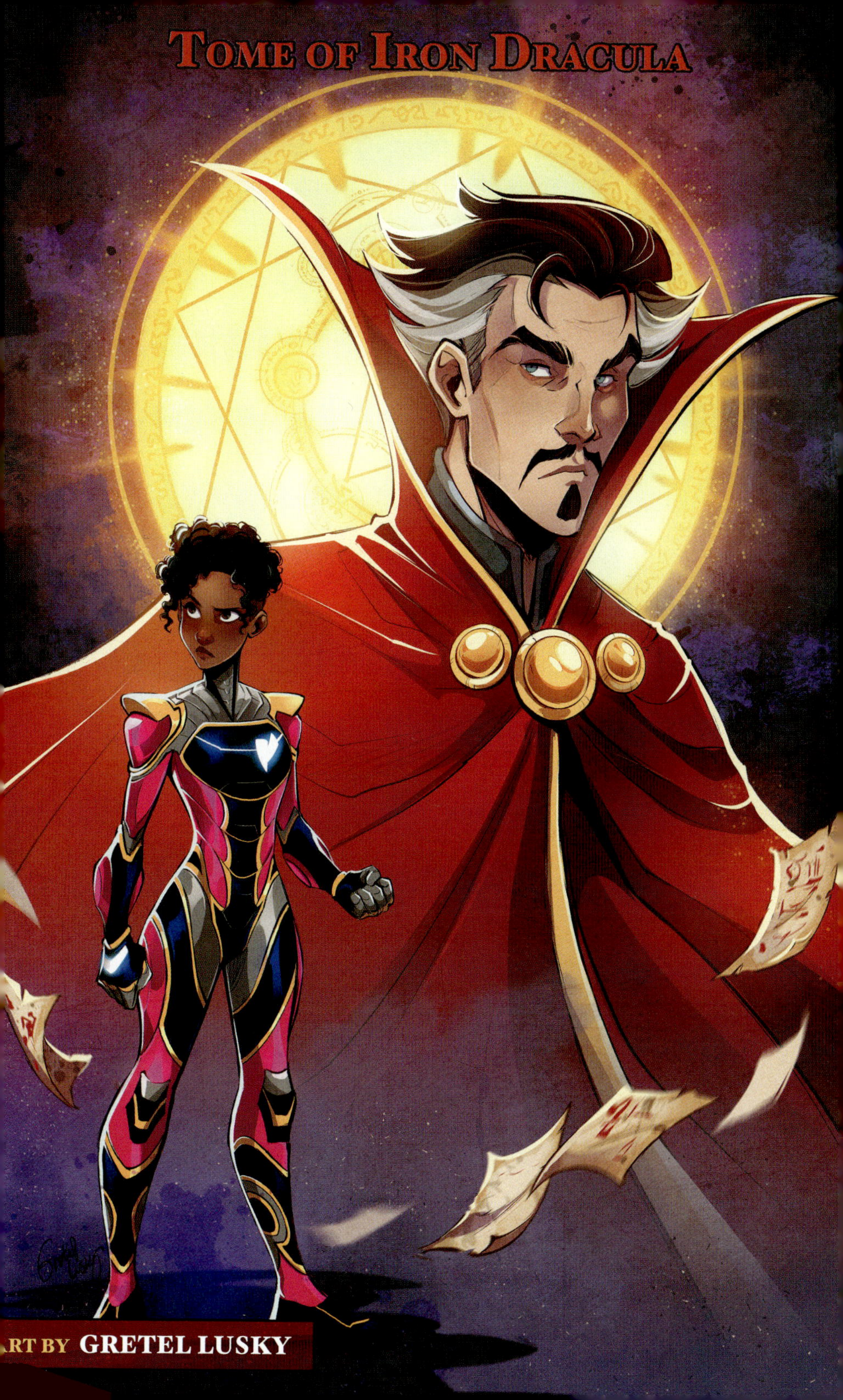

ART BY GRETEL LUSKY

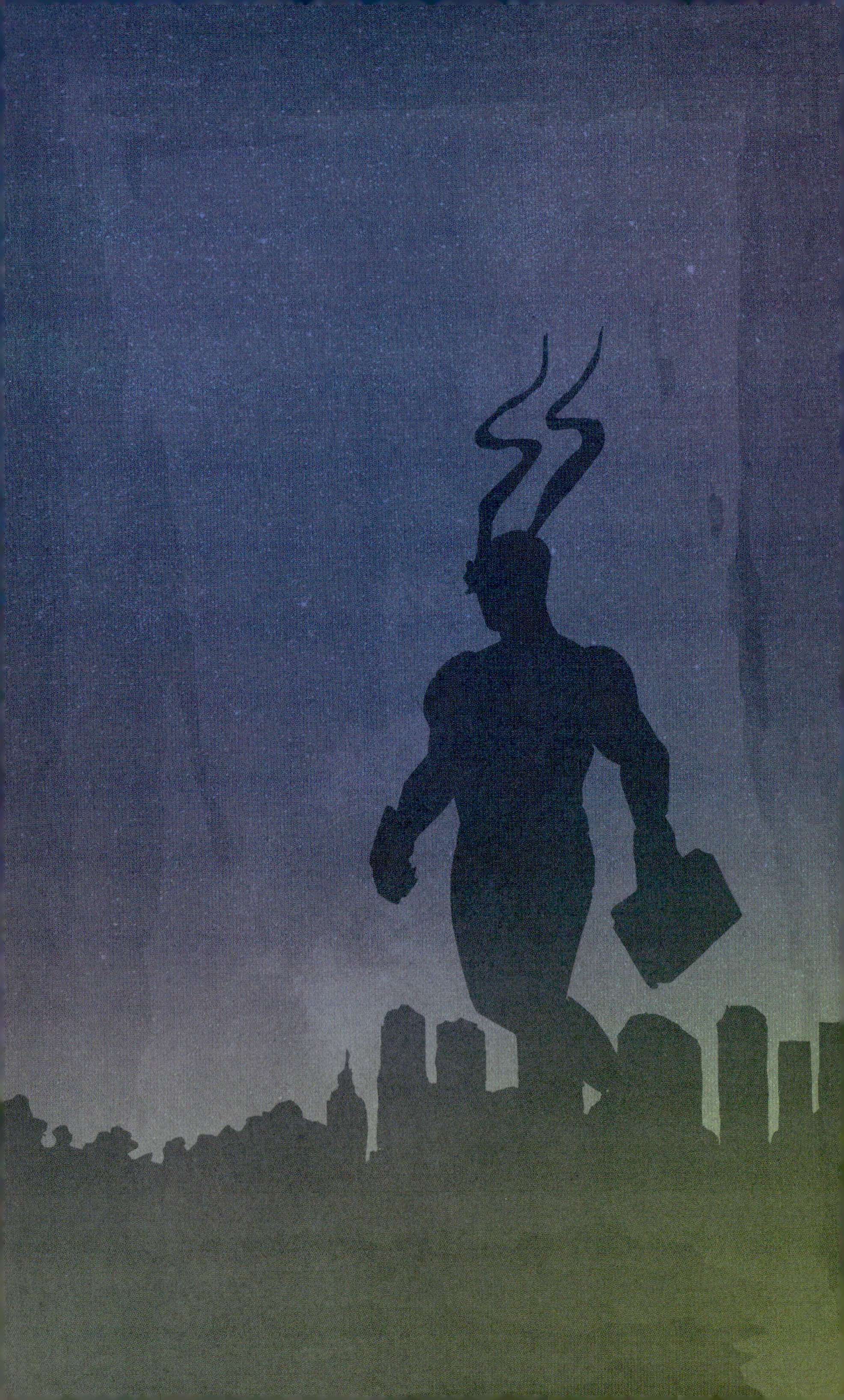

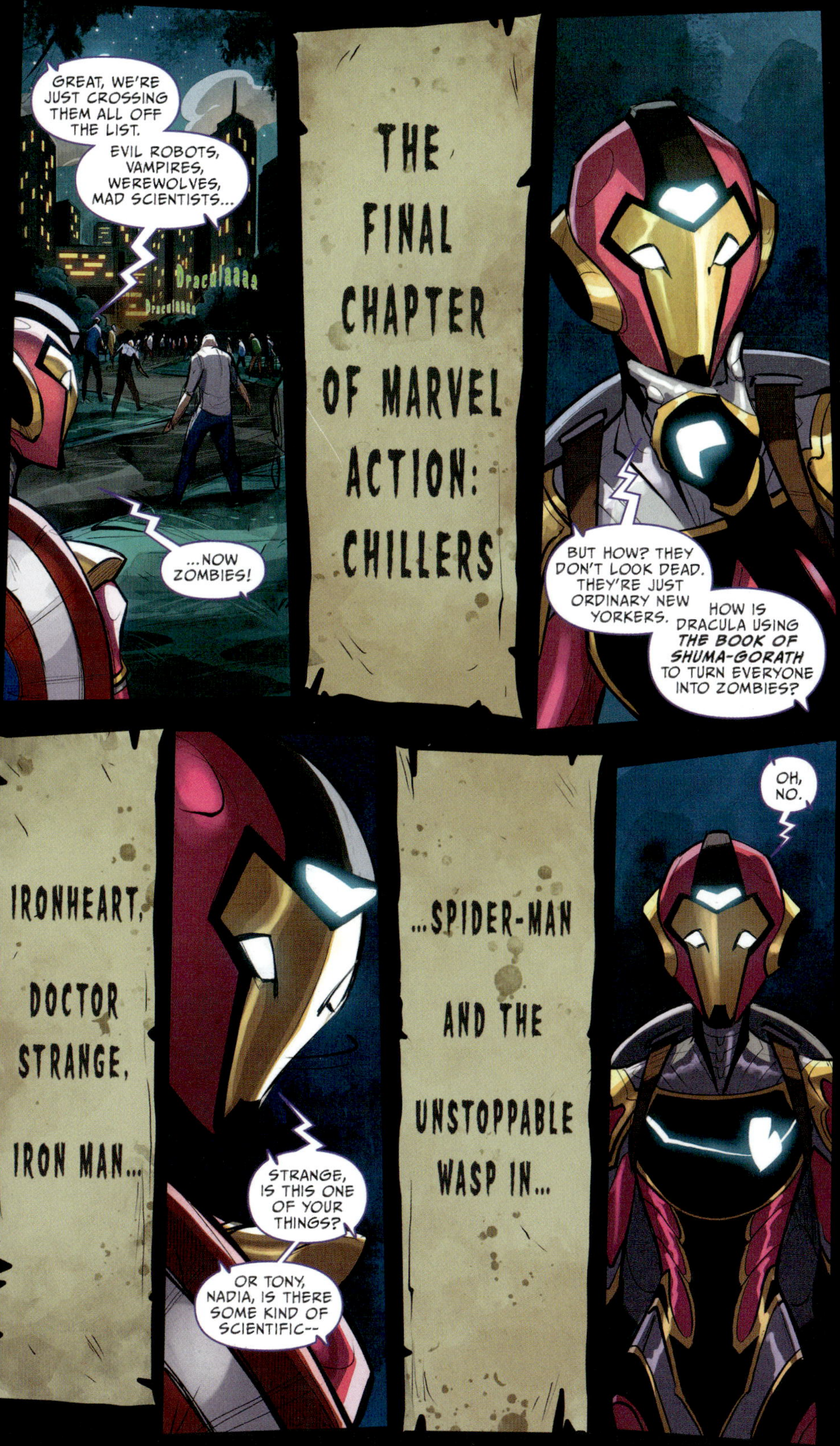
GREAT, WE'RE JUST CROSSING THEM ALL OFF THE LIST.
EVIL ROBOTS, VAMPIRES, WEREWOLVES, MAD SCIENTISTS...
Draculaaaa
...NOW ZOMBIES!
THE FINAL CHAPTER OF MARVEL ACTION: CHILLERS
BUT HOW? THEY DON'T LOOK DEAD. THEY'RE JUST ORDINARY NEW YORKERS.
HOW IS DRACULA USING *THE BOOK OF SHUMA-GORATH* TO TURN EVERYONE INTO ZOMBIES?
IRONHEART, DOCTOR STRANGE, IRON MAN...
STRANGE, IS THIS ONE OF YOUR THINGS?
OR TONY, NADIA, IS THERE SOME KIND OF SCIENTIFIC--
...SPIDER-MAN AND THE UNSTOPPABLE WASP IN...
OH, NO.

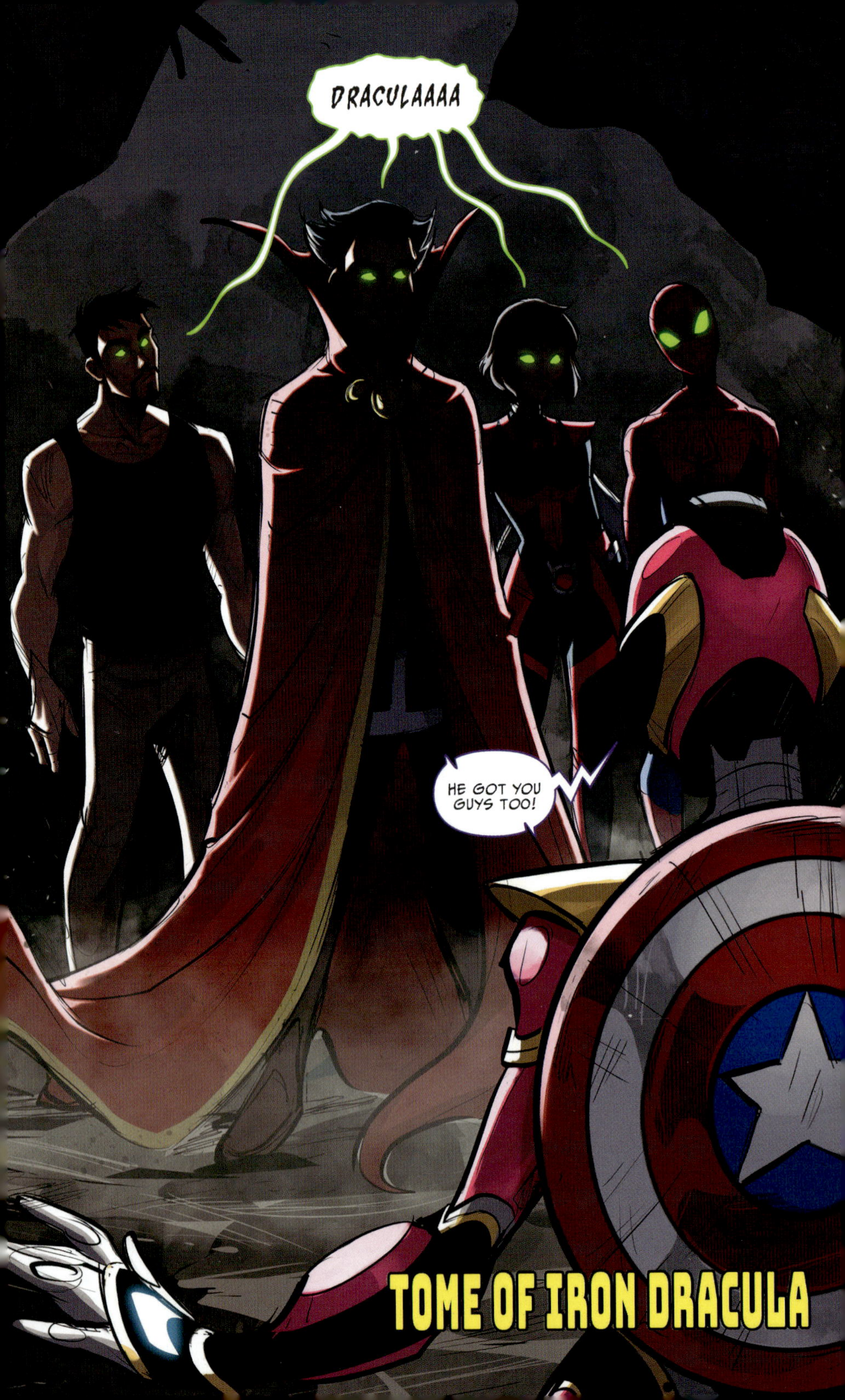
DRACULAAAA
HE GOT YOU GUYS TOO!
TOME OF IRON DRACULA

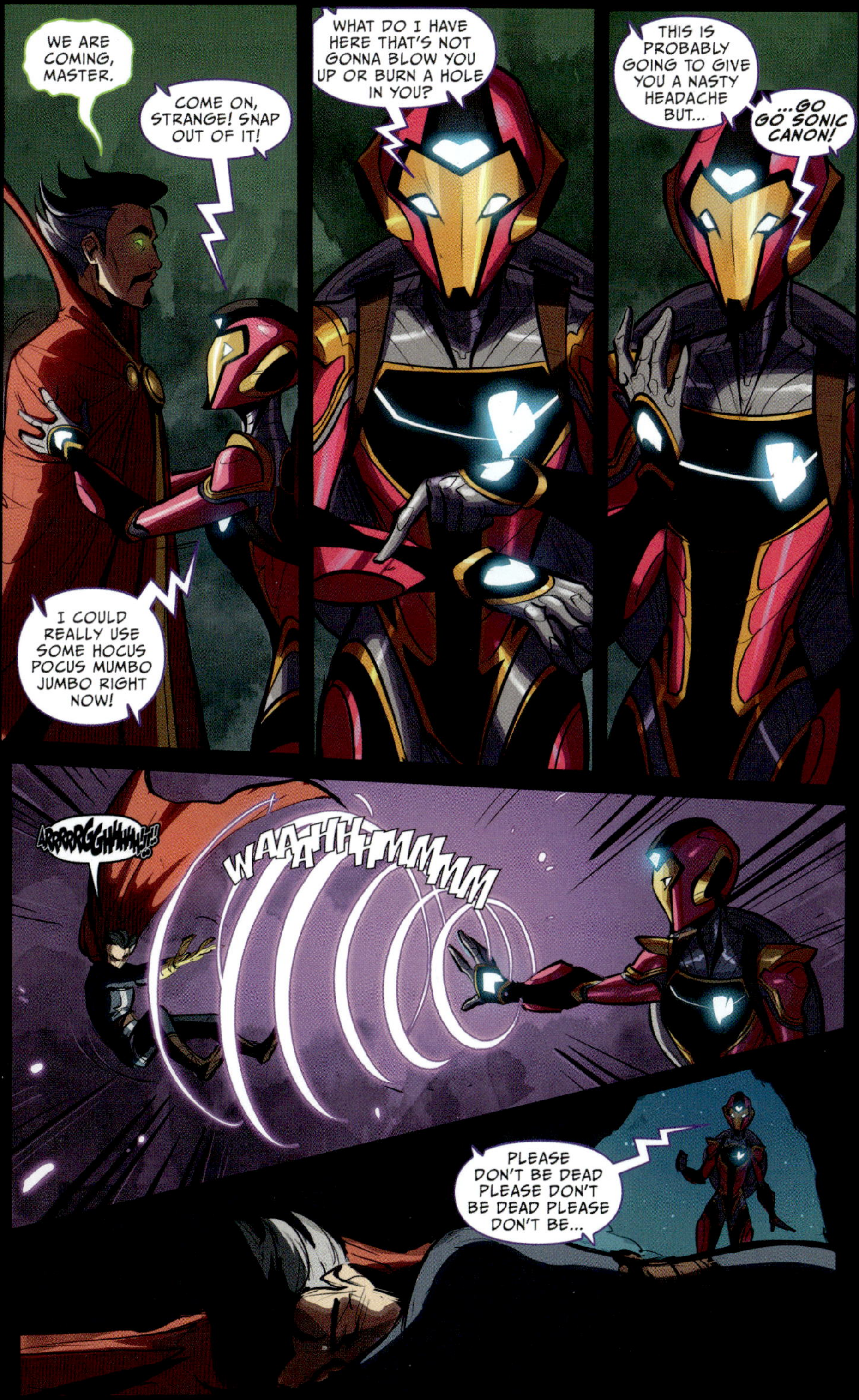
WE ARE COMING, MASTER.
COME ON, STRANGE! SNAP OUT OF IT!
I COULD REALLY USE SOME HOCUS POCUS MUMBO JUMBO RIGHT NOW!
WHAT DO I HAVE HERE THAT'S NOT GONNA BLOW YOU UP OR BURN A HOLE IN YOU?
THIS IS PROBABLY GOING TO GIVE YOU A NASTY HEADACHE BUT...
...GO GO SONIC CANON!
ARRRRRGGHHHHH!!
WAAAHHHMMMM
PLEASE DON'T BE DEAD PLEASE DON'T BE DEAD PLEASE DON'T BE...

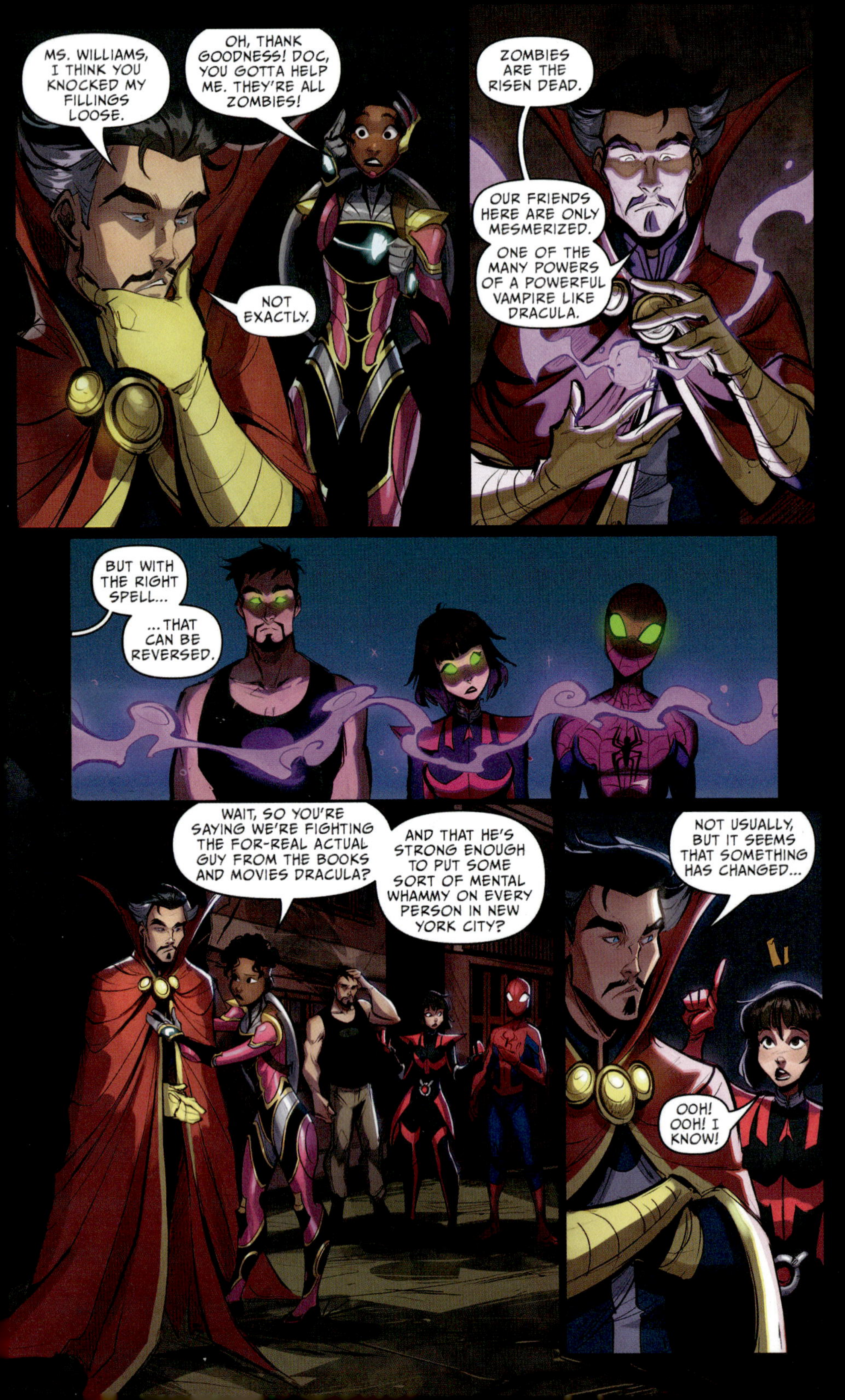
MS. WILLIAMS, I THINK YOU KNOCKED MY FILLINGS LOOSE.
OH, THANK GOODNESS! DOC, YOU GOTTA HELP ME. THEY'RE ALL ZOMBIES!
NOT EXACTLY.
ZOMBIES ARE THE RISEN DEAD.
OUR FRIENDS HERE ARE ONLY MESMERIZED.
ONE OF THE MANY POWERS OF A POWERFUL VAMPIRE LIKE DRACULA.
BUT WITH THE RIGHT SPELL...
...THAT CAN BE REVERSED.
WAIT, SO YOU'RE SAYING WE'RE FIGHTING THE FOR-REAL ACTUAL GUY FROM THE BOOKS AND MOVIES DRACULA?
AND THAT HE'S STRONG ENOUGH TO PUT SOME SORT OF MENTAL WHAMMY ON EVERY PERSON IN NEW YORK CITY?
NOT USUALLY, BUT IT SEEMS THAT SOMETHING HAS CHANGED...
OOH! OOH! I KNOW!

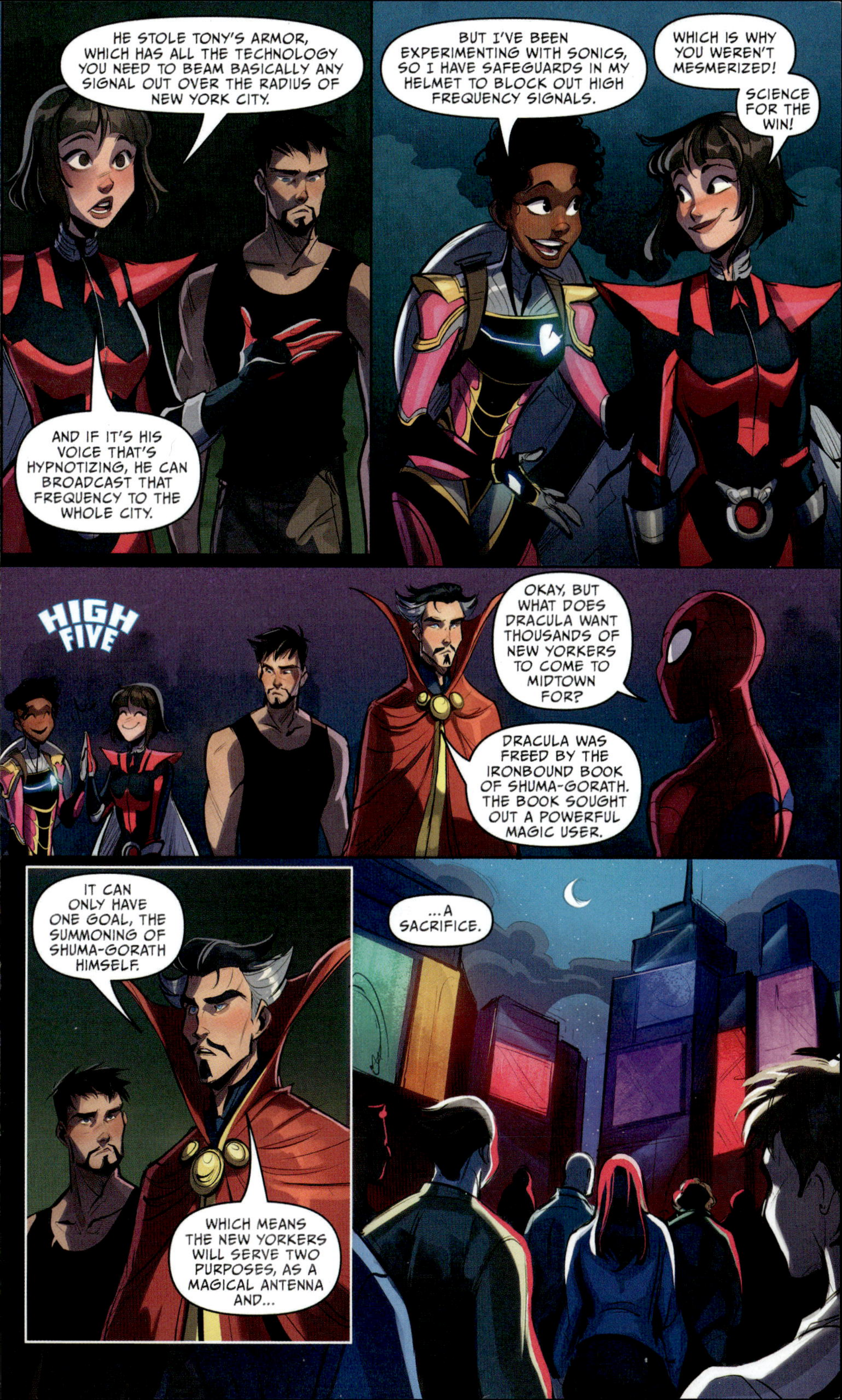
HE STOLE TONY'S ARMOR, WHICH HAS ALL THE TECHNOLOGY YOU NEED TO BEAM BASICALLY ANY SIGNAL OUT OVER THE RADIUS OF NEW YORK CITY.
AND IF IT'S HIS VOICE THAT'S HYPNOTIZING, HE CAN BROADCAST THAT FREQUENCY TO THE WHOLE CITY.
BUT I'VE BEEN EXPERIMENTING WITH SONICS, SO I HAVE SAFEGUARDS IN MY HELMET TO BLOCK OUT HIGH FREQUENCY SIGNALS.
WHICH IS WHY YOU WEREN'T MESMERIZED!
SCIENCE FOR THE WIN!
HIGH FIVE
OKAY, BUT WHAT DOES DRACULA WANT THOUSANDS OF NEW YORKERS TO COME TO MIDTOWN FOR?
DRACULA WAS FREED BY THE IRONBOUND BOOK OF SHUMA-GORATH. THE BOOK SOUGHT OUT A POWERFUL MAGIC USER.
IT CAN ONLY HAVE ONE GOAL, THE SUMMONING OF SHUMA-GORATH HIMSELF.
WHICH MEANS THE NEW YORKERS WILL SERVE TWO PURPOSES, AS A MAGICAL ANTENNA AND...
...A SACRIFICE.

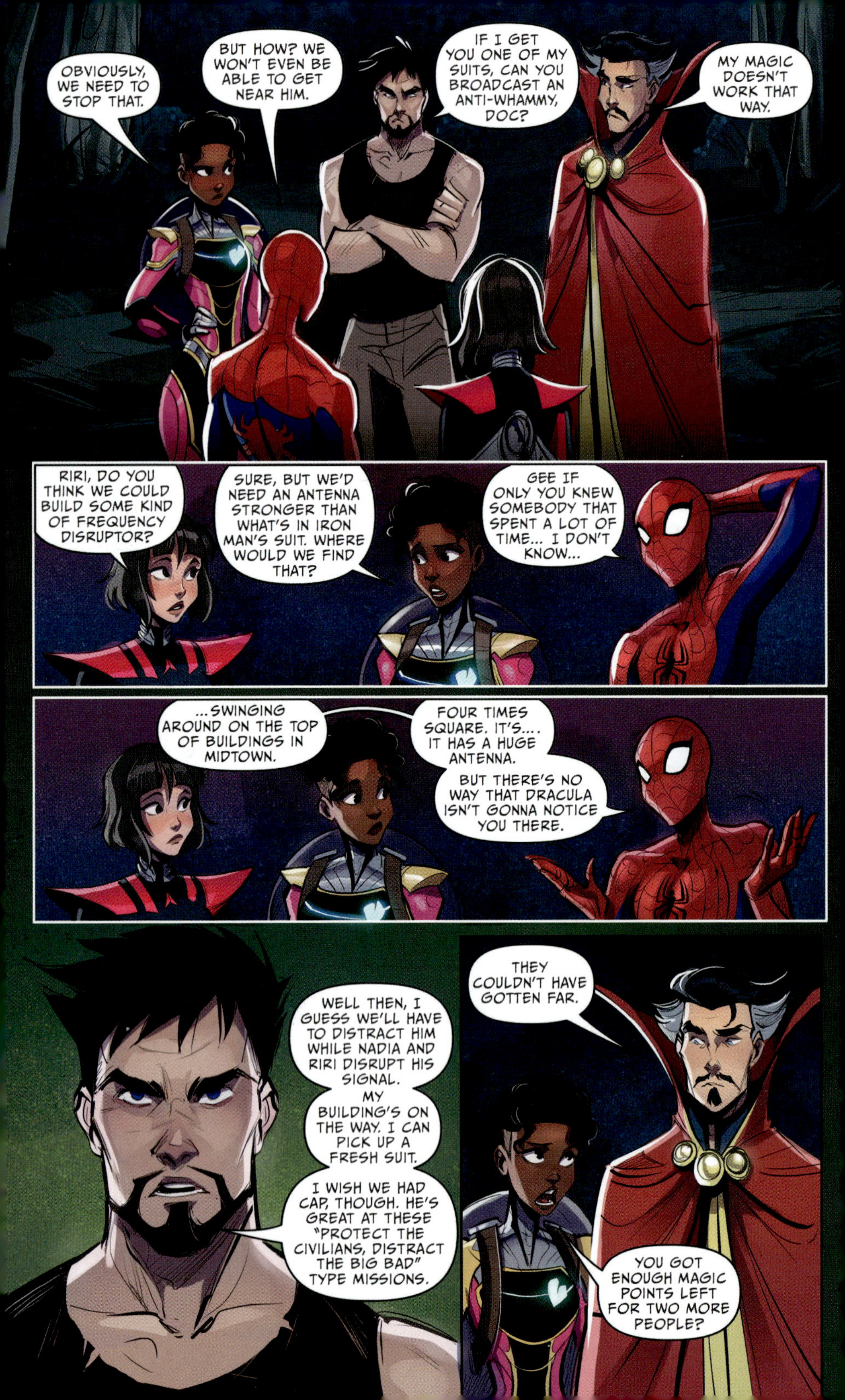

OBVIOUSLY, WE NEED TO STOP THAT.
BUT HOW? WE WON'T EVEN BE ABLE TO GET NEAR HIM.
IF I GET YOU ONE OF MY SUITS, CAN YOU BROADCAST AN ANTI-WHAMMY, DOC?
MY MAGIC DOESN'T WORK THAT WAY.
RIRI, DO YOU THINK WE COULD BUILD SOME KIND OF FREQUENCY DISRUPTOR?
SURE, BUT WE'D NEED AN ANTENNA STRONGER THAN WHAT'S IN IRON MAN'S SUIT. WHERE WOULD WE FIND THAT?
GEE IF ONLY YOU KNEW SOMEBODY THAT SPENT A LOT OF TIME... I DON'T KNOW...
...SWINGING AROUND ON THE TOP OF BUILDINGS IN MIDTOWN.
FOUR TIMES SQUARE. IT'S.... IT HAS A HUGE ANTENNA.
BUT THERE'S NO WAY THAT DRACULA ISN'T GONNA NOTICE YOU THERE.
WELL THEN, I GUESS WE'LL HAVE TO DISTRACT HIM WHILE NADIA AND RIRI DISRUPT HIS SIGNAL.
MY BUILDING'S ON THE WAY. I CAN PICK UP A FRESH SUIT.
I WISH WE HAD CAP, THOUGH. HE'S GREAT AT THESE "PROTECT THE CIVILIANS, DISTRACT THE BIG BAD" TYPE MISSIONS.
THEY COULDN'T HAVE GOTTEN FAR.
YOU GOT ENOUGH MAGIC POINTS LEFT FOR TWO MORE PEOPLE?

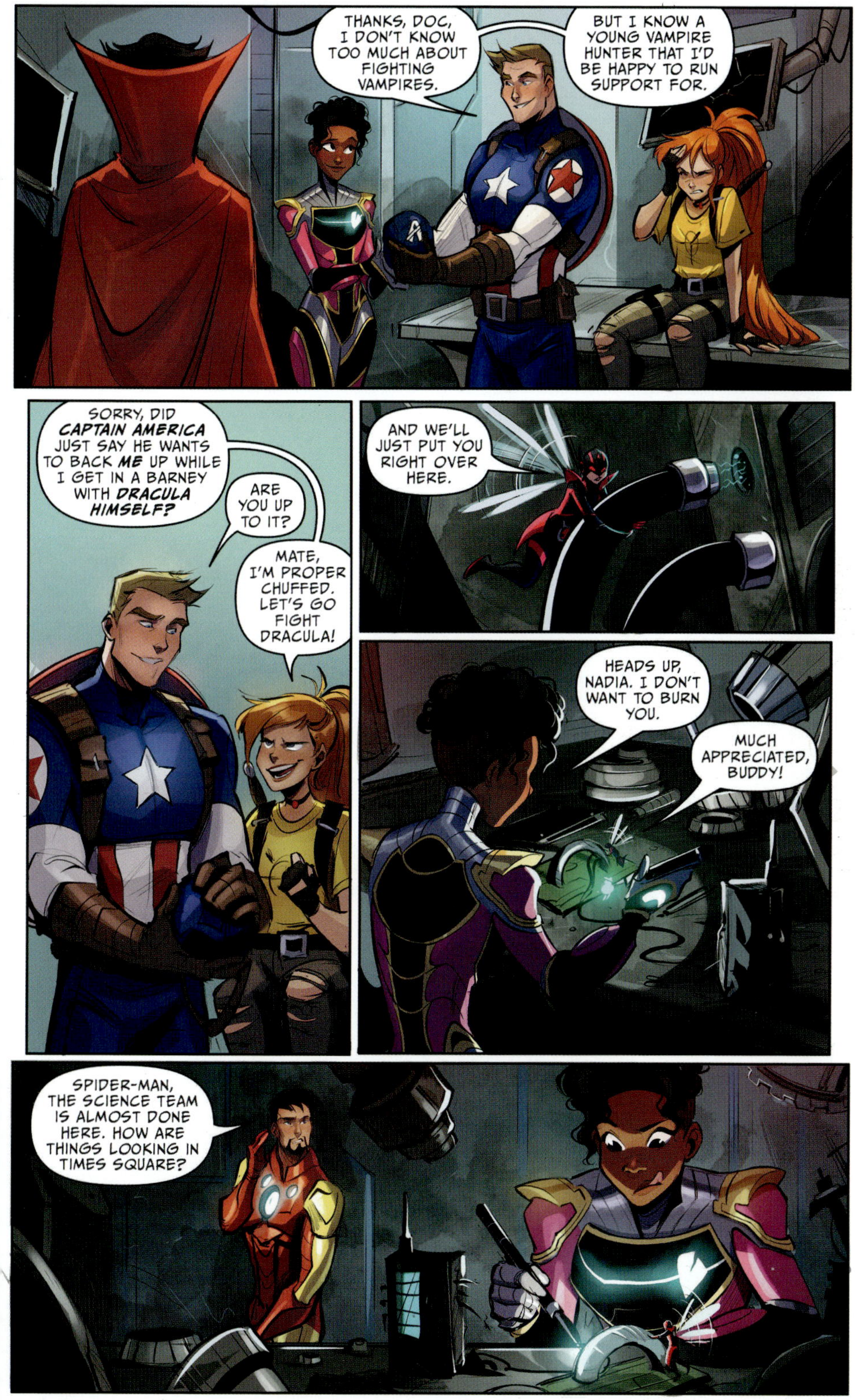
THANKS, DOC, I DON'T KNOW TOO MUCH ABOUT FIGHTING VAMPIRES.
BUT I KNOW A YOUNG VAMPIRE HUNTER THAT I'D BE HAPPY TO RUN SUPPORT FOR.
SORRY, DID CAPTAIN AMERICA JUST SAY HE WANTS TO BACK ME UP WHILE I GET IN A BARNEY WITH DRACULA HIMSELF?
ARE YOU UP TO IT?
MATE, I'M PROPER CHUFFED. LET'S GO FIGHT DRACULA!
AND WE'LL JUST PUT YOU RIGHT OVER HERE.
HEADS UP, NADIA. I DON'T WANT TO BURN YOU.
MUCH APPRECIATED, BUDDY!
SPIDER-MAN, THE SCIENCE TEAM IS ALMOST DONE HERE. HOW ARE THINGS LOOKING IN TIMES SQUARE?

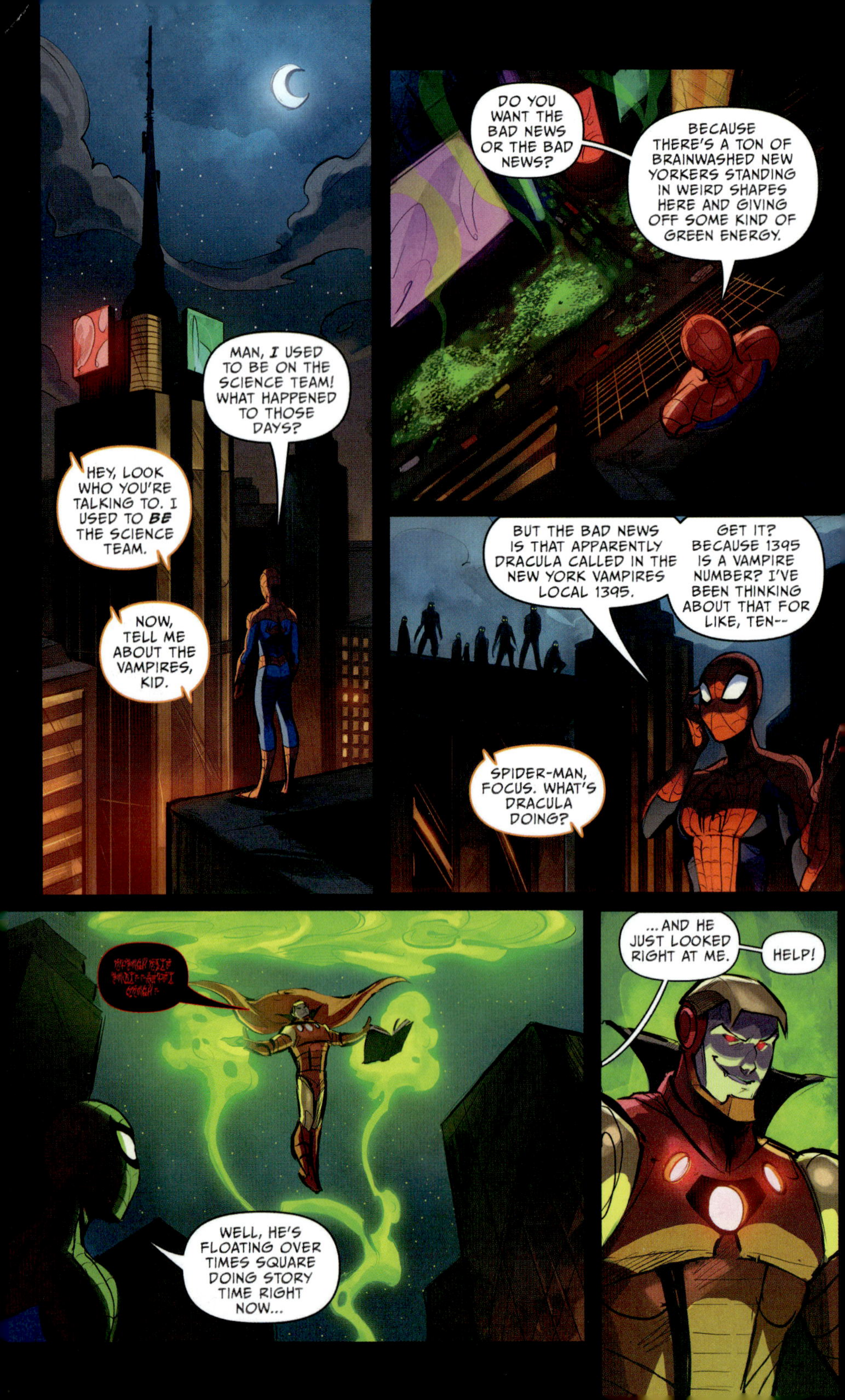
MAN, *I* USED TO BE ON THE SCIENCE TEAM! WHAT HAPPENED TO THOSE DAYS?
HEY, LOOK WHO YOU'RE TALKING TO. I USED TO ***BE*** THE SCIENCE TEAM.
NOW, TELL ME ABOUT THE VAMPIRES, KID.
DO YOU WANT THE BAD NEWS OR THE BAD NEWS?
BECAUSE THERE'S A TON OF BRAINWASHED NEW YORKERS STANDING IN WEIRD SHAPES HERE AND GIVING OFF SOME KIND OF GREEN ENERGY.
BUT THE BAD NEWS IS THAT APPARENTLY DRACULA CALLED IN THE NEW YORK VAMPIRES LOCAL 1395.
GET IT? BECAUSE 1395 IS A VAMPIRE NUMBER? I'VE BEEN THINKING ABOUT THAT FOR LIKE, TEN--
SPIDER-MAN, FOCUS. WHAT'S DRACULA DOING?
WELL, HE'S FLOATING OVER TIMES SQUARE DOING STORY TIME RIGHT NOW...
...AND HE JUST LOOKED RIGHT AT ME.
HELP!

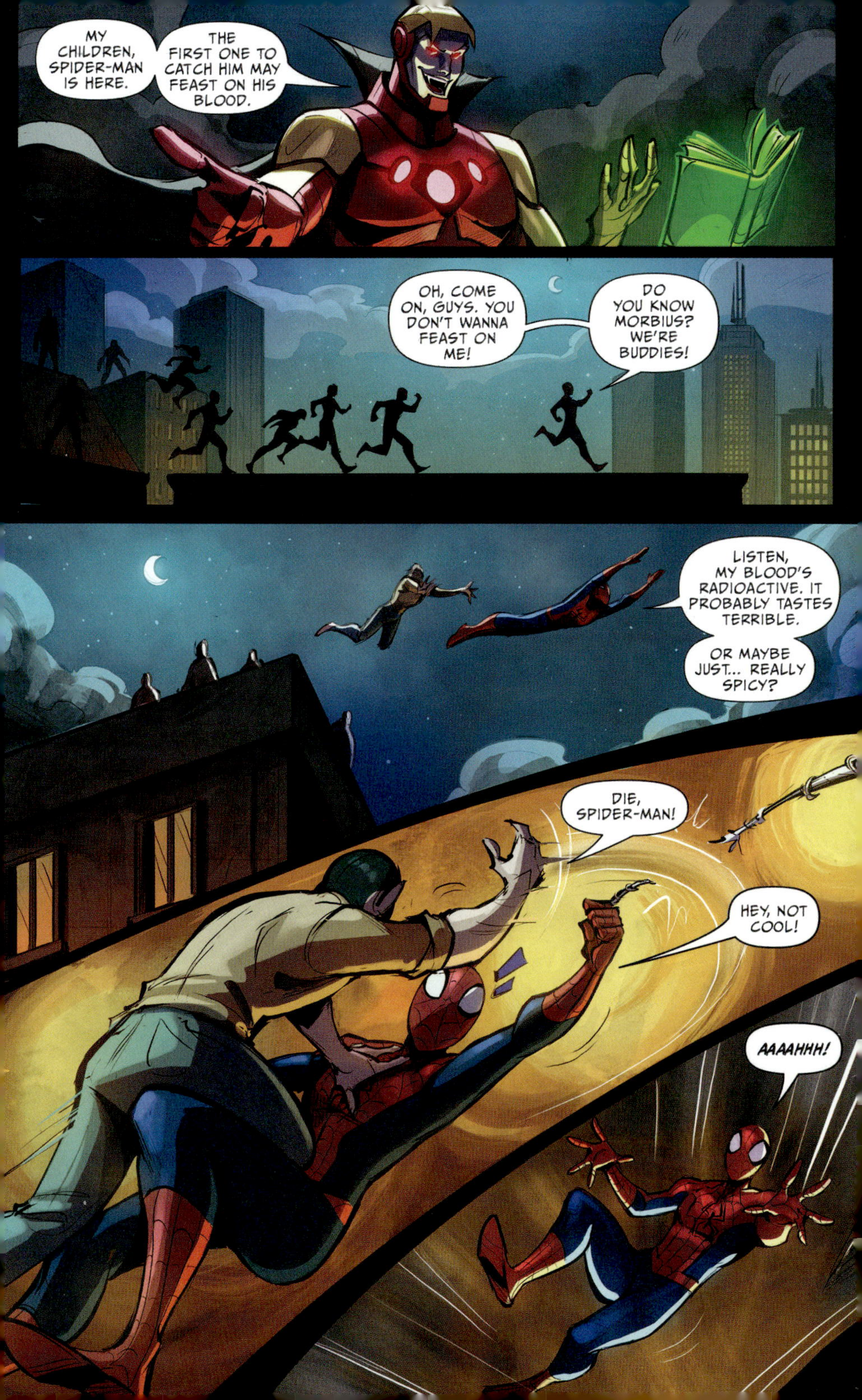
MY CHILDREN, SPIDER-MAN IS HERE.
THE FIRST ONE TO CATCH HIM MAY FEAST ON HIS BLOOD.
OH, COME ON, GUYS. YOU DON'T WANNA FEAST ON ME!
DO YOU KNOW MORBIUS? WE'RE BUDDIES!
LISTEN, MY BLOOD'S RADIOACTIVE. IT PROBABLY TASTES TERRIBLE.
OR MAYBE JUST... REALLY SPICY?
DIE, SPIDER-MAN!
HEY, NOT COOL!
AAAAHHH!

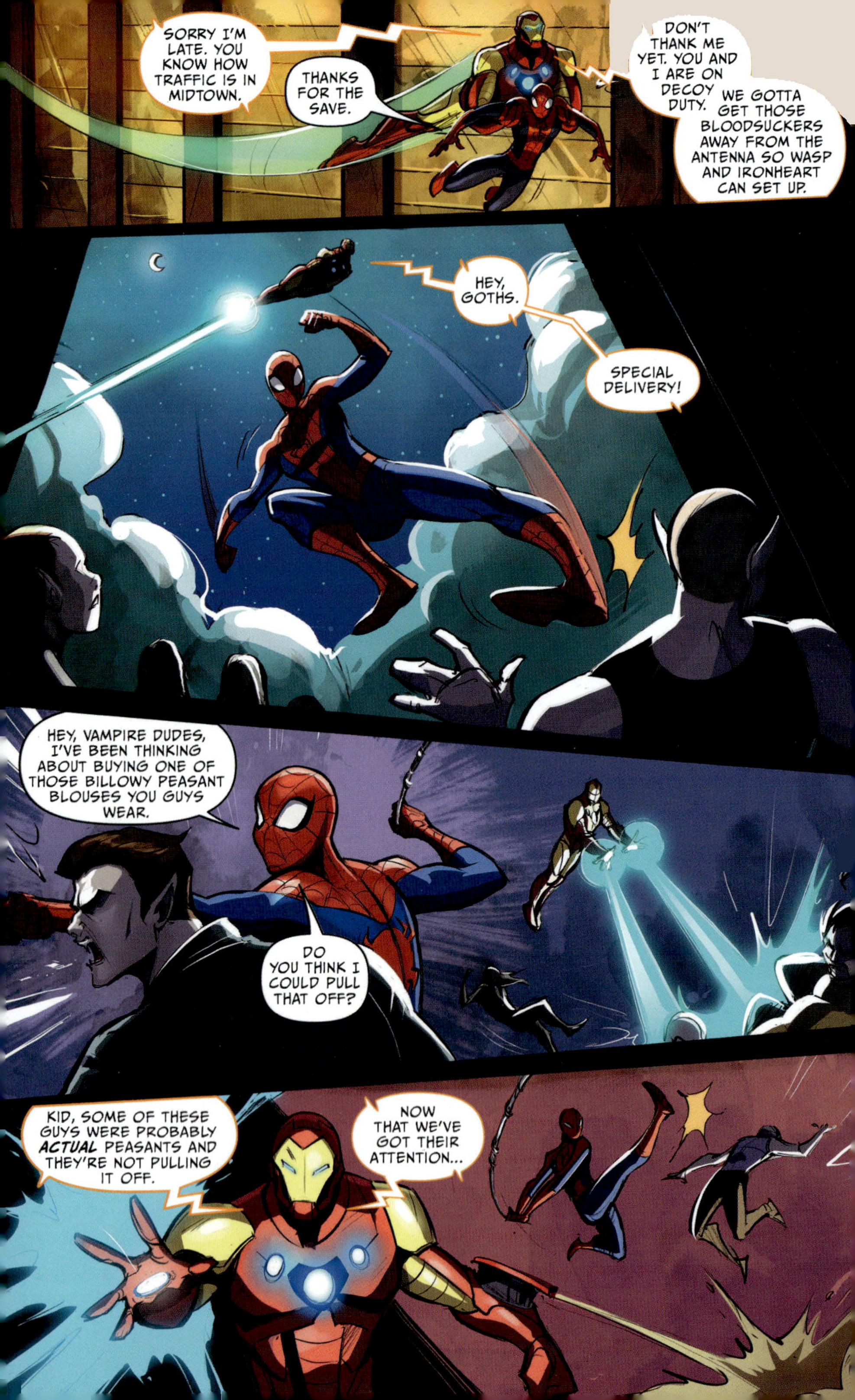

SORRY I'M LATE. YOU KNOW HOW TRAFFIC IS IN MIDTOWN.
THANKS FOR THE SAVE.
DON'T THANK ME YET. YOU AND I ARE ON DECOY DUTY.
WE GOTTA GET THOSE BLOODSUCKERS AWAY FROM THE ANTENNA SO WASP AND IRONHEART CAN SET UP.
HEY, GOTHS.
SPECIAL DELIVERY!
HEY, VAMPIRE DUDES, I'VE BEEN THINKING ABOUT BUYING ONE OF THOSE BILLOWY PEASANT BLOUSES YOU GUYS WEAR.
DO YOU THINK I COULD PULL THAT OFF?
KID, SOME OF THESE GUYS WERE PROBABLY ***ACTUAL*** PEASANTS AND THEY'RE NOT PULLING IT OFF.
NOW THAT WE'VE GOT THEIR ATTENTION...

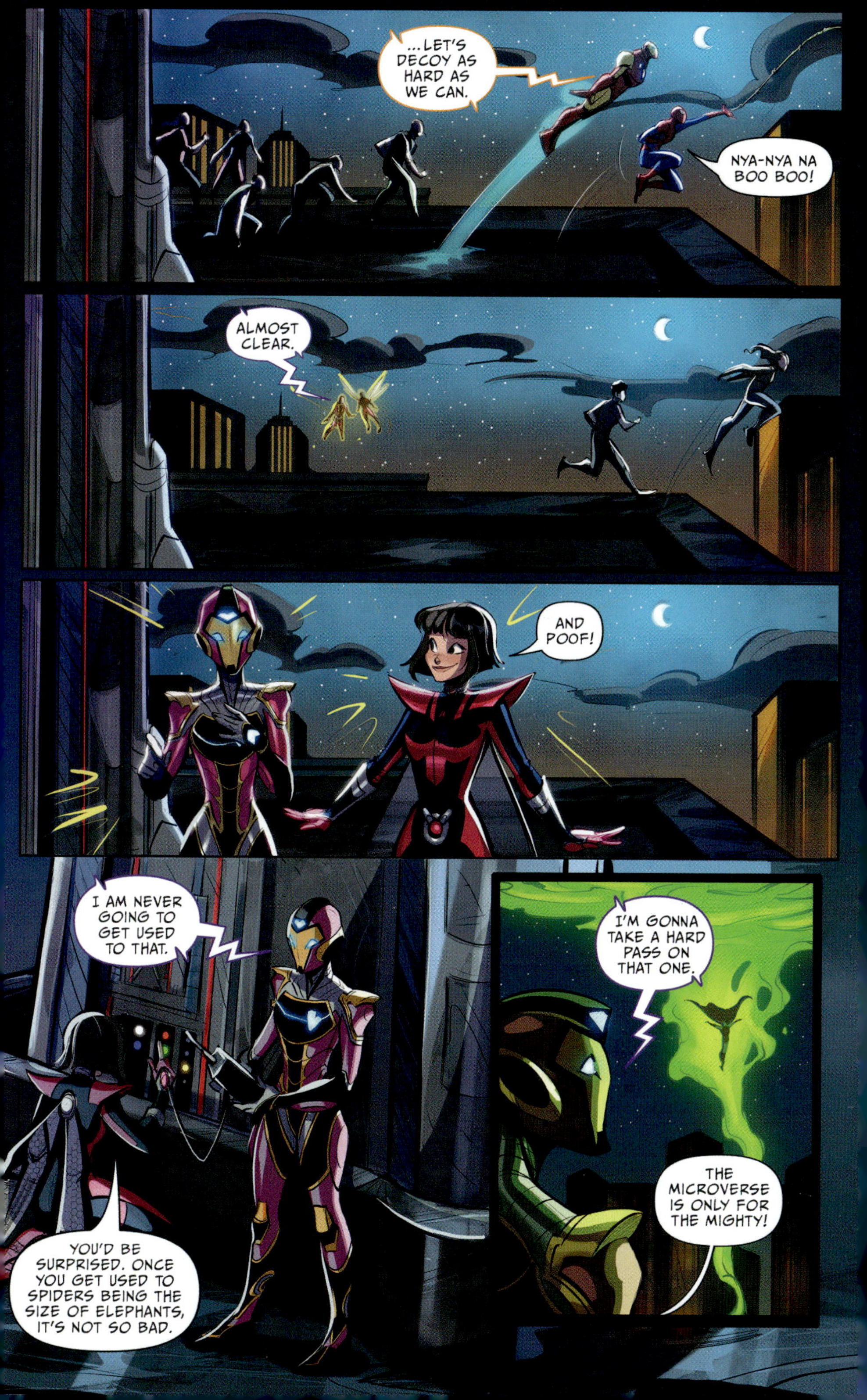
...LET'S DECOY AS HARD AS WE CAN.
NYA-NYA NA BOO BOO!
ALMOST CLEAR.
AND POOF!
I AM NEVER GOING TO GET USED TO THAT.
YOU'D BE SURPRISED. ONCE YOU GET USED TO SPIDERS BEING THE SIZE OF ELEPHANTS, IT'S NOT SO BAD.
I'M GONNA TAKE A HARD PASS ON THAT ONE.
THE MICROVERSE IS ONLY FOR THE MIGHTY!

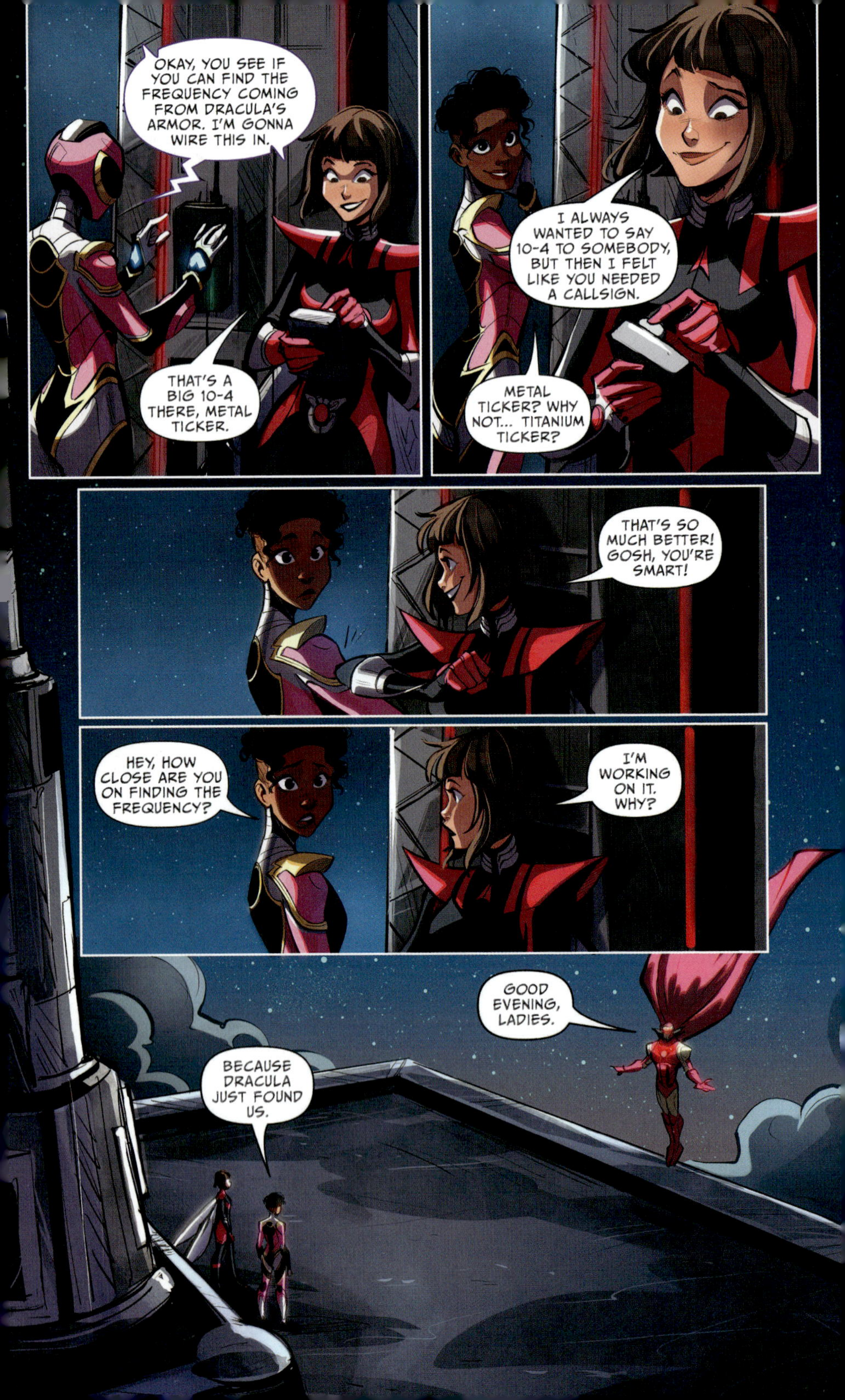
OKAY, YOU SEE IF YOU CAN FIND THE FREQUENCY COMING FROM DRACULA'S ARMOR. I'M GONNA WIRE THIS IN.
THAT'S A BIG 10-4 THERE, METAL TICKER.
I ALWAYS WANTED TO SAY 10-4 TO SOMEBODY, BUT THEN I FELT LIKE YOU NEEDED A CALLSIGN.
METAL TICKER? WHY NOT... TITANIUM TICKER?
THAT'S SO MUCH BETTER! GOSH, YOU'RE SMART!
HEY, HOW CLOSE ARE YOU ON FINDING THE FREQUENCY?
I'M WORKING ON IT. WHY?
GOOD EVENING, LADIES.
BECAUSE DRACULA JUST FOUND US.

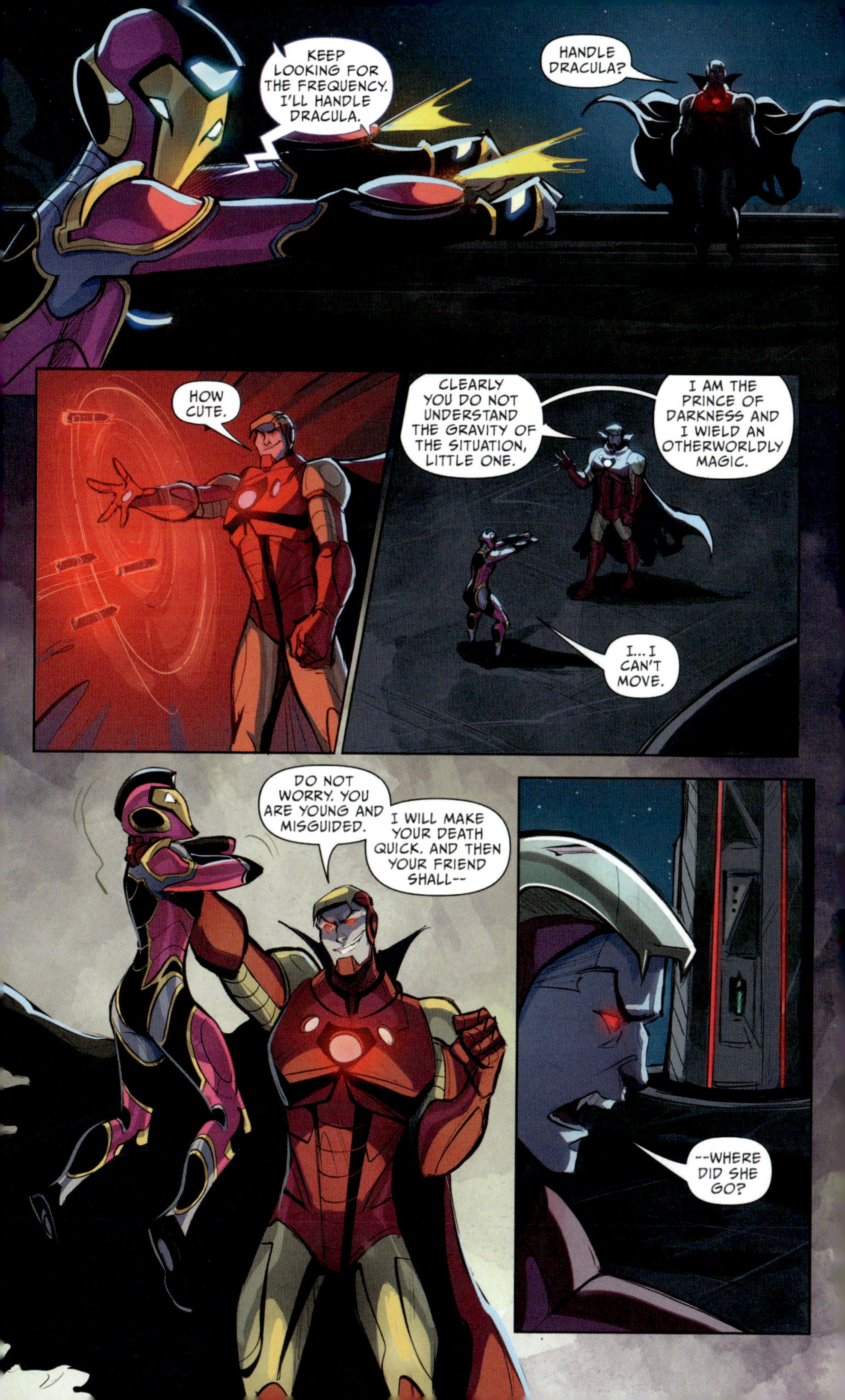
KEEP LOOKING FOR THE FREQUENCY. I'LL HANDLE DRACULA.
HANDLE DRACULA?
HOW CUTE.
CLEARLY YOU DO NOT UNDERSTAND THE GRAVITY OF THE SITUATION, LITTLE ONE.
I AM THE PRINCE OF DARKNESS AND I WIELD AN OTHERWORLDLY MAGIC.
I... I CAN'T MOVE.
DO NOT WORRY. YOU ARE YOUNG AND MISGUIDED.
I WILL MAKE YOUR DEATH QUICK. AND THEN YOUR FRIEND SHALL--
--WHERE DID SHE GO?

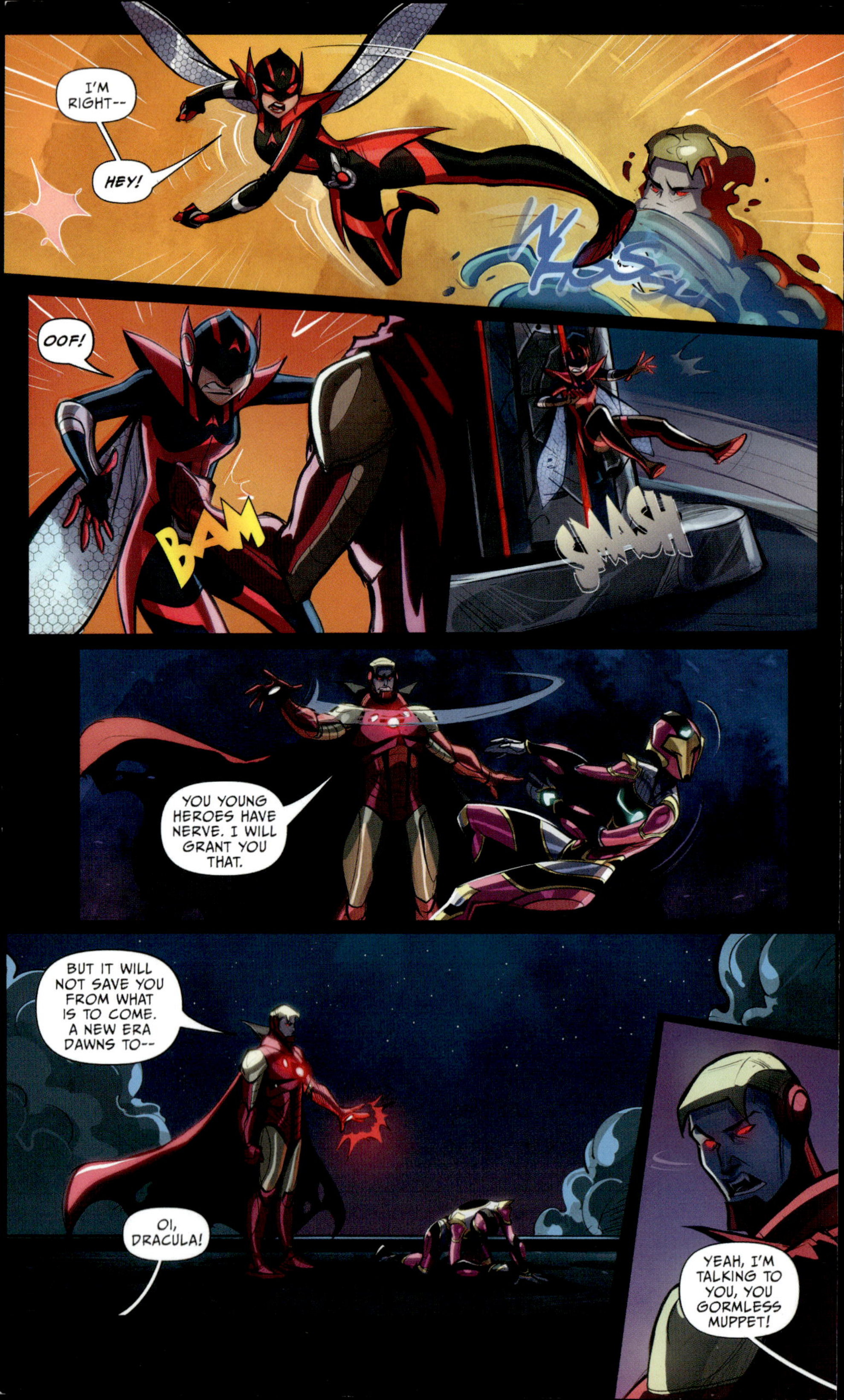
I'M RIGHT--
HEY!
WHOSH
OOF!
BAM
SMASH
YOU YOUNG HEROES HAVE NERVE. I WILL GRANT YOU THAT.
BUT IT WILL NOT SAVE YOU FROM WHAT IS TO COME. A NEW ERA DAWNS TO--
OI, DRACULA!
YEAH, I'M TALKING TO YOU, YOU GORMLESS MUPPET!

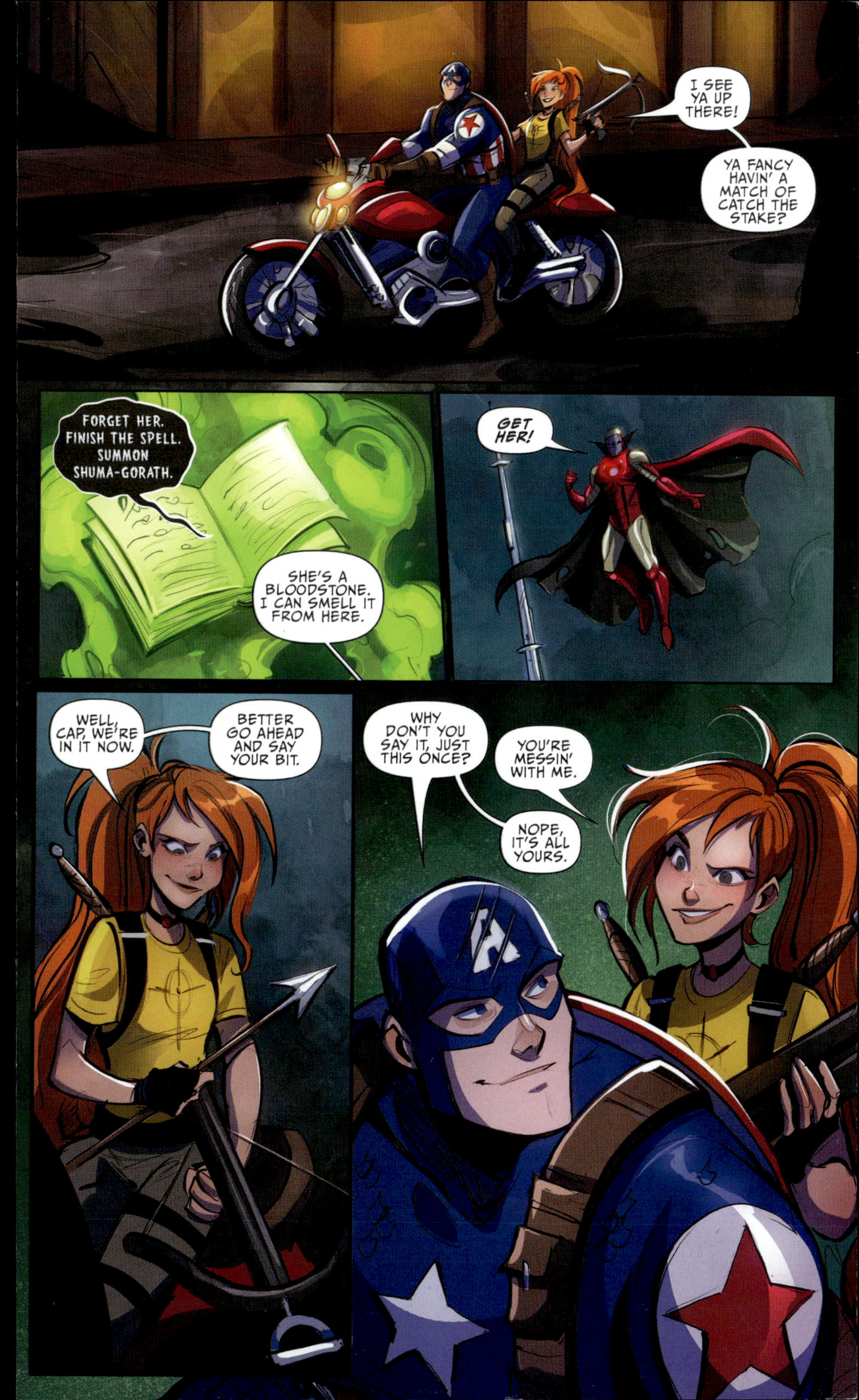
I SEE YA UP THERE!
YA FANCY HAVIN' A MATCH OF CATCH THE STAKE?
FORGET HER. FINISH THE SPELL. SUMMON SHUMA-GORATH.
SHE'S A BLOODSTONE. I CAN SMELL IT FROM HERE.
GET HER!
WELL, CAP, WE'RE IN IT NOW.
BETTER GO AHEAD AND SAY YOUR BIT.
WHY DON'T YOU SAY IT, JUST THIS ONCE?
YOU'RE MESSIN' WITH ME.
NOPE, IT'S ALL YOURS.

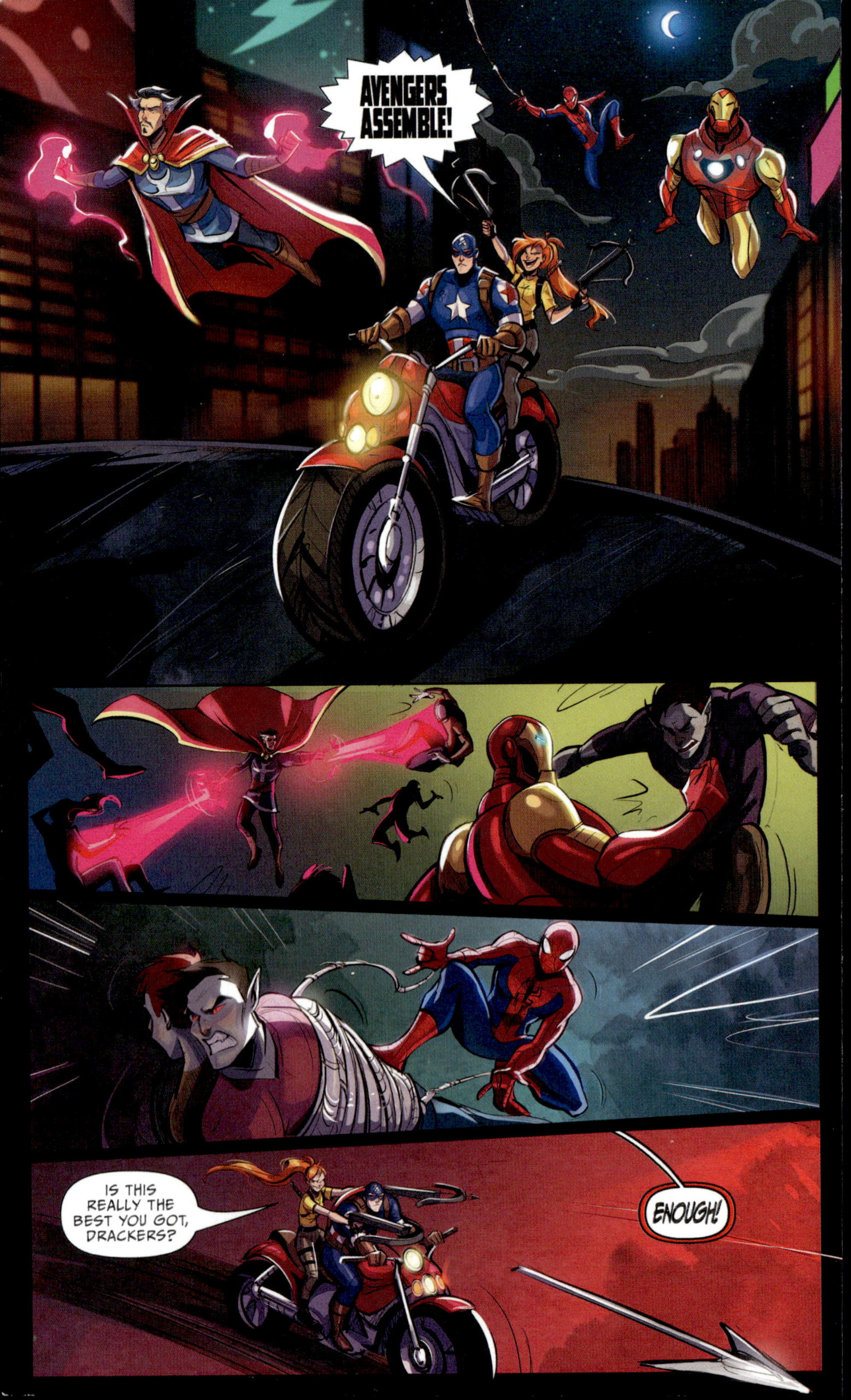
AVENGERS ASSEMBLE!
IS THIS REALLY THE BEST YOU GOT, DRACKERS?
ENOUGH!

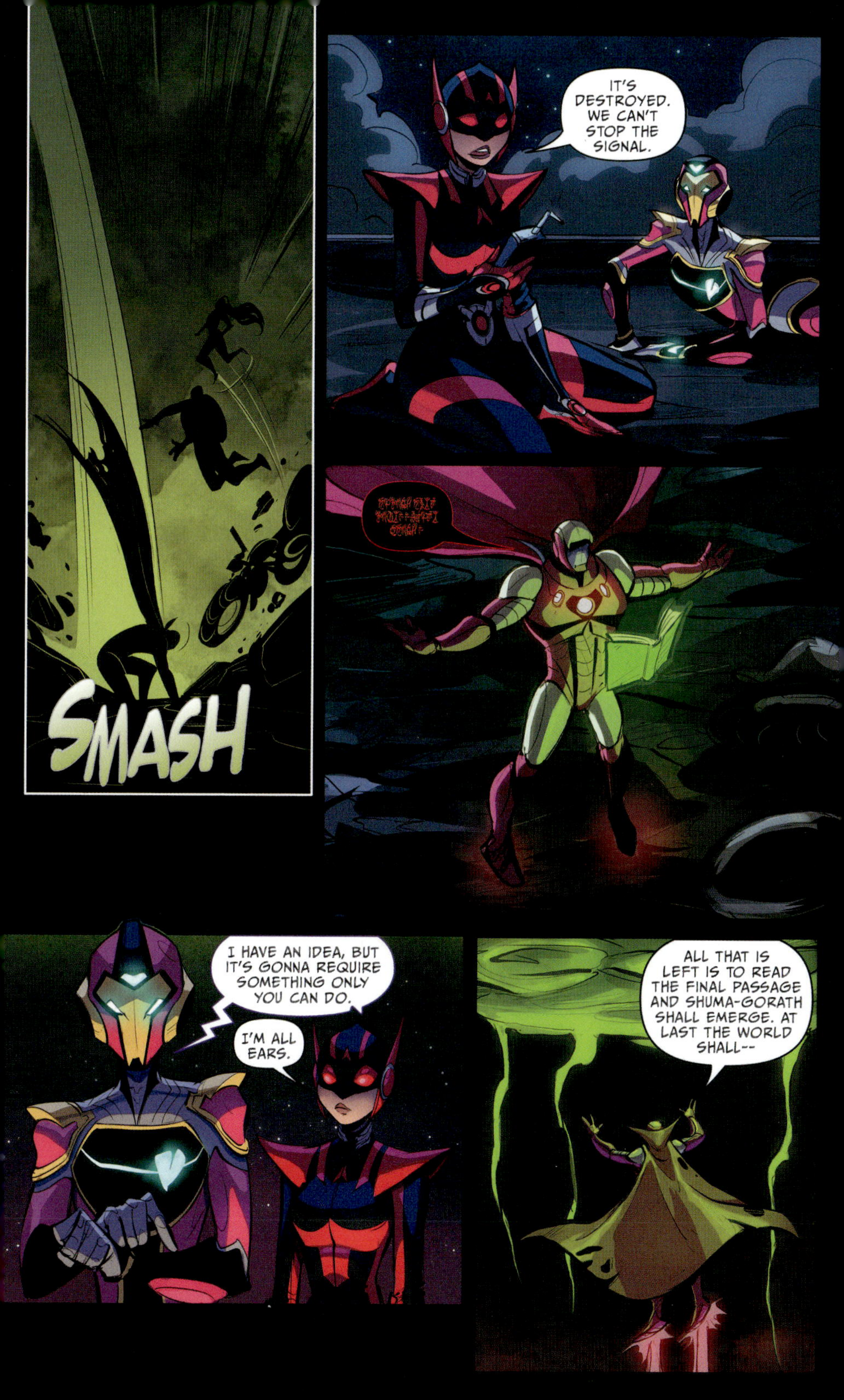
SMASH
IT'S DESTROYED. WE CAN'T STOP THE SIGNAL.
I HAVE AN IDEA, BUT IT'S GONNA REQUIRE SOMETHING ONLY YOU CAN DO.
I'M ALL EARS.
ALL THAT IS LEFT IS TO READ THE FINAL PASSAGE AND SHUMA-GORATH SHALL EMERGE. AT LAST THE WORLD SHALL--

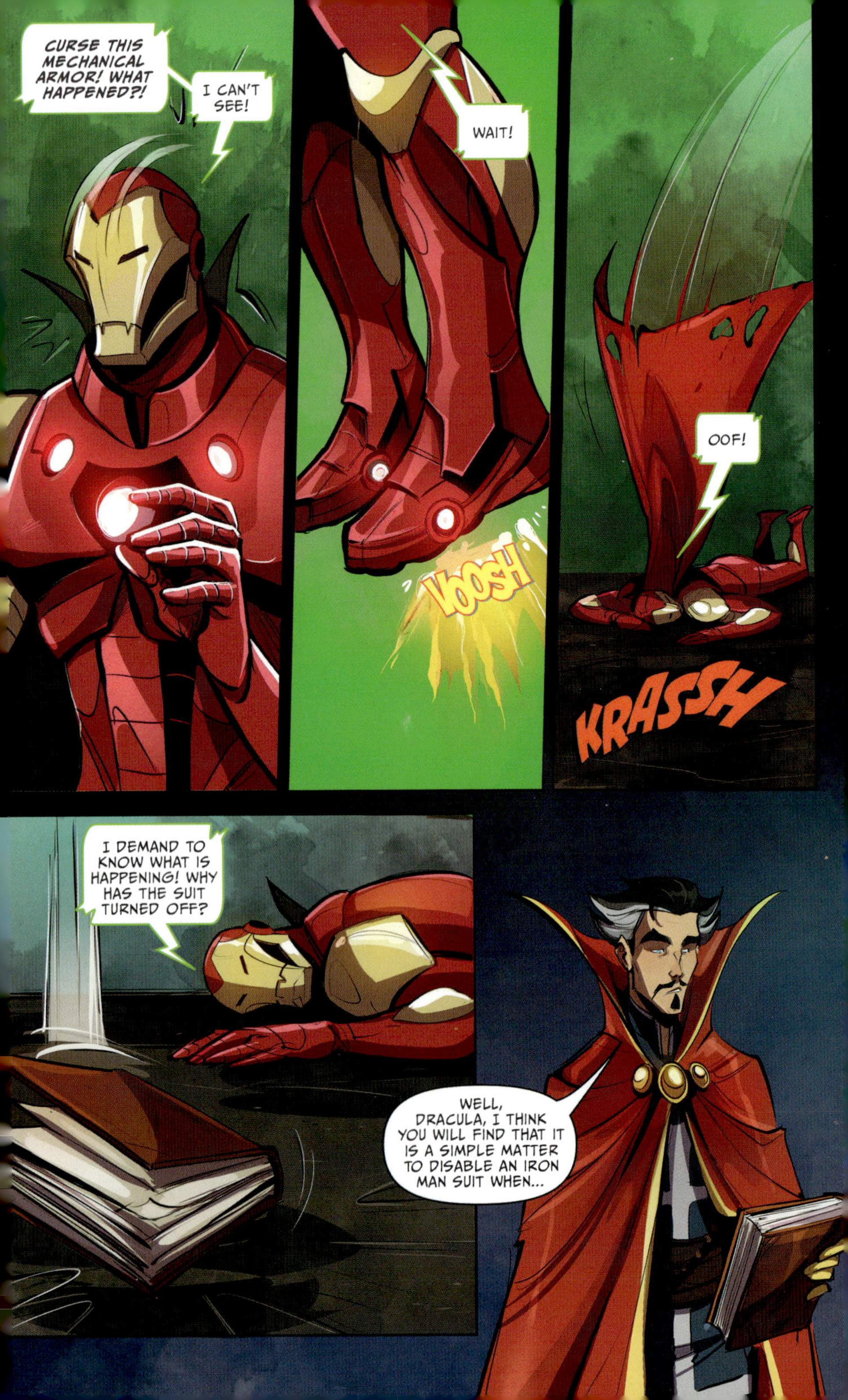
CURSE THIS MECHANICAL ARMOR! WHAT HAPPENED?!
I CAN'T SEE!
WAIT!
VOOSH
OOF!
KRASSH
I DEMAND TO KNOW WHAT IS HAPPENING! WHY HAS THE SUIT TURNED OFF?
WELL, DRACULA, I THINK YOU WILL FIND THAT IT IS A SIMPLE MATTER TO DISABLE AN IRON MAN SUIT WHEN...

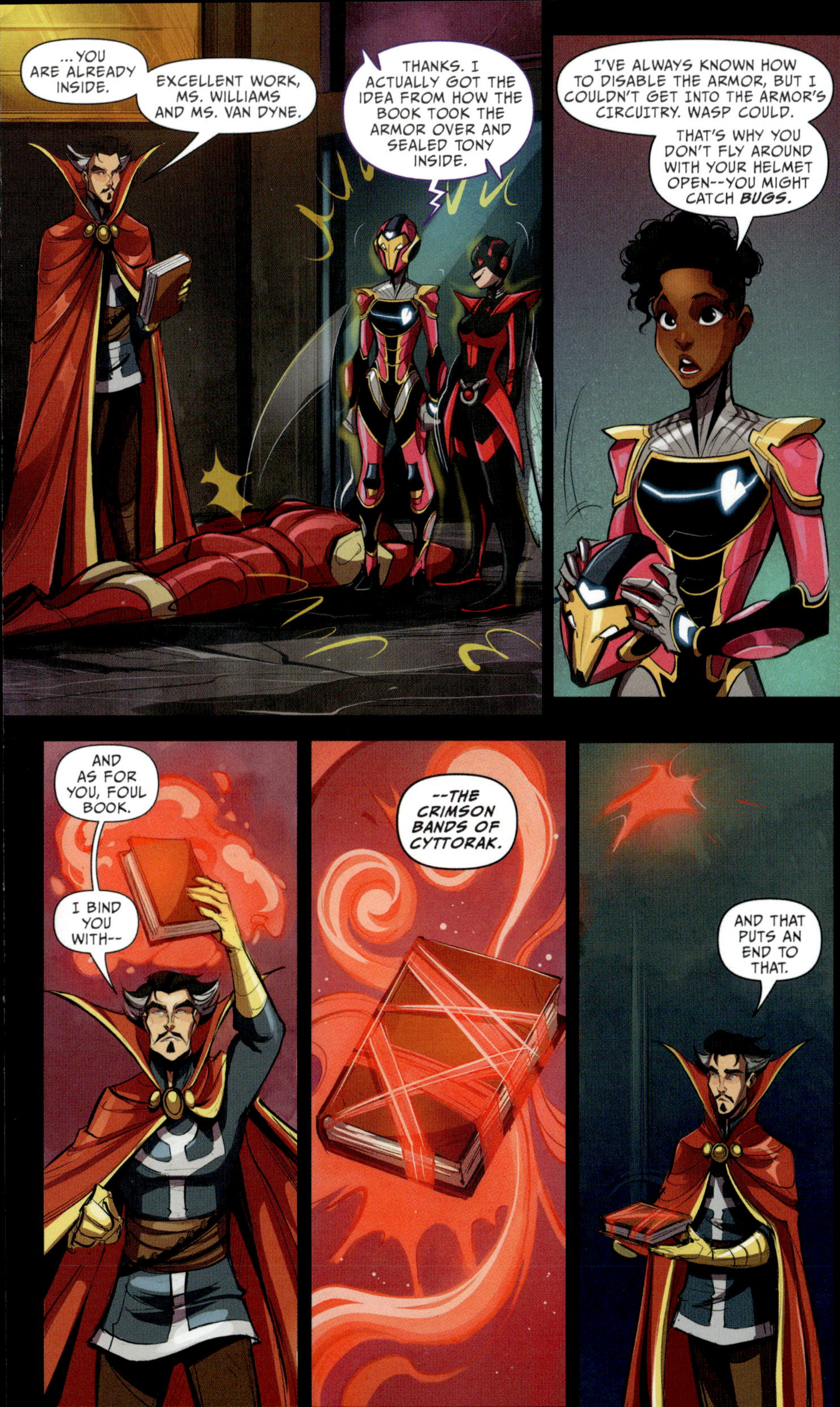
...YOU ARE ALREADY INSIDE.
EXCELLENT WORK, MS. WILLIAMS AND MS. VAN DYNE.
THANKS. I ACTUALLY GOT THE IDEA FROM HOW THE BOOK TOOK THE ARMOR OVER AND SEALED TONY INSIDE.
I'VE ALWAYS KNOWN HOW TO DISABLE THE ARMOR, BUT I COULDN'T GET INTO THE ARMOR'S CIRCUITRY. WASP COULD.
THAT'S WHY YOU DON'T FLY AROUND WITH YOUR HELMET OPEN--YOU MIGHT CATCH BUGS.
AND AS FOR YOU, FOUL BOOK.
I BIND YOU WITH--
--THE CRIMSON BANDS OF CYTTORAK.
AND THAT PUTS AN END TO THAT.

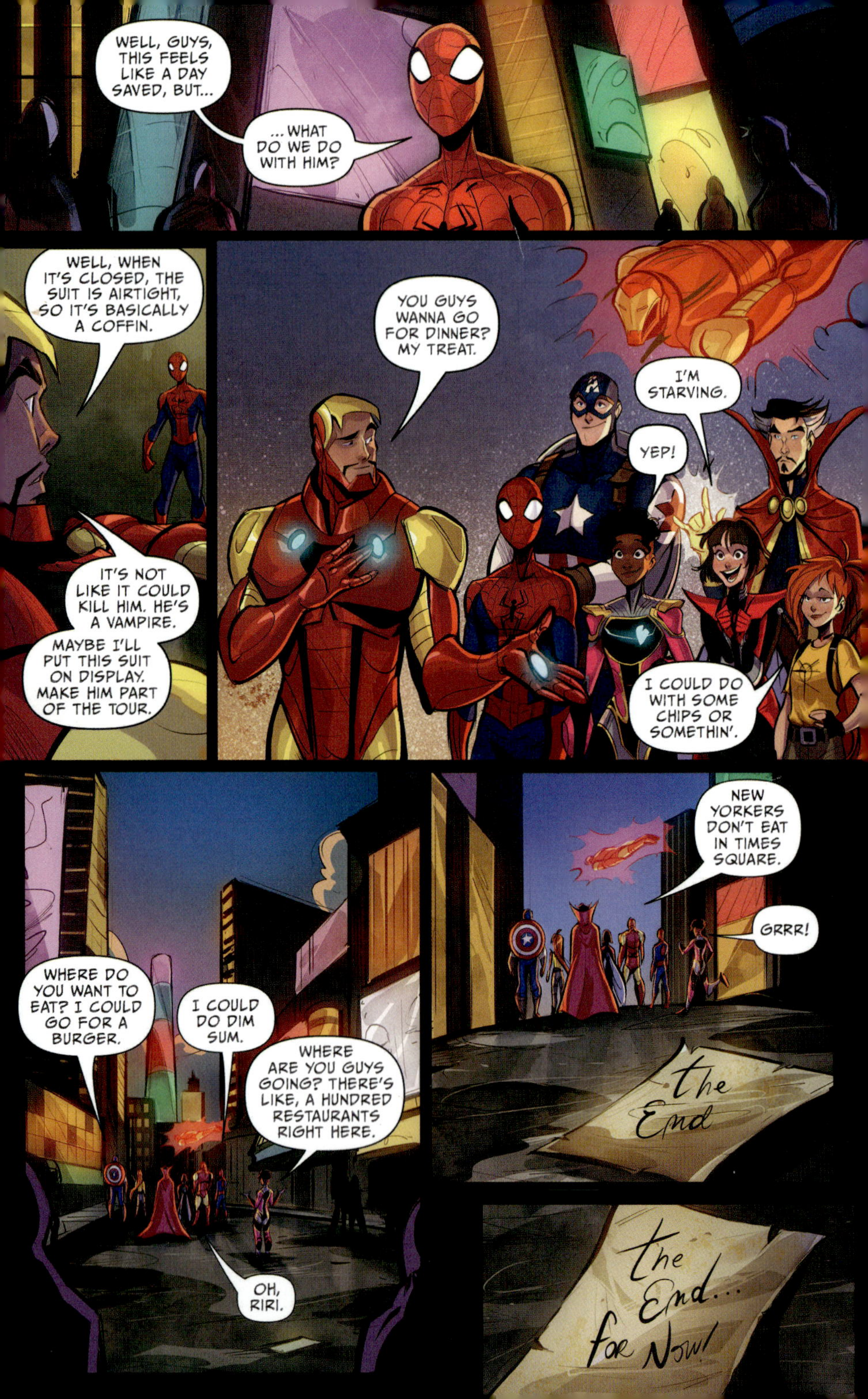
WELL, GUYS, THIS FEELS LIKE A DAY SAVED, BUT...
...WHAT DO WE DO WITH HIM?
WELL, WHEN IT'S CLOSED, THE SUIT IS AIRTIGHT, SO IT'S BASICALLY A COFFIN.
IT'S NOT LIKE IT COULD KILL HIM. HE'S A VAMPIRE.
MAYBE I'LL PUT THIS SUIT ON DISPLAY. MAKE HIM PART OF THE TOUR.
YOU GUYS WANNA GO FOR DINNER? MY TREAT.
I'M STARVING.
YEP!
I COULD DO WITH SOME CHIPS OR SOMETHIN'.
WHERE DO YOU WANT TO EAT? I COULD GO FOR A BURGER.
I COULD DO DIM SUM.
WHERE ARE YOU GUYS GOING? THERE'S LIKE, A HUNDRED RESTAURANTS RIGHT HERE.
OH, RIRI.
NEW YORKERS DON'T EAT IN TIMES SQUARE.
GRRR!
the End
the End... for Now!

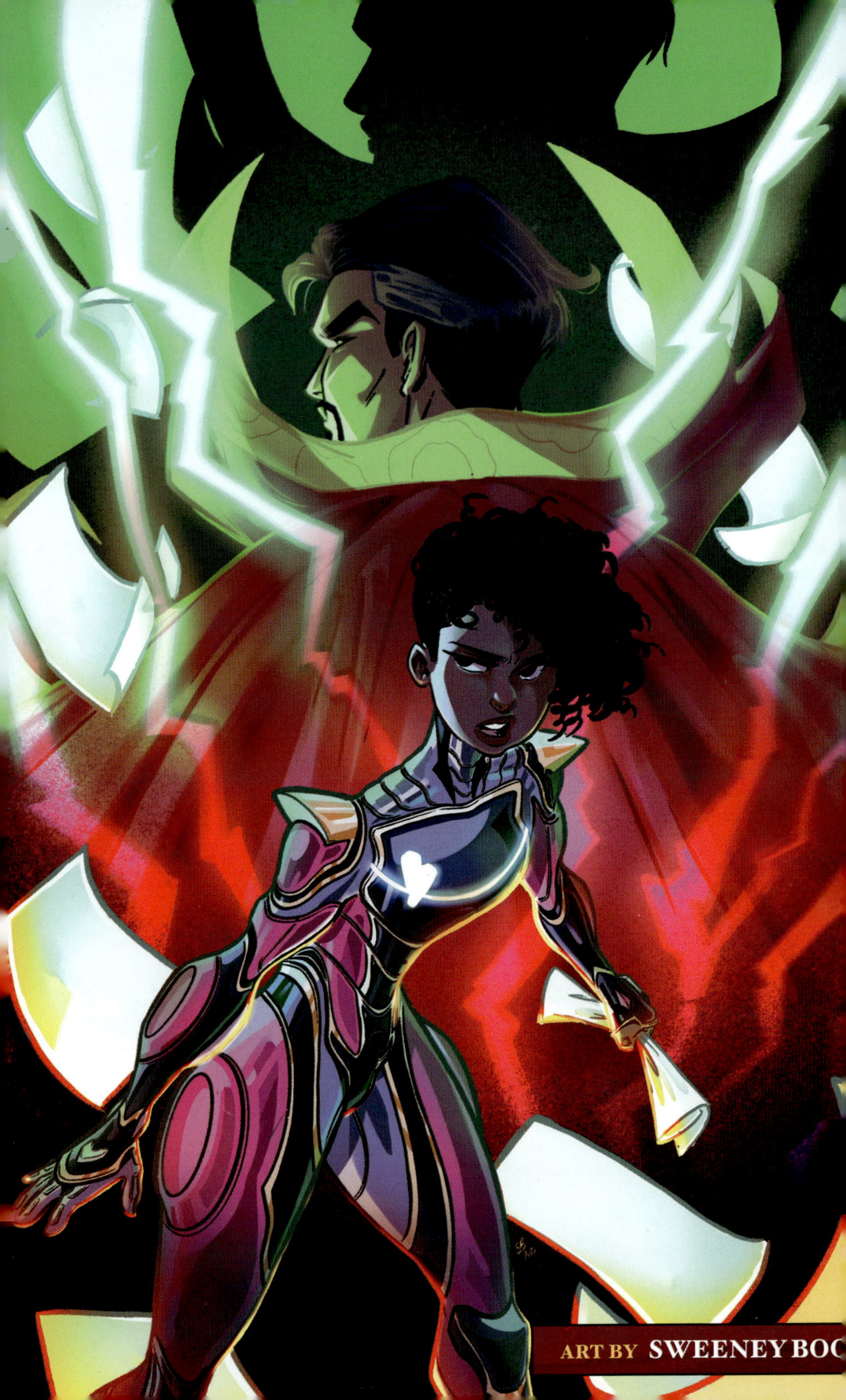

ART BY SWEENEY BOO

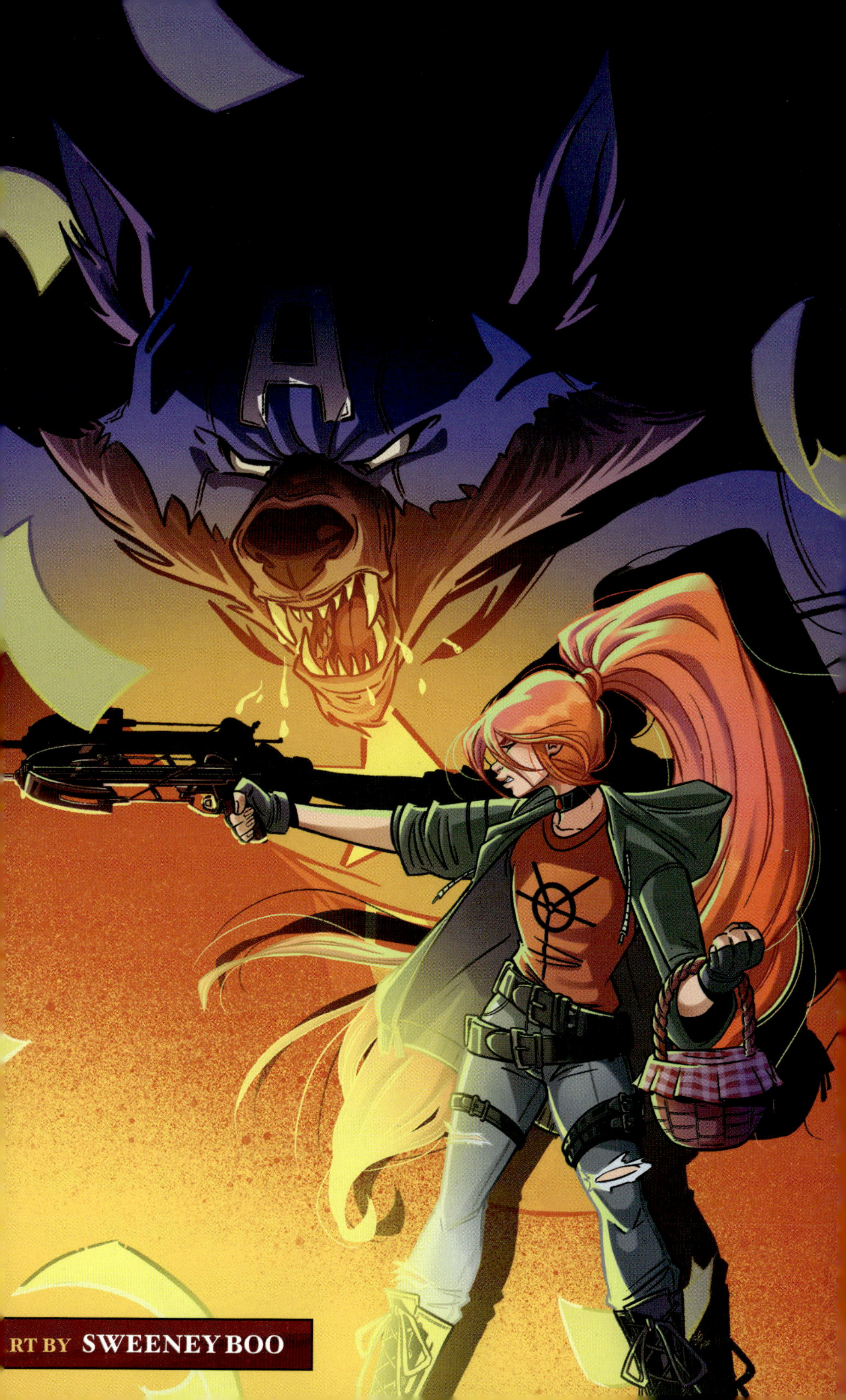
RT BY SWEENEY BOO

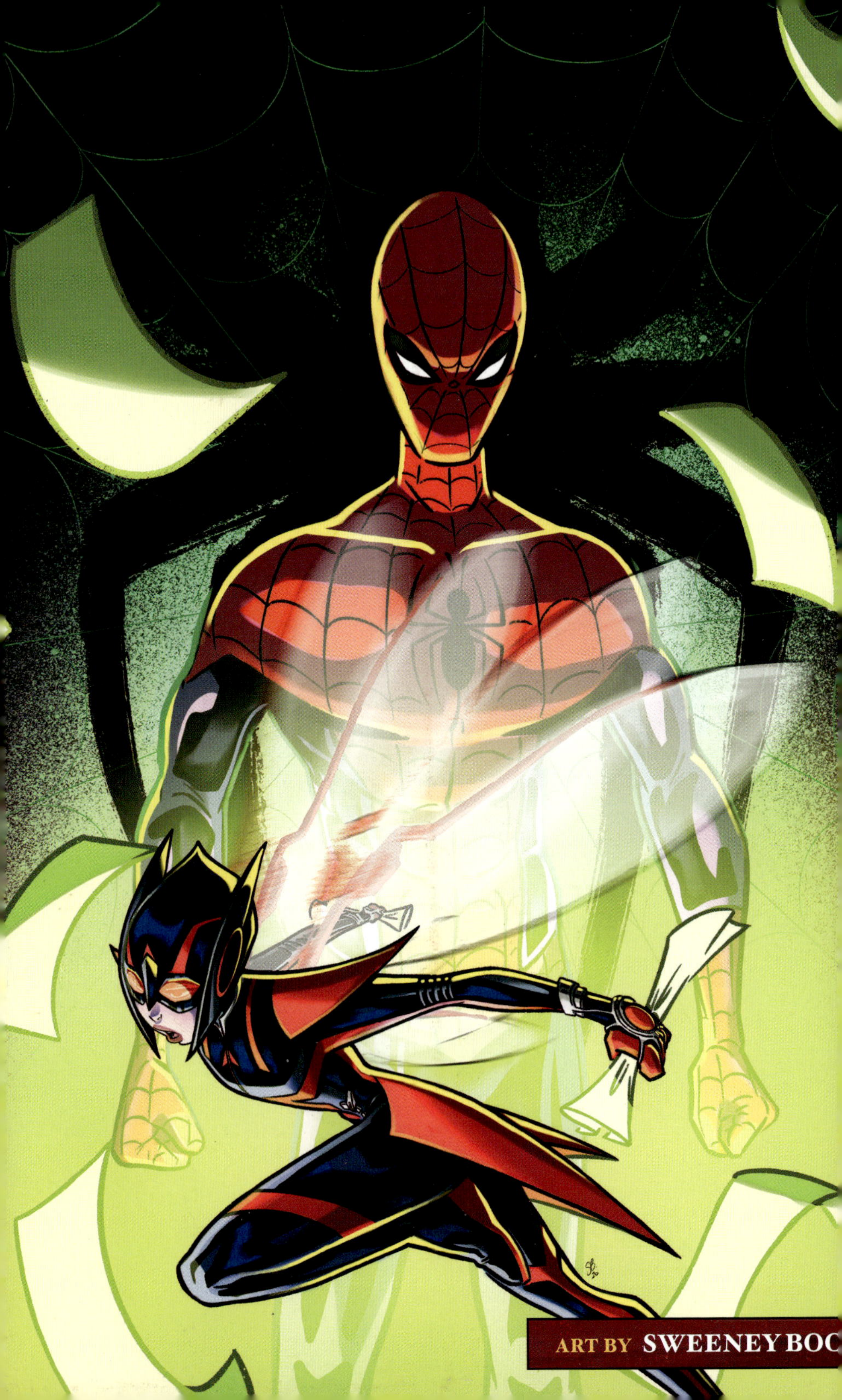

ART BY SWEENEY BOC

ART BY SWEENEYBOO

Cover Artist
Gretel Lusky

Letterer
Valeria Lopez

Series Editor
Elizabeth Brei

Collection Editors
Alonzo Simon
& Zac Boone

Collection Designer
Jessica Gonzalez

MARVEL ACTION: CHILLERS. SEPTEMBER 2021. FIRST PRINTING. © 2021 MARVEL. All Rights Reserved. The IDW logo is registered in the U.S. Patent and Trademark Office. IDW Publishing, a division of Idea and Design Works, LLC. Editorial offices: 2765 Truxtun Road, San Diego, CA 92106. Any similarities to persons living or dead are purely coincidental. With the exception of artwork used for review purposes, none of the contents of this publication may be reprinted without the permission of Idea and Design Works, LLC. IDW Publishing does not read or accept unsolicited submissions of ideas, stories, or artwork. Printed in Korea.

Originally published as MARVEL ACTION: CHILLERS issues #1–4.

Special thanks to Lauren Bisom and Caitlin O'Connell for their invaluable assistance.

ISBN: 978-1-68405-825-9   24   23   22   21   1   2   3   4

Marvel Publishing:

VP Production & Special Projects: Jeff Youngquist
Editor, Juvenile Publishing: Lauren Bisom
Associate Editor, Special Projects: Caitlin O'Connell
VP, Licensed Publishing: Sven Larsen
SVP Print, Sales & Marketing: David Gabriel
Editor In Chief: C.B. Cebulski

Nachie Marsham, Publisher
Blake Kobashigawa, VP of Sales
Tara McCrillis, VP Publishing Operations
John Barber, Editor-in-Chief
Mark Doyle, Editorial Director, Originals
Erika Turner, Executive Editor
Scott Dunbier, Director, Special Projects
Mark Irwin, Editorial Director, Consumer Products Mgr
Joe Hughes, Director, Talent Relations
Anna Morrow, Sr. Marketing Director
Alexandra Hargett, Book & Mass Market Sales Director
Keith Davidsen, Senior Manager, PR
Topher Alford, Sr Digital Marketing Manager
Shauna Monteforte, Sr. Director of Manufacturing Operations
Jamie Miller, Sr. Operations Manager
Nathan Widick, Sr. Art Director, Head of Design
Neil Uyetake, Sr. Art Director Design & Production
Shawn Lee, Art Director Design & Production
Jack Rivera, Art Director, Marketing

Ted Adams and Robbie Robbins, IDW Founders

Facebook: facebook.com/idwpublishing
Twitter: @idwpublishing
YouTube: youtube.com/idwpublishing
Instagram: @idwpublishing